I0609257

William Westall

For Honor and Life

A Novel

William Westall

For Honor and Life
A Novel

ISBN/EAN: 9783337031862

Printed in Europe, USA, Canada, Australia, Japan

Cover: Foto ©Andreas Hilbeck / pixelio.de

More available books at **www.hansebooks.com**

A Novel

.

BY

WILLIAM WESTALL

AUTHOR OF

"HER TWO MILLIONS" "A FAIR CRUSADER"
"A PHANTOM CITY" "BIRCH DENE" ETC.

NEW YORK

HARPER & BROTHERS PUBLISHERS

1894

CONTENTS

CHAP.

FOR HONOR AND LIFE

———✦———

CHAPTER I

A LANCASHIRE LAD

My father was a born Switzer, of Canton Berne, and came of a family which for generations had produced soldiers of fortune, most of whom served in the Swiss regiments of the French kings.

Others of the Von Astors, who were ever a prolific race, took to the professions and to trade. Among these was a certain Frederic von Astor. Having a shrewd head for business and a turn for science, he betook himself to Elsass, studied practical chemistry, and served a long apprenticeship to the arts of dyeing and calico printing. After a while he received an invitation to proceed to Lancashire, where he obtained an important position in the house of Peel, Yates & Co. But Frederic Astor was too enterprising to serve long in a subordinate capacity. He dropped the "von," set up for himself, married a Lancashire wife, and became a British subject and my father.

Of his three brothers, one was in the French Guards, another in the army of Holland, the third in the army of Naples. My maternal grandfather was also a soldier ; he served with distinction at Dettingen, Fontenoy, Culloden, and Quebec.

So I came of a fighting stock on both sides of the house, and it seemed to be in the nature of things that I also should desire to be a soldier, and seek to win the bubble reputation at the cannon's mouth.

But it was also in the nature of things that my father, a man of peace from his youth up, should want me to become a calico printer and succeed to the fine business he had built up. Wherefore it came to pass that when, in my seventeenth year, I left Giggleswick Grammar-school, where I acquired a smattering of Latin, Greek, arithmetic, and the use of the globes, and attained to great proficiency in bird's-nesting, boxing, foot-ball, and cricket, I was ordered to begin my career "at the works." I pleaded hard with my father to let me begin it in the army. But he said that was all nonsense, I must buckle to business. So to parody Gibbon, I sighed as a would-be soldier and obeyed as a son.

I made my *début* in the designing-room, and as I had a turn for sketching, and my father did not "tie me to the bell," and I was allowed to spend a good deal of time out of doors, riding after the harriers, running after the otter-hounds, and what not, I did not find the life altogether intolerable. But one day when I was busy in the designing-room my father chanced to come in, and seeing me hard at work laid his hand on my head and commended me for my industry.

"What are you drawing, Fritz?" says he, looking over my shoulder. "*Ach Himmel!* Soldiers! Who ever heard of soldiers as a pattern for calico printing? This won't do at all. I must put you to something more practical. You shall go into the color-shop and dye-house. The morning in the one, the afternoon in the other."

The change pleased me. I was getting tired of sitting on a stool and bending over a desk. The next day I went into the color shop and made a horrid mess of my hands and clothes. But I liked the dye-house best, and had rare sport larking with the men, going with them to the croft, getting up wheelbarrow races, and, when the weather was warm, bathing in the dye-becks.

But this part of my career was brought to an abrupt termination by an untoward incident. One afternoon I profited by my father's temporary absence to get up a pitched battle in one of the crofts between the dye-house lads and a contingent of tier boys. The weapons were wet pieces, rolled up and used like flails. I led the tier boys, who were considered to be the weaker party. We had a glorious fight, and I think we should have beaten the dyers if in the very thick of the engagement my father had not appeared on the scene with a horsewhip in his hand.

Then there were wild cries of "Th' mayster! th' mayster!" and both armies dispersed in dire dismay and left me in sole possession of the field.

My father was very angry, and said that for the future he should keep me in the counting-house, under his own eye, and I was too much ashamed of myself to offer any vain excuses.

I went into the counting-house accordingly, and made an honest attempt to master the mysteries of book-keeping, in the which, however, I failed so signally that as a last resort my father resolved to give me a trial at the "Manchester end." Though he had come to the conclusion that I should never shine as a calico printer, he entertained a lingering hope that I might be turned into a tolerable if not a brilliant salesman.

I rather liked the new departure. A bedroom was provided for me at the warehouse, but I spent much of my time at home, and in riding, driving, and coaching on the twenty miles of road between Manchester and the works, or "shop," as Lancashire folk call a calico-printing factory. All the same I did some work. I was introduced to the customers, and gave some of them a dinner at the White Bear. I even booked a few orders, and my too sanguine parent informed our chief salesman that he thought I was on the right track at last.

It did not last long, however. One morning when I had charge of the warehouse, while the salesmen were making their rounds, a customer came in boiling with rage, and complained that we were sending him nothing but "jobs." Everything was wrong. length, width, reed. picks ; the colors were as bad as they could be, and the printing was worse. Considering this to be an imputation on the honor of the firm, I told the fellow roundly that the pieces were perfect and that he was a fool, and when he gave me an impertinent answer, kicked him down-stairs and half-way across Mosely Street.

This proved to be the final incident of my commercial career. My father gave up for good and all the attempt to convert me into a business man, and was so angry at my latest escapade that he did not speak to me for a month. Nevertheless, I continued to make occasional visits to the "shop," and one Thursday (somebody being on the sick-list) I was asked to go to Manchester on the following day for the wage money.

I complied with alacrity. It was a job that suited me, and early next morning King Corkery was put into the gig and I started for Manchester. The horse was so called because he had been bought at Preston Fair from a dealer who rejoiced in the name of Corkery O'Brien, and said he was descended from an Irish king.

Corkery was an excellent animal. No journey was too long for him. He would do his eight miles an hour, up hill and down dale, all day long, but faster than that he declined to go under any circumstances, and had never been known to gallop even when out at grass.

As it was a three-months' pay, and the sum I had to bring back large, I armed myself with a pair of horse-pistols, which I put in a holster strapped to the right-hand rail of the gig.

I got the money in two large bags, securely padlocked, which were put under the gig seat, and when King Corkery had had a good feed and three hours' rest I set out on my homeward journey. For the greater part of the way all went well. I gruelled the King at Bury, then drove steadily on through hilly Haslingden, which was as cold as it generally is, past Baxenden, and down into Accrington.

By this time it was at the edge of dark, but being within two miles of home, and considering myself and my money quite safe, I pulled Corkery into his slowest trot, so that I might take him home cool.

I had been jogging on in this style for three or four minutes when two men, who seemed to spring from the ground, and had, no doubt, been lying in the ditch bottom, caught my horse by the head and brought him to a stand.

Then one of them came to the gig side and presented a pistol at my head.

"We know what you have got there," said he. "Out with it, or you are a dead man. Two bags."

"Very well," I answered. "Better lose my money than my life. Wait half a minute while I open the boot."

While speaking I stooped, as though to comply with his demand, at the same time drawing and cocking one of my pistols. Then, quickly rising, I let fly at the footpad who was holding Corkery. The horse made a plunge that threw the villain on his back, and, as a second shot rang through the air, bounded off at full gallop.

The King went like mad. Stopping him was out of the question, even if I had wanted to stop him. The gig swayed so wildly from side to side that it was a wonder we did not capsize, or go bodily into Hynburn Brook, which bordered the road.

But the old horse, though terribly scared, knew what he was about, and five minutes after the encounter he turned into the farm-yard at my father's house, and stopped at the stable door, trembling violently, and shaking his head as though he had taken leave of his senses.

Before I could alight, old Wiggin, the groom, came running with a lantern.

"What's up?" he exclaimed. "Owd Corkery hasn't been taking th' boggart" (bolting) "sure-ly. Bithmon has he! Why, he is aw of a swat, his heyd's covered wi' blood—and dom me if th' top of one of his ears hasn't getten knocked off! Whativer's been to do?"

At this moment my father, who had been on the lookout for me, came into the yard.

"Glad to see you safe back, Fritz," said he. "Got the money all right? But, God bless me, what has happened to King Corkery? I thought you knew better than to bring a horse back in this state."

"Why, he is th' same hissel," put in Wiggin, holding up the lantern. "Look at him. Dom me, if there isn't blood on his face and a hoyle in his hat."

"You have been attacked! Are you hurt, boy?" asked my father, anxiously.

"No anyhow, not much – I didn't know" (taking off my hat and feeling my head). "It's only a scratch."

"Very nearly a kill, though. Look at these holes; the bullet went through your hat. Thank God you are no worse. How did it happen and when? And the wage money?"

When I had answered my father's questions he put his arm round my neck and led me towards the house.

"You have saved me fifteen hundred pounds, dear boy,"

said he. "That is good, but better still is it that you have shown courage and presence of mind. Make light of it to your mother. She has been blaming me, and rightly, for letting you go alone for the wage money. We shall have to make a soldier of you after all. It is in your blood. We cannot compete with nature, and nature evidently designed you for a man of war. All the same, I don't like the idea of buying you a commission. It seems wrong that a man should pay for the privilege of serving his country. However, your Uncle Daniel is coming next week. We will talk it over with him. I wonder who those fellows were—not regular highwaymen, I am sure. Most likely neighbors, maybe our own men."

And so it proved, or rather was presumed, for as, owing to the darkness, I had been unable to recognize my assailants, I could not swear to them. Nevertheless there was every reason to believe—reasons amounting to moral certainty—that the delinquents were two of our own block printers temporarily short of a job, who, having heard of my errand to Manchester, planned to rob and, if need were, to murder me. Both were men of indifferent character. On the day in question their movements were suspicious, and for a week afterwards one of them, known as Jack-off-th'-Shelf, kept his bed, and when he reappeared carried his arm in a sling, having, as he said, lamed his shoulder by falling down-stairs.

We all thought that the bullet that hit King Corkery's ear had gone through Jack's arm. But, as there was no direct evidence connecting him with the offence, he saved his neck, for had his confederate and himself been prosecuted to conviction, they would have had to swing from the battlements of Lancaster Castle.

CHAPTER II

My Uncle Daniel held a captain's commission (which gave him the rank of colonel in the army) in the Royal Swiss Guard of France. He was a tall, handsome, brown-visaged man, decorated with the cross of St. Louis, and a thorough soldier, and for me, and I think for my father, his visit, his conversation, and his stories were highly enjoyable. He had next to no English, but as I had picked up from my father a fair knowledge of colloquial German, and from my sisters' governess a smattering of French, I understood him perfectly. We became fast friends from the first day of our acquaintance (I had not seen him before). He warmly sympathized with my ambition to become a soldier, and met my father's objection to buying a commission in the British army by offering to obtain me one without purchase, in his own or some other Swiss regiment.

"But he is English," objected my father.

"The English son of a Swiss father. Besides, it is quite enough that he is a Von Astor, and my nephew. Since the time of Francis I. there has always been at least one of the family in the Royal Guard, and as no questions will be asked about Fritz's nationality, none need be answered."

My father accepted this proposal all the more readily that he was an enthusiastic admirer of the great French Revolution, which was just then in the earlier stage of its wild career. He believed that the rest of Europe would follow the example of France, that we were at the beginning of a new era, an era of peaceful progress and universal brotherhood, and though I might become a soldier I should never need to fight.

In the light of subsequent events this may seem rather absurd, but at that time there were few liberal-minded men who did not cherish similar illusions, and nobody, so far as I know, foresaw that Europe was on the eve of a cataclysm such as had not occurred since the downfall of the Roman empire.

For the rest my father behaved very handsomely, gave me an ample outfit, and promised to supplement my pay in such sort as to enable me to live like an officer and a gentleman. But he wisely insisted that before entering a regiment I should spend three or four terms at a military college, in order to better my knowledge of the French tongue, and learn something of the theory of my future calling.

So I went with my uncle to France, and after eighteen months of strenuous study and practical work at Angers joined the Swiss Guard. I could have had an immediate appointment as ensign in a line regiment; but my uncle thought, and I agreed with him, that I had better go into the Guards, though I had to wait for my commission, and serve meanwhile as a gentleman volunteer.

This was in 1791, and since I left England the conditions and prospects of France had undergone a portentous change. The revolutionary flood was rising higher and higher, and threatened ere long to overwhelm the throne and sweep away the last vestiges of the ancient institutions of the land.

Whatever my uncle may have thought, he had little to say about politics, but the condition of the army gave him great concern. It was simply going to pieces. The privates elected their officers and then refused to obey them. The French Guards and several other regiments mutinied. The

Swiss regiment of Chateauvieux broke into open revolt at Nancy, and the mutiny was only suppressed after an action in which five hundred men were killed and wounded. The ringleaders were tried by court-martial, seven of them shot and forty sent to the galleys. But a few months later the prisoners were liberated and brought to Paris, hailed by the populace as heroes and martyrs, and received with honor by the National Assembly.

These things sorely grieved the officers and men of the Swiss Guard. Their only consolation was that the mutineers, being mostly from Geneva and the Welcher Schweiz (the French-speaking cantons), were no true Switzers.

"God alone knows what will be the end of it all," said my uncle, sadly. "But our course is clear. We have sworn to defend the king against his enemies, and defend him we shall, even though we have to lay down our lives to the last man. Whatever may betide, the Swiss Guards will be true to their salt."

This was the sentiment of every man in the regiment, for *noblesse oblige*, and privates as well as officers were "gentlemen of the Swiss Guard," jealous of their honor and proud of their fidelity to the flag under which they served.

As touching myself I regarded the outlook foreshadowed by my uncle without misgiving, rejoicing rather than otherwise at the idea of a fight *à outrance* with the truculent mob that held Paris in terror. But I thought as a youth who had not yet fronted or even seen death.

I also possessed a full measure of youthful vanity, and was so proud of my new clothes that I had a portrait of myself taken in full dress uniform and sent to my father. It depicts a tall, broad-shouldered young fellow of nineteen or twenty, dressed in a scarlet cutaway coat, with long lappets, white inside and folded back, blue collar and facings, with white button-holes and silver buttons, white waistcoat, belt, breeches, and leggings, the last coming above the knee. His cocked hat is trimmed with silver, his hair powdered, and his arms are sword, musket, and bayonet.

When I had gone through a course of drill at Courbevoie, at that time the regimental depot, I went to Paris and took up my quarters in the barracks at the Tuileries, where the main body was then stationed for the protection of their majesties.

I saw them often. Louis XVI. was a stout, clumsily built man with a good-natured yet weak face, and bore himself so unlike a king that I could hardly believe that he came of a kingly race. We of the Swiss Guard had afterwards bitter cause to regret that France had not been blessed with a more masterful monarch, and ourselves with a more resolute chief.

But Marie Antoinette was a right queenly woman, whose high qualities more than atoned for her husband's defects. She had a noble face and an imposing presence, and a manner so gracious and winning that all who knew her loved her. Her majesty took great interest in her guards, and knew all the officers and many of the privates by name.

One day, when we were mustered for parade in the *cour royale* of the palace, she beckoned to my uncle and spoke a few words to him; whereupon he beckoned to me, and, the honor being quite unexpected, and myself unused to the etiquette of courts, I stepped forward in some confusion.

"So this is your nephew, Captain d'Astor? *Quel beau garçon!*" (what a fine young fellow), said the queen. "What is his name?"

"Frederick, madame; but we generally call him Fritz."

"Well, Monsieur Fritz, you bear an honored name, and I am sure you will prove worthy of it. These are trying times, and we have many enemies and few friends."

I was deeply moved, for Marie Antoinette's voice was troubled, and her beautiful eyes were filled with tears.

"I would die for your majesty!" I exclaimed passionately.

".Ah, no! Don't speak of dying. Rather live for us, for the king, my children — and me."

And then she gave me her hand to kiss, and I returned to my place in the ranks, proud of the honor which had been conferred on me, and treasuring the queen's words in my heart.

But our fidelity to the king made us hated alike by the Jacobins of the National Assembly and the populace of Paris, and when political excitement ran high the Guards were either confined to barracks or sent away for a few days, lest their appearance in the streets should give offence to the rabble and lead to trouble, and it was against regulations to go beyond the precincts of the palace at any time, except in twos and threes. Men who went out alone were apt never to return.

Yet I contrived to see a good deal of Paris, luckily, for the time came when a knowledge of its topography, and of the manners and customs of its inhabitants, was a matter of life and death to me.

Accompanied by my comrade Glutz, a volunteer like myself, with whom I had struck up a warm friendship, now and then by Sergeant Sternberg, who knew his way about as well as a rag-picker or a police-officer, I walked the streets of Paris for hours at a time. These excursions were generally made in the evening, when we were least likely to attract attention; and as we were armed, and, I dare say, looked dangerous customers to tackle, we were seldom molested.

Nevertheless we could not always avoid awkward rencontres, and one night, but for Sternberg's coolness and presence of mind, we should have been forced into a fight from which it was hardly possible we could have escaped with our lives. It fell out that, as we turned out of the Rue Feydeau into the Rue St. Marc, we encountered two or three score of sans-culottes,* who, though our scarlet coats were hidden under our cloaks, recognized us at sight, probably by reason of our white gaiters and military bearing.

These sans-culottes, a term signifying without breeches, though not necessarily without trousers, were for the most part the dregs of the population, idlers and vagabonds, armed and paid by the municipality, and dressed, or half-dressed, as they pleased.

Having been strictly enjoined by our officers to behave with circumspection and give no occasion for offence, we wanted to go on quietly, but the ruffians barred the way, brandishing their weapons and yelling " Down with the Swiss! To the devil with all aristocrats!"

As it would have been both ignoble and dangerous to turn back, we kept our ground, and Glutz. who was as brave as a lion, threw back his cloak and laid his hand on his sword.

" Quietly," whispered the sergeant in German. " Twenty to one are long odds : let us see whether they mean mischief before we try fighting.

" You are of the Swiss Guard ?" said the head ragamuffin, coming forward as though he were going to eat us. He had no coat, and his shirt-sleeves were rolled up to the elbows ; on his head was a Phrygian cap, which might easily have been mistaken for a red nightcap, and he carried a firelock and a sabre.

---

* At the beginning of the revolution the nobles stigmatized their opponents as *sans-culottes*, a designation which so delighted " the men of the people " that they adopted it as a title of honor, and it eventually became the name of a party, but did not survive the Terror.

"We are," answered Sternberg, curtly.

"Men who would fire on the people at a tyrant's bidding deserve to die. Would you fire on the people at Louis Capet's bidding?"

"I know nothing of tyrants, but I know my duty, and if my commanding officer ordered me I should fire on my own father."

"Or me?"

"Certainly. For choice I would much rather fire on you than my father, and I am quite ready to do it now" (pointing to his pistols).

On this the others laughed boisterously, and after saying we were brave fellows, who knew no better, bade us go on.

"After you, gentlemen, if you please," said the sergeant, doffing his hat. "We Switzers never turn our backs — on our friends."

The sans-culottes laughed again and marched off, while we stood aside with our backs to the wall.

"Why should we wait?" asked Glutz, innocently.

"Thunder and lightning! Don't you see?" growled Sternberg, in his rough vernacular. "If we let them get behind us we might be brained before we could turn round."

CHAPTER III

MOB LAW

ALL this time, that is to say from October, 1791, when they fled from Paris and were arrested at Varennes, to August, 1792, when they were removed to the Temple, the royal family were under strict surveillance at the Tuileries. The king was continually watched lest he should make a second attempt to quit the kingdom; neither he nor the queen could take the air without being followed by gendarmes, who never let them out of sight, and insulted by the unmannerly crowds who thronged the gardens of the palace, and beset the gates of the Cour Royale.

The king's deposition was openly demanded both in the National Assembly and the streets. On the 20th of June the mob broke into the palace, forced his majesty to put on a cap of liberty, assailed him with scurrilous abuse, and threatened him with death.

After this the downfall of the monarchy was merely a question of time.

In the sense that during these trials the king showed no fear, he may be said to have behaved nobly. On the other hand, he displayed none of the qualities by which causes are won and kingdoms saved. His saintly submission to cruel enemies and adverse fate hastened his doom. The royal martyr turned his cheek to the smiters, and they smote again and yet again.

Meanwhile the Swiss Guards were sent hither and thither, and matters were so arranged by the ministers, or by some sinister influence behind them, that at the times when our services were most needed at Paris we were generally elsewhere.

In the month of July my company was at Courbevoie, which is about a league beyond the bridge of Neuilly.

Though it was not easy to obtain leave, we went into Paris twice. But the declaration of war against Austria and Prussia, and inflammatory speeches by unscrupulous demagogues, had raised popular excitement to fever point, and on the first of these occasions Glutz and myself—who, owing to the heat of the weather, could not well wear our cloaks— were so ill received that we deemed it prudent to turn back before worse befell us.

We could not have gone in mufti without civilian passes, which we did not possess, nor wearing side-arms and pistols, with which it would have been unwise to dispense.

The second time we managed better. Sergeant Sternberg and Corporal Waldteufel, of our company, had made friends with some National Guards; and one evening, when the latter were not to be on duty, they lent us their uniforms—two for Glutz and myself, two for Sternberg and Waldteufel, who were to be of the party.

We had leave from 6 P.M. until midnight, and took a fiacre as far as the Rue St. Honoré, and after supping at a café in the Rue du Luxembourg began our walk, a walk which was marked by a startling adventure—an adventure which, judged by its consequences, proved to be one of the most momentous incidents of an eventful life.

Though France just then was like a seething volcano, though she was in the throes of a revolution, threatened by civil war and foreign invasion, Paris, her heart and brain, seemed as gay and careless as ever. The theatres were open, the cafés full, the shops doing a roaring trade, the boulevards and public gardens thronged with pleasure-seeking crowds. Nobody either questioned or noticed us, for though the citizen soldiers of the National Guard were less popular with the masses than the sans-culottes, they were respected.

We strolled on until we reached a part of the town where we met few people of fashion, a quarter of narrow streets, poor dwellings, and sombre walls, pierced with blind alleys and wide gateways, leading into warehouses and workshops.

Here and there was a lamp hanging from a rope which stretched across the street, and could be raised or lowered by means of pulleys attached to the walls. But when there was a moon, and on short summer nights, these lamps were not lighted.

By this time the sky had become overcast with clouds and it was almost dark, though we could still see some little distance ahead and had no difficulty in finding our way.

" Hadn't we better be making towards Courbevoie ?" said Glutz. " Time is getting on, and it looks as though it would rain, and for my part I don't find these dark and dirty old streets particularly amusing. *Donner Wetter !* It is raining. I felt a drop on my face."

" And if you did, what then ? You are surely not like a French dandy, more afraid of a shower of rain than a shower of bullets," growled Sternberg in his deep guttural. '' All the same—thunder and lightning, what is that ?"

" Shouts and the trampling of many feet, and the gleam of weapons," said I, peering into the darkness. " Coming this way, too."

" *Was ist los* " (what is up), " I wonder ? Anyhow, we don't want to get mixed up in a row that might make us overstay our leave, and you know how straitly the Herr Hauptman, your respected uncle, charged us to keep out of scrapes. So let us slip into this gateway and wait till these shouters go by."

On this sage advice we promptly acted. The gateway was in deep shade, and formed a coigne of vantage from which we could see without being observed.

2

CHAPTER IV

TO THE LANTERN

THE hubbub grew louder, the din more hideous—men shouting, women screaming, arms clashing.

"To the lantern with him! Down with all aristocrats! Down with Madame Veto!" (the queen)." To the lantern with him!" were the first articulate cries that reached our ears.

" *Gott im Himmel!* They are going to hang somebody," muttered Glutz, pointing to a lamp which was swaying in the wind a few yards from where we stood.

This was likely enough. In those days the populace of Paris were in the habit of utilizing lamp ropes for the removal of obnoxious individuals. Hanging without trial or judgment was the sanction of mob law.

Meanwhile the advance guard of the procession had reached the gateway, and a queer procession it was—dishevelled women, wicked-looking lads, wild-visaged men, and a horde of sans-culottes, hustling along a bareheaded man bound with cords, whose blood-streaked face and torn clothes showed that he had been engaged in a desperate struggle.

The crowd halted under the lamp.

"To the lantern with him!" shrieked the women.

"He would not say, 'Down with Madame Veto!'" Give him a swing in the air!" shouted the men.

"Down with all aristocrats! Stick his head at the end of a pike!" cried the boys.

One of the murderers began to lower the rope.

"Cannot we rescue him?" I asked my companions.

" I am afraid not , they are too many and the sans-culottes are armed. Besides, it would be against orders," said the sergeant, dubiously.

" What are orders when a man's life is at stake ?"

" Let us try, in God's name !" exclaimed Glutz, tightening his belt.

" A rush would do it. The miscreants would be too much surprised to offer an effective resistance, and if there is a way out at the back of this yard, we could escape before they realized what had happened."

This in German.

" There is a way out," answered a voice behind us in the same language.

" Who are you ?" I demanded, turning sharply round.

" A Switzer, like yourselves, and the porter in charge of this warehouse. But there is not a moment to lose. If you rescue that poor gentleman I will help to shut the gate when you return, and show you the way out afterwards."

" Good ! What say you, Sternberg and Waldteufel ?"

" We are with you, Herr von Astor," answered both the men in a breath, drawing their swords.

" Good again ! Now, all together, and remember that our object is to rescue him and get away, and do no more fighting than is absolutely necessary. Charge !"

And then we made our rush. Two of the sans-culottes were already adjusting the rope round their victim's neck. With a mighty kick, Waldteufel, who was a very giant of a fellow, sent one of them sprawling. Glutz dashed his sword-hilt in the other fellow's face, and with a swift cut of mine I severed the prisoner's bonds.

" Back to the gateway !" I said, taking his arm and hurrying him along.

For a minute or two the crowd stood stock-still, as though they had been struck with paralysis, and then, realizing what had happened, made a dash at the gate, which we were in the act of closing.

If they got in our doom was sealed, and, taking aim between the bars, I shot the two leaders down, one after the other. This checked their followers for a few seconds, and while they hesitated we shut and bolted the gates.

"It will take them ten minutes to break in, at the very least," said the friendly Switzer. "This way, gentlemen."

We went off at the *pas gymnastique* (quick march), followed by a dozen musket-shots and the curses of the crowd, neither of which did us any harm.

The warehouse yard was bounded at the bottom by a high wall.

"On the other side of that wall you will be safe—for the present," said the porter. "But I advise you to get out of the neighborhood quickly, there will be a devil of a hue-and-cry after you. Push that cask against the wall, then climb to the top and drop on the other side."

"But what will you do?" I asked, as Sternberg gave the rescued man a leg up.

"I shall pretend that those ruffians have wakened me out of a sound sleep, and ask what the mischief they mean by trying to break the gate in."

"And your name? You have done a brave, generous deed, and I shall never forget you or it."

"Peter Bauer, *aus* Unterwalden. But over with you, Meinherr. Don't you hear them hammering at the gate? And I must put this cask out of sight before they get in."

I grasped the honest fellow's hand, sprang on the cask, and the next moment I was among my companions.

"Are we all here?" I asked.

"All," answered Sternberg.

"Do you know where we are?"

"Not exactly, but—"

"I do," put in the ex-prisoner, "and if you will allow me to lead the way—whither would you like to go?"

"Anywhither, so long as we throw that *canaille*" (riff-raff) "off the scent."

"*Allons!* March!"

After a rapid walk of fifteen minutes through a net-work of gloomy streets and narrow lanes our guide slackened his pace and turned to me.

"Now we are safe," he said. "I defy them to overtake us. We are close to the Latin Quarter, but, as a bareheaded man attracts attention, would you do me the favor to step into that old-clothes shop at the corner and get me a hat? —the shabbier the better."

I went into the shop and bought the gentleman an old hat.

"Thank you," he said in English.

"God bless me! Are you English?" I exclaimed in my native tongue.

"No, I spoke inadvertently. But the fact is I have just returned from London, where I fell into the habit of saying 'Thank you.' May I, without being indiscreet, inquire to whom I am indebted for saving my life at the very moment I had given myself up for lost? It was well and bravely done."

"My name is Astor, and my companions are Messieurs Glutz, Sternberg, and Waldteufel."

"These are German names; you speak German and English and yet wear the uniform of the National Guard."

"We are of the Swiss Guard, monsieur," I said, coldly, for I was getting tired of being asked everything and told nothing.

"I am glad to hear it, and, now I know you to be as loyal as you are chivalrous and brave, I shall deal as frankly with you as you have dealt with me—which means that I place in your hands the life you have so nobly saved. I used to be the Vicomte de Lancy; at present I call myself by my family name of Boulanger" (Baker), "which is plebeian enough for a member of the Jacobin Club. I am a loyal servant of the king and queen, whose release from their gilded prison I would give my life to effect. This night I was in the Faubourg St. Jacques on business—political business—and having occasion to call at a cabaret frequented by workmen, I had the ill-luck to be recognized and denounced by a sans-culotte who had once been my coachman. I succeeded in getting away, but was followed, and after a hot chase fell into the toils. My captors offered to let me go if I would shout 'Down with Madame Veto!' and join in singing the 'Carmagnole.' But this I could not do, even to obtain my liberty. Then two proposals were made—one to take me to the nearest police-station, the other to hang me at the nearest *lanterne*. The assassins carried the day, and were only prevented from carrying out their design by your courage and address, for which, gentlemen of the Swiss Guard, I tender you my warmest thanks."

And the Vicomte de Lancy doffed his hat and made us a courtly bow. He was somewhat below middle height and slightly built, and, as well as I could make out in the moonless gloom, had regular features, a fair skin, and brown curly hair. As touching his age, he seemed to be about thirty, although by daylight he would probably look younger. Before we parted he took me aside.

"A word in your ear," he whispered. "Though I am compelled to keep in the shade, under pain of losing my head or taking an air bath, I know something of what is going on. Not all who bow the knee to Baal worship him in their hearts. You understand. Well, I have information —from a sure source—that the chiefs of the Jacobin Club and the commune of Paris have resolved to consummate the destruction of the monarchy, proclaim the republic, and lodge their majesties and the royal family in a fortress or a dungeon. The attempt is to be made within a month, perhaps sooner. The Tuileries will be attacked by an armed force, consisting of sans-culottes and Marseillais, under the command of Santerre. Should the Swiss Guard remain stanch and fire on the people they are to be destroyed to the last man—if the insurrection succeeds. But if proper measures be taken for the defence of the palace, and the National Guard, the gendarmerie, and yourselves be true, the insurgents will be defeated and the kingdom saved."

"We, at least, shall be true — on that you may stake your existence; and so, I think, will the others," I answered.

"Good! I am glad to hear you say so. And now, dear friends, farewell — this night has made us friends, has it not? We may meet again, but whether we do or not I shall never forget that I am your debtor for life."

And then we shook hands and the *ci-devant* vicomte went his way and we went ours, *en fiacre*, and passed the sentry on guard at Courbevoie barracks as the clocks went twelve.

CHAPTER V

A FORLORN HOPE

On the following morning I told my uncle, strictly as my uncle, of our adventure of the previous night, as also what I had heard from the gentleman who called himself Boulanger. I thought it right that my uncle should be informed of this, and I could not tell him a part without telling him the whole.

"It is well this has not come before me officially, or I should have to take notice of it in a way you might not find agreeable," he said, with a grim smile. "You should not have disguised yourselves as National Guards, and you had no business to meddle with those sans-culottes."

"Wouldn't you meddle, uncle, if you saw a poor devil on the point of being hanged, the rope actually round his neck—wouldn't you make an attempt to save him?"

"A man in his individual capacity may, of course, if he thinks fit, risk his life to save that of another. But you belong to the regiment, and have no right to compromise it even to save a dozen lives; and if you had failed in your attempt and fallen into the hands of those cutthroats the regiment would have been seriously compromised. The Jacobins would have demanded your heads, possibly the disbanding of the regiment. They have audacity enough for anything, those fellows. I hope the National Guards whose clothes you borrowed will keep their own counsel, else there may be trouble even yet."

"I am sure they will, for their own sakes," quoth I, and then by way of changing the subject inquired what my uncle thought of the information I had received from M. Boulanger.

"I dare say the gentleman is right," was the answer. "I have heard similar rumors from other quarters, though none so definite as this. It is no news that the Jacobins and sans-culottes hate the regiment. They have done that for a long time, and no wonder! We are the only impediment to the accomplishment of their designs."

"You forget the National Guard and the gendarmerie."

"The National Guard are merely a loosely disciplined local militia, commanded by office-clerks and shopkeepers; they would almost certainly refuse to fire on the people, as it is the fashion to call the rabble, even in defence of the Constitution, and as the old soldiers composing the gendarmerie have mutinied once they may mutiny again. They elect their own officers, too, and men who elect their own officers cannot be trusted to obey them. The outlook is not encouraging, either for the king or ourselves. The regiment cannot survive the monarchy. They must stand or fall together. . . . If I could have foreseen these things, Fritz, I should not have let you join the regiment. But being a volunteer you can resign without dishonor. Had you not better do so? and I will ask your father, as a favor to me, to buy you a commission in the British army."

"What! leave you and the regiment because danger threatens! Never while I live!" I exclaimed, indignantly.

My uncle smiled approvingly. The regiment was his pride and delight. What wife and children and home are to other men, the regiment was to him. He esteemed its honor and reputation more than his own life, and was as loyal to it as a faithful lover to an adored mistress. With him it was "the regiment" *par excellence*. Only occasionally did he speak of it as the Swiss Guard.

"I like your spirit, lad," he said. "It is that of a true

soldier. Well, let it be so, and I am sure that whatever happens you will do your duty." And then he added, lowering his voice, " Did the king possess the spirit of a drummer-boy we could save him even yet. If he would summon us to the palace, and let us make a clean sweep of the riff-raff who keep him a prisoner in his own palace, and disperse at the point of the bayonet the first mob of howling sans-culottes that appears in the Place du Carrousel, we should hear no more of demands for his dethronement, and plots to destroy the monarchy and set up a republic. But it is no use talking. Louis XVI. has not the spirit of a brooding hen, much less of a drummer-boy, and as likely as not will yield without a struggle."

" And then ?"

" Thunder and lightning ! The deluge, the disbanding of the regiment, the reign of the rabble and the ruin of France."

This was the first time my uncle had spoken to me so freely of politics, and he straitly enjoined me to make no mention of our conversation to any of my comrades, an injunction which I need hardly say that I carefully observed.

The next day he went to the War Office, and on his return informed me, to my great delight, that I was to be promoted to a vacant ensigncy, of course in the regiment, and that I should be gazetted in the course of a few days.

Another piece of information which he brought was less satisfactory. It was contained in a newspaper called *The People's Friend*, and related to our rescue of Mr. Boulanger. But the account it gave of the occurrence was so grotesquely exaggerated that had the affair been less serious I should have been highly amused. It was headed " Rescue of a Prisoner by Aristocrats and Prussians disguised as National Guards," and told how several patriots, having recognized in the Faubourg St. Jacques the *ci-devant* Vicomte de Lancy, counter-revolutionist, returned emigrant, and emis-

sary of Coburg and Pitt, they very properly arrested him,
and were conveying him to a police-station when they were
suddenly set upon by a hundred men in the uniform of the
National Guard. After a terrible conflict, in which at least
ten of the aggressors were killed or badly wounded, and
four of the patriots sorely hurt, the prisoner was rescued
and the aristocrats got clean away. As several of the latter
had been heard to utter exclamations in German, there would
be no doubt that some of them, at least, were Prussians.

It was added that the police were investigating the affair,
and would spare no efforts to ascertain by whose connivance
they had been enabled to enter Paris, and to clothe themselves in the uniforms of the National Guard.

"I am glad the account is so grossly exaggerated. It
will render discovery all the more difficult, and I should be
very sorry for the regiment to be compromised," observed
my uncle. "If those men of the National Guard whose
uniforms you borrowed were to blab—"

"What would happen?" I asked.

"I am afraid you and Sternberg and the others would
happen to lose your heads, and the king would be requested
perhaps required, to disband the regiment. It would have
been better to let the ex-vicomte hang."

Captain von Astor seemed so much put out that I deemed
it inexpedient to say that I did not agree with him. And
it was well I did not, for the catastrophe which he appre-
hended very nearly came to pass. Either our friends of the
National Guard were not quite so discreet as they ought to
have been, or by a sufficiently easy process of deduction the
police got on the right track. The story of a hundred
Prussians and aristocrats rescuing a prisoner and then utterly disappearing was too absurd for belief. They could
neither have got into Paris nor have obtained a hundred uniforms without the police being informed, and the latter had

doubtless convinced themselves by independent inquiry that the number was ridiculously overstated. Then, the only troops in or about Paris who spoke German were the Swiss Guard, and though their uniform was very different from the uniform of the National Guard, they might easily be confounded at night by men who were too much surprised to observe accurately.

Be that as it may, we were suspected, and a few days after the rescue Major Bachmann, the acting commander of the regiment, was informed of the fact and requested to aid in the discovery of the culprits.

The old soldier answered bluntly that the only aid he could render was to parade the regiment, and so afford the gentlemen of the police and their witnesses an opportunity of identifying the supposed offenders.

The offer was accepted, and at a time agreed upon half a dozen gendarmes and twice as many villanous-looking sans-culottes, with their sabres by their sides and wearing Phrygian caps and carmagnoles (blouses with tricolored sashes) appeared in the barrack-yard, and the regiment was paraded for their inspection.

I was on tenter-hooks. So were Glutz, Sternberg, and Waldteufel. For, though it was hardly conceivable that we should be identified, it was clearly on the cards that the scoundrels might pick one of us out by pure chance, and as in that case the picked man would have to give an account of his movements on the night in question, detection would be inevitable.

But fortune did not serve us so ill. The sans-culottes (who were now ready to swear that the rescuers wore the uniform of the Swiss Guard) pitched on men who, as was proved by the evidence of the non-commissioned officer on duty at the time, had answered to their names at roll-call and never left the barracks afterwards.

Our adversaries retired discomfited, yet unconvinced. But the story, as told by the patriots and police, got wind, and, I fear, did much to envenom the feeling against us which bore such terrible fruit later on.

July passed, and August—the fatal August of 1792—began amid sinister rumors and evil omens. The secret imparted to me by M. Boulanger had become a matter of common knowledge. The preparations for the rising were too extensive to be concealed, and the Jacobin leaders made no attempt to conceal them. Within a few days the Tuileries was to be attacked by a force composed of sans-culottes, Marseillais, the armed patriots of the sections, and as many of the National Guard as could be persuaded to take part in the insurrection.

The authorities, on their part, made as though they meant to defend the palace and protect the king, but the only force at their disposal were the Swiss Guard and the National Guard, whose fidelity was doubtful. Moreover, the government did all in their power, short of openly siding with the insurgents, to aid and encourage them. On the 4th of August we were warned to hold ourselves in readiness to march into Paris, and the same night the regimental colors were buried in the barrack cellar in order that, whatever happened, they should not fall into the hands of the rebels.

On the following day the strength of the regiment was weakened by three hundred men, sent into Normandy, as was given out, to assist in the collection of taxes. In the meanwhile we had been deprived of our field-guns, and the reiterated requests of the colonel for further supplies of small-arms ammunition were peremptorily refused.

At ten o'clock on the night of August 8th we received orders to be at the Tuileries at three on the following morning, and two hours later we set out in full marching order, but with only thirty rounds of ball cartridge per man.

It was not a gay march. Forlorn hopes seldom are gay, and we were the forlorn hope of the monarchy. We had none of the elation which men feel who fight for hearth and home and the altars of their sires. We were going to fight against terrible odds for a doomed monarch and a lost cause. Our animating motives were soldierly honor and loyalty to the regiment; only a sense of duty held us together. The officers had been deprived of the power to enforce discipline. The men knew that they would be received with open arms by the patriots and rewarded by their chiefs. Yet I saw no sign of faltering; not a valid man was absent at roll-call; not a man fell out of the ranks as we marched through the silent city over which hovered the angel of death.

Few of these sturdy Switzers, worthy descendants of the heroes of Morgarten and Morat, were ever again to see the smoke of their villages or hear the yodling of the herdsmen in their native mountains.

CHAPTER VI

FOR HONOR

THE château of the Tuileries was a great and splendid palace, forming, with its dependencies, an irregular quadrangle. The main building, which stood at right angles to the river Seine, had two fronts, one looking towards the gardens, the other towards the Place Carrousel, now a vast open square, at that time bordered by mean houses and tortuous streets.

On this side of the palace were three courts, known respectively as the royal, the princes', and the Swiss, so called because it contained the lodgings of the Swiss Body Guard.

The courts were separated from each other by high walls, and from the Place Carrousel by a similar barrier, lodge-gates, and guard-houses.

Beyond the gardens was the Place Louis XV., afterwards Revolution Place, now Concord Place. Farther still were the Champs Elysées (Elysian Fields), a large and beautiful park, planted with trees and shrubs, interspersed with shady walks and picturesque villas set in fair gardens.

The north side of the gardens was lined with trees and terraces, and between them and the Rue St. Honoré were many buildings, among them the military riding-school, which had been converted into a chamber for the National Assembly.

These particulars are necessary for a right comprehension of what follows.

The 9th of August was a day of preparation for the combat which apparently had now become inevitable, although. according to report, the king's ministers were advising him to renounce all idea of resistance and to take refuge with his family in the National Assembly.

But to this course, which would have been a virtual abdication, the queen was strongly opposed, saying that, for her part, she would rather be nailed to the walls than leave the palace. The supreme command of the defence was vested in General Mandat, a brave and capable officer, and if his plans had not been thwarted by treachery and himself basely betrayed, the main body of the insurgents would never have reached the precincts of the palace.

The regiment, numbering some eight hundred men, under the command of Colonel Maillardoz and Majors Bachmann and Salis, was divided into detachments, which were placed in the three courts and the vestibule of the palace. The main body, that to which I belonged, was posted in the royal court.

During the evening we were joined by two thousand National Guards, who brought with them five field-pieces. Most of these men, as also a detachment of gendarmes, were stationed on the garden side of the palace, and the guns were unlimbered in the Cour Royale.

At twelve o'clock the calm of a beautiful summer night was broken by the ringing of alarm-bells all over Paris, succeeded after a short interval by the beating of the *générale* and the *rappel;* the former calling the insurgents to arms, the latter summoning the National Guard to defend the king and the Constitution.

The insurrection had begun, and it remained to be seen whether the measures taken by General Mandat to prevent the threatened attack on the Tuileries, by intercepting the rebels at the bridges and on the quays, would be successful.

Most of the officers passed the night in the royal apartments; the men bivouacked in the courts.

At four o'clock in the morning General Mandat received an order to proceed without delay to the City-hall, to take the final instructions of the municipality, who controlled, in the last resort, the movements of the National Guard. After some hesitation he went, accompanied by his son and an aide-de-camp. Within an hour the aide-de-camp returned in hot haste, and reported that General Mandat had been murdered on the steps of the City-hall, and that the patriots were parading his head at the end of a pike. He reported further that the artillery placed by the general's orders on the quays and bridges had been withdrawn, and that the gunners had joined the rebels.

This ominous news was communicated only to the officers, who, fearing that it might discourage the regiment and encourage our allies of the National Guard to follow the example of their mutinous comrades, kept it to themselves.

At six o'clock the king, accompanied by some of his courtiers, two of his ministers, and Colonel Maillardoz, came into the Cour Royale to inspect the troops. He wore a violet velvet coat, the Bourbon badge of mourning. His eyes were bloodshot and the lids dark and swollen, as though he had passed a sleepless night. His countenance was composed, yet there was an occasional nervous twitching about the corners of his mouth which bespoke anxiety and apprehension, and his pathetic, almost helpless smile as the regiment presented arms and shouted " Live the king !" went to our hearts.

But the cannoneers of the National Guard kept a gloomy silence, and when his majesty passed to the garden side of the palace their comrades greeted him with cries of " Live the nation !" and as he returned from his inspection he was followed by shouts of " Live the sans-culottes ! Down with the veto ! Down with the king ! Down with the queen."

3

These were the troops who had come to take part with us in the defence of the château!

At seven o'clock the word went round that Louis XVI. had decided, despite the queen's opposition, to withdraw with his family to the Assembly. We could hardly believe it, but when one hundred and fifty men of the regiment and three hundred grenadiers of the National Guard were told off as his escort doubt was no longer possible. The queen, her two children, and several ladies of the court went with him, also Baron von Erlach, who commanded the detachment, Colonel Maillardoz, and the two majors.

When they were gone Captain von Durler, who had been left in command of the regiment, now reduced to six hundred and fifty men, invited my uncle and myself and several other officers to breakfast with him in one of the royal apartments, whence, as it overlooked the Cour Royale and the Place Carrousel, we could see what went on there.

"This beats everything. What next, I wonder?" said my uncle, as we took our seats at the table.

Though the wit of the remark was not very obvious, it set the table in a roar. But it was rather the occasion than the remark that was the cause of our mirth. We were laughing at the fiasco which had just taken place, and to relieve our feelings after the suspense and excitement of the night.

"Well," observed somebody, "it is rather droll to think that we came here expecting to die in defence of his sacred majesty, and make the Tuileries the Thermopylæ of the monarchy."

"His sacred majesty has run away, and we shall live to fight another day," put in one of the lieutenants. "When do we return to Courbevoie? What are your orders, Captain von Durler?"

"To remain where we are until further orders, and not let ourselves be forced."

"So! The king is coming back, then?"

"He will never come back," said my uncle, gravely. "His departure is a virtual abdication. The king who yields to the menaces of the mob without striking a blow for his crown is a king no longer. There is nothing more for us to do."

"Except to obey orders," observed Captain von Durler.

"Of course. Except to obey orders. That goes without saying."

"We shall have no fighting, then?" I said in a tone which I dare say savored somewhat of discontent; for though I knew, theoretically, that fighting is a terrible thing which it is always well to avoid when you can do so with honor, I could not help feeling a little disappointed that we were not to have a brush with the sans-culottes, whom I cordially hated and would have liked to see well punished.

"I can guess your thoughts, Fritz," returned my uncle, dryly. "Like all young soldiers you want to be doing. But what is the use of wasting the lives of our brave fellows in a cause which does not concern them, and for a king who has deserted them?"

"But if the insurgents try to force us?"

"In that case we must resist. Military honor forbids us either to run away or lay down our arms. But the insurgents won't attempt to force us. Why should they? We are not the government. The king and his ministers are at the National Assembly, let them go there. Let them—"

Here my uncle's words were drowned by a great uproar—shouts, yells, words of command, the beating of drums. We all ran to the balcony overlooking the Carrousel and the courts. The Place was thronged with a mob of Marseillais, sans-culottes, National Guard, men of the people, armed and unarmed, and some women. They were demanding admission into the Cour Royale; several had got astride of the wall.

"My orders are to avoid a combat," said Captain von Durler. "I shall withdraw the regiment into the château. To your posts, gentlemen!"

We all followed him down-stairs, and in a few minutes we had our men and a platoon of faithful National Guards in the palace; some were posted in the vestibule, others on the grand staircase and the stairs leading to the chapel, the remainder at the windows of the apartments on the first floor.

Meanwhile, somebody had opened the gate of the Cour Royale, and the rebels poured in, fraternizing with the gunners of the National Guard. A number of the sans-culottes carried their caps on the point of their pikes and bayonets in token of amity, shouting "Long live the Swiss!" These, coming up to the palace, entered the vestibule and called on the regiment to join them "in the name of unity and fraternity." To prevent the ruffians from mounting the staircase, we barricaded it with a beam of wood.

By this time the advance guard of Santerre's army, which numbered some thirty thousand citizen-soldiers, was marching into the Carrousel in columns of companies and close order, and presently several of their officers pushed their way into the vestibule, and asked us to surrender to the nation.

One of these gentlemen, a certain Westermann, from Elsass, addressing the soldiers in German, exhorted them to lay down their arms and depart in peace, and accused the officers of desiring to make the regiment resist for the gratification of their own vanity.

Sergeant Sternberg gave him his answer.

"We are Swiss," said he, "and Switzers only lay down

their arms with their lives. The proposal is an insult. If you want the regiment to march away or disband—and we desire nothing better—let it be done legally. But without orders we shall neither quit our post nor lay down our arms."

Captain von Durler had already spoken in the same sense.

"We don't want to hurt you," he said. "All we want to do is to be let alone and obey our orders, which are to remain here and not allow ourselves to be forced. We would rather be your friends than your enemies; but if you attack us we shall resist to the last extremity."

Finding that we were not to be seduced from our duty the patriots changed entreaties for threats, saying that it was ridiculous to suppose that a few hundred Switzers could resist thirty thousand patriots in arms, and that if we did not surrender they would give us no quarter. They howled, yelled, cursed, and brandished their weapons like people possessed. An officer of Santerre's seized our leader's arm, and threatened him with his sabre.

"If he strikes, shoot him," said Captain von Durler to a soldier near him, whereupon the officer lowered his sword and loosed his hold.

Another lunged at the captain with his pike. Von Durler warded off the stroke with his hand, for even yet he had not drawn his sword, fearing, probably, that the action would be construed as a signal for battle. But the patriots, ascribing our patience to fear, redoubled their insults, calling us hired assassins, satellites of the tyrant, and shouting "Down with the Swiss!" Some dashed up to the barricade and shook their fists in our faces. At length, when the uproar was at its height and it seemed as though the howling maniacs were going to storm the barricade, one of them discharged a pistol.

The effect was startling. Our men brought their pieces to the present. One of the sergeants, thinking we were going to be rushed, shouted "Fire!" The muskets went off, and with a wild yell the sans-culottes bolted from the building, tumbling over each other in their eagerness to escape. The people in the upper rooms gave them a volley from the windows, and at the same time Santerre opened fire from the Carrousel and the Cour Royale, both with small-arms and artillery, and the action became general.

One of the first to fall on our side was the lieutenant who less than an hour before had said we should live to fight another day.

Seeing that unless the rebel artillery were silenced our position would soon become untenable, Captain von Durler ordered a charge, and himself led the way. The struggle for the guns was short and decisive. It was a confused hurly-burly, a fierce hand-to-hand fight; and so great was my excitement, so dense and thick the smoke, that I can recall little of what happened to my comrades, and not much of what happened to myself.

A big Marseillais came near spitting me with his pike, but I got within his guard and ran him through the throat. Several of our men were killed among the guns. Waldteufel clubbed his musket, and with a single sweep of it floored three sans-culottes. We cleared the Cour Royale in two minutes, then charged through the gate and captured the artillery in the Carrousel. But as we could not carry the guns away, the men broke several ramrods in pieces and used them as spikes. And then, as we were only two hundred and the rebels numbered thousands, we made our way back, unpursued by the enemy, but suffering much from the fire of two guns in a garden opposite the Swiss Court, which ploughed up our ranks with grape-shot and laid many a poor fellow low.

At this juncture a number of Marseillais, who had been lurking about the palace, seeing that we were running short of ammunition, issued from their hiding-places and attacked us fiercely. These we charged and dispersed at the point of the bayonet, and once more cleared the main court, which by this time was covered with dead and wounded men, and enveloped in so thick a cloud of smoke that we could scarcely see.

As we re-entered the vestibule of the palace, still unpursued, M. d'Hervilly (an officer of the old army, who was afterwards killed at Quiberon) came running bareheaded and breathless. " His majesty wants you at the Assembly," he gasped. " You are to go thither immediately."

" Good !" said Von Durler, and at once gave orders for the men to be rallied for the retreat, and bade me run upstairs, inform my uncle, who commanded there, of the new order, and tell him to descend into the vestibule, and form his people in column for the march across the garden.

The arrangements for the retreat were made completely, deliberately, and without confusion. Since we had driven out the Marseillais, not an insurgent had dared to show himself in the Cour Royale. Two of the captured guns, which had not been discharged, were wheeled into the vestibule, pointed towards the main gate, and placed in charge of two grenadiers, who volunteered to remain behind and use them against any of Santerre's men who should venture into the court before we were clear of the building. It has been said since that the "patriots," as they called themselves (I call them cowardly cutthroats), captured the Tuileries. It is not true. To take possession of an unoccupied house is not to capture it. We had repulsed the attack at every point, and our sole reason for withdrawal was the king's order. If Louis XVI. had remained with us, instead of going to the Assembly and taking with him three hundred good soldiers (most of whom were afterwards basely murdered), the French monarchy had not fallen on that fatal day, neither would his majesty have had to lay his head on the block six months later.

Captain von Durler's column marched first, and no sooner were they in the grounds than we of the rear-guard, who were waiting a few minutes in order that none might be left behind, heard a great shouting, followed on the instant by the rattle of musketry.

"My God! What on earth can that be?" I cried in amaze.

"It is what I feared," said my uncle. "Those treacherous scoundrels in the garden terraces who were to have aided us in the defence are attacking Von Durler. We have been fighting for honor, men" (raising his voice); "now we shall have to fight for our lives. March!"

CHAPTER VII

WHEN we debouched into the garden, drums beating and flags flying, the first column was some two or three hundred yards ahead of us, and the National Guard who lined the terraces and buildings to our right were mowing them down with discharges of musketry, to which our men, having exhausted their slender store of ammunition, were unable to reply. Nevertheless they kept their ranks and marched as steadily as if they were on parade.

When the rear-guard emerged from the palace they were received in like manner. We were also attacked from behind by some of the bolder spirits of Santerre's army, who had stolen across the Cour Royale under cover of the smoke, and gained the gardens by the vestibule of the Tuileries.

Like the first column, and for the same reason, we could not reply. Men fell out every minute, and no sooner was a man down than the wolfish sans-culottes finished him with their pikes, stripped him, and cut off his head. The line of retreat was strewn with naked, decapitated bodies.

When Von Durler's column reached the first fountain in the great alley it wheeled to the right *en route* for the National Assembly, to which access was gained by descending a staircase and crossing a road. But the first column was still nearly three hundred, the second nearly two hundred strong, and as it would have taken a long time for so many to defile through a narrow opening, and we should be exposed all the while to a hot fire, our assailants being heavily massed in that quarter, we continued our course down the

great alley, with the intention of passing into the Place Louis
XV., over the swinging bridge at the bottom of the garden,
whence we might reach the Assembly by the Rue St. Honoré, or, if the way thither were barred, return to Courbevoie.

We were presently out of the bullet storm from the terraces, and the sans-culottes were too busily occupied with
despoiling our dead comrades to give us much trouble.

The brave fellows in the ranks, who had been greatly
discouraged by having to retreat and being unable to fight,
responded to the " *Vorwärts !*" of their officers by giving a
cheer and breaking into a run. We hoped that our ordeal
was nearly over, but all felt that the sooner we were out of
the Tuileries gardens the better.

We were still going at the double-quick, and had nearly
reached the great octagon basin at the end of the great
alley when the bugler sounded a halt.

The men stopped and stood at ease.

"The swinging bridge is occupied in force," said Captain
von Astor. "Go on and reconnoitre, Fritz, you and Sergeant Sternberg. Keep as much in cover as you can."

The command was promptly obeyed. We crept from tree
to tree and from bush to bush, yet rapidly withal, until we
reached a point where, in order to reconnoitre effectually,
we had to show ourselves in the open." The occupiers of
the bridge and its approaches were National Guards, ranged
en bataille. They fired on us at sight.

This was enough. We hurried back to the main body and
reported what we had seen. I estimated the strength of the
enemy in sight at three to four hundred.

"No matter how many there are," said my uncle. " We
must either cut our way through them, or stop here to be
made targets of first and have our heads cut off afterwards.
We are between two fires."

It was true ; the sans-culottes in our rear were creeping

forward again and beginning to shoot at us from behind the chestnut-trees.

A score or so of our fellows had still a cartridge, some two cartridges, apiece, taken from the pouches of their dead comrades and fallen foes.

These were placed in front, with instructions to reserve their fire until they could see the whites of the Frenchmen's eyes, and after delivering it to charge.

I took this opportunity to tear from the staff the flag I had been carrying and fasten it round my body.

Captain von Astor's plan was to draw the enemy's fire, which he reckoned they would deliver as soon as we came within range; then, after pausing an instant, to let the first line give them a volley in return, advance at the *pas de charge*, and force the bridge at the point of the bayonet before the rebels had time to reload their pieces.

The plan was carried out to the letter. When my uncle waved his sword and cried " *Vorwärts, meine Kinder !*" (Forward, my children), the men marched on with their muskets at the trail.

The National Guard opened fire as we had expected, but as we were in open order and the trees shielding us somewhat, it was less destructive than it might have been. A minute afterwards the first line delivered their volley, and then, with a wild cheer, closed up and made for the bridge.

It was our last chance, and a far more forlorn hope than the fight for the guns in the Cour Royale. There were enemies in front of us, enemies behind us, enemies to the right of us, enemies to the left of us, all well supplied with ammunition, while we had none.

We went straight for the bridge, and with mien so resolute that I believe the people immediately opposed to us would have given way if they could; but those in the rear refusing to budge, the files in front were forced to fight, and they fought as desperately as men do when they are at bay.

Acting on a hint from one of my comrades, I emptied my pistols before using my sword, and was so fortunate as to drop an enemy to each shot. The next moment the press became so great that I could not draw my sword. While I was thus practically disarmed, a little Frenchman made a thrust at me with his bayonet, and though I wriggled to one side, it pierced the fleshy part of my thigh. Then it was my turn. Laying my hands on his shoulders and squeezing his windpipe with my thumbs I pushed him down under the feet of the combatants, and there he lay, unable to rise. Foes and friends were wedged together in a seemingly inextricable mass, each party trying to thrust the other back by main force, until Waldteufel, who towered a full foot above the Frenchmen's heads, again clubbed his musket, and after beating them to the ground, walked on over their prostrate bodies.

For us who followed him the way was now comparatively clear, and ten minutes after the first onset we were in the Place Louis XV., but with terrible gaps in our ranks. While the head of the column was forcing the bridge, those in the rear were waging an unequal contest with the main body of the National Guard, who poured volley after volley into them, and, as no quarter was given, not one of ours lived to tell the tale.

But it soon became apparent that we who survived had escaped from one danger only to fall into another. At the north side of the great square and hard by the Rue Royale was a body of mounted gendarmes, whose duty it was, as guardians of the peace, to join their strength to ours and render us all the aid in their power. We formed and marched in their direction, for that way lay the Rue St.

Honoré, which we should have to traverse in order to reach the Assembly.

At the same time they marched towards us, as we hoped with friendly intent, but when the foremost of them began to unsling their carbines and shout, " Live the nation !" we knew what to expect.

"Left wheel ! Quick march ! To the statue !" ordered my uncle.

Then turning to me (the only officer of the rear-guard besides himself left alive) he added : " Those rascals are going to attack us, and as they have horses and cartridges and we neither, they have us at their mercy. The pedestal of the statue will afford us some little protection, and from that point we must make a dash for the Champs-Elysées, and scatter among the trees. It is our only chance. Are your pistols loaded ?"

" Yes."

" Well, take my advice, and use them only in the last extremity—to save your life or another's. What have you done with the flag ?"

" Torn it in pieces, and thrown the fragments away."

" Good! The traitors may murder us, but they will get no trophies."

Meanwhile the gendarmes were nearing us, yet slowly withal, and some hung back, as though they had not quite made up their minds what to do. This was fortunate, for had they charged resolutely we should have been cut down to a man, being as yet not half-way across the square.

But soon the leaders, throwing hesitation aside, put their horses to the trot, and when they were within range halted and opened fire with their carbines, whereupon Captain von Astor bade our fellows break their ranks, race for the statue, and there rally. Several of them had gone down at the first volley, others were killed or wounded by the way, and my dear lion-hearted uncle fell at the very foot of the statue, shot through the back.

Kneeling down beside him, I raised his head and in-quired whether he was much hurt.

" To the death," he murmured, "to the death. But I die like a soldier, and the regiment—the regiment has done its duty. Save yourselves as best you can—the Champs-Ely-sées—take my pistols. Give my love to your father. Tell him the regiment, the—honor of the regiment—"

These were Captain von Astor's last words. After kiss-ing him I laid his head gently down, and, taking the pistols, gave one to Sternberg, the other to Waldteufel.

Again our assailants held back, either because they were moved by some feeling of compunction or conscience, or, not being sure that we were without ammunition, feared to come to close quarters.

Their hesitation might be our salvation. Not a moment was to be lost.

" To the Champs-Elysees !" I cried, " to the Champs-Elysées ! Hide among the trees, and then every man for himself. Scatter and run for your lives."

The poor fellows needed no second bidding. They went off like a pack of hounds on a burning scent. I waited for a few seconds, making it a point of honor to be the last. To that momentary pause I probably owed my life.

When the gendarmes divined our object they started in hot pursuit, some trying to overtake, others to intercept the fugitives, who made the mistake of going too straight and keeping too much together, a mistake which I avoided by turning in another direction and then doubling.

I had been one of the best sprinters of my time at Giggles-wick, and felt sure that in a short run I could outpace the coarse-bred, overweighted horses ridden by the gendarmerie, and I luckily got a fair start before any of them singled me out for pursuit. But I no sooner set my face towards the Fields than an officer of the corps, who had emerged from the Cours de la Reine, turned his horse in the same direction, with the evident intention of intercepting me. If he had come straight on I might have evaded him by making another double. Instead of that he took a line at right angles to mine, and if we both went on it was inevitable that we should meet at the apex of the triangle. We were nearing each other every second, and, to make matters worse, a band of sans-culottes, coming from the gardens, were after me in full cry.

Turning back or taking another course was therefore out of the question. What should I do? My first idea was to slacken my pace, let my man come up, kill or disable his horse with a pistol-shot, then run on and gain the Fields.

But this was to lose precious time. Moreover, when I had disabled the horse I should still have to deal with the rider, and he was fresh and myself half-blown; after him, with the several other gendarmes who had joined in the chase, to say nothing of the sans-culottes.

Then in my extremity I bethought me of another plan, a plan which though bolder was no more hazardous and promised better results. When my adversary and myself came within a few yards of each other I feigned distress, ran laboriously, stumbled and reeled as though I were quite exhausted and could do no more. On this the gentleman checked his horse and drew a pistol from his holster. But as he was cocking it I whipped mine from my belt and gave him a shot point blank which stopped further operations on his part. Whether he was mortally or only slightly wounded I never knew, for as he lurched forward, dropping his pistol, I caught his bridle with one hand and his leg with the other, threw him out of the saddle, and leaping into his place went off at full gallop, followed by half a dozen gendarmes and the bullets and blasphemies of a hundred howling sans-culottes.

CHAPTER VIII

UP A TREE

My borrowed mount carried me splendidly. My pursuers were nowhere. The distance between us increased at every stride of my horse, and I felt confident that, barring accidents and the unforeseen, I should reach Courbevoie without further trouble.

Unfortunately, as it appeared at the time—fortunately, as it turned out—the unforeseen happened. Just as I was congratulating myself on my good-luck and the way being clear, I saw, turning into it from a side road near the Arc de Triomphe de l'Étoile, a mob of at least two or three hundred people, among whom were several horsemen. In those days it was unsafe even for a quiet citizen to encounter a Paris mob. They might take exception to something in the cut of his clothes, or some peculiarity in his bearing or his face, accuse him of being an aristocrat or a spy, and either hale him to the nearest police-station, or hang him out of hand. On that day of riot and rebellion mobs were likely to be more truculent and blood-thirsty than usual, and my appearance was decidedly against me. I was hatless, black with powder and red with blood, I wore the hated uniform of the Swiss Guard, and behind me were clattering the traitorous gendarmes. If there had been only a score or so in front of me I might have charged through them and taken my chance, but against two or three hundred I should have no chance.

There was nothing for it but to take to the wood, and evade my pursuers by dodging among the trees—if I could.

The moment I had thus decided I wheeled my horse to
the right and put him at one of the two ditches which at
that time bounded the main alley of the Champs-Elysées.
He did the jump gallantly, but as the trees and bushes rendered progress on horseback difficult, I dismounted and
took to my feet, first appropriating the unhorsed officer's
remaining pistol.

But whither should I betake myself?   The gendarmes
and sans-culottes were not far off; the mob I had seen near
the Arc de Triomphe would doubtless join in the chase, and
the hoarse cries, mingled with occasional musket-shots towards the Place Louis XV., showed that some of my comrades had escaped into the Fields and were coming in
my direction, pursued by their ruthless foes.   Moreover, the
Fields were of no great extent, every rod of the ground
would be quested, every thicket explored, and to appear in
any of the contiguous thoroughfares were to court detection,
and detection meant death.

Whither should I betake myself?   At any rate, it would
not do to stand still.   The cutthroats whom I had just
evaded were within earshot—I could hear their shouts; so
I went on, running where running was possible, walking and
creeping where it was not, dodging from bush to bush and
from tree to tree—in short, doing all I could to throw the
sleuth-hounds off the scent.   But their cries, now loud, now
faint, then loud again, were ever in my ears.   They seemed
to come from everywhere, and I twisted and turned like a
hunted hare.

At length I came to a wall, a garden wall.   On the other
side might be safety.   I would get over and throw myself
on the hospitality of the people who lived there, for where
there was a garden there must be a house.   But the wall
was high—ten feet at least—and smooth, offering not a
vestige of foothold.   Still, by a vigorous effort I might reach

the top with my hands, raise myself up, and drop on the other side.

I had come to this conclusion and was about to make the attempt when I spied a door, half hidden by a bush.

If the door were open, or I could push it open!

And then something like a miracle happened. The door was drawn a few inches ajar, and at the opening appeared the startled face of a young girl, an almost angelic face, as it appeared to me at that moment. But the instant she caught sight of me the door went to with a bang, and as I bounded forward the bolts were shot into their sockets and the key was turned in the lock.

"For Heaven's sake, let me in!" I cried. "I am a hunted man. Scores of sans-culottes and gendarmes are at my heels, the wood is beset, and if I am caught I shall be torn to pieces."

"O *mon Dieu!* But who are you?"

"An officer of the Swiss Guard. Nearly all my comrades have been murdered in the gardens and on the Place. The king has left the Tuileries—"

The door opened again.

"Enter! Quick, quick, before they come!" said the young girl, excitedly.

I needed no second bidding; the next moment I was inside, and the door was once more bolted and locked.

The young girl to whom I owed my life (for escape without her help had been wellnigh, if not altogether, impossible) had a face whose fascination and charm it were difficult to exaggerate. Her eyes, shaded with long lashes, were large and dark, her hair and strongly marked eyebrows black as night, her features as clearly cut as those of a Greek cameo, and her complexion was singularly delicate and pure. But what most struck me was her expression, so full of sympathy and pity, yet, considering the circumstances, strangely devoid of fear.

"Oh, you are wounded "' she said, compassionately.

In my excitement I had almost forgotten the bayonet wound in my thigh, and now observed for the first time that my white breeches were stained with blood. I had also got a cut on my head which, albeit slight, had bled freely, and I dare say gave me a grewsome look.

"Not seriously," I answered, "and when I have rested awhile, and the coast is clear and night falls, I shall be quite able to walk to Courbevoie."

"But where shall I hide you meanwhile? The servants are not to be trusted, and if the miscreants should come— and they are coming, don't you hear their shouts?—if they should search the house and find you there it would be terrible for you, terrible for us all, and my mother is an invalid."

"In that case I will go at once."

"No, no, a thousand times no! What do you take me for, monsieur? Do you think a soldier's daughter could refuse an asylum to a wounded officer who has been fighting for the king? And some gentlemen of the Swiss Guard once rendered my Uncle Claude a great service. I expect him here this night, and he will be able to devise something. But the question is what to do now? Where to put you?"

"Is there no out-house?"

"Would you be safe in an out-house if those wretches were to make a search? Stay! I have it! I have it!" clapping her hands with delight. "Charles II. of England escaped from his enemies by hiding in an oak-tree; why should not you escape from yours by hiding in that chestnut-tree? From that bench you can easily reach the lower branches and swing yourself up."

"The very thing!" I exclaimed. "How shall I thank you enough, mademoiselle?"

" By mounting quickly. Don't you hear the shouts? In a few minutes your pursuers will be here. When they are gone I shall let you know. Go, go, not another word!"

Yet another word I spoke, advising that, in the event of the gendarmes demanding admission, they should be admitted without either delay or demur, and invited to satisfy themselves by ocular demonstration that their suspicions were baseless.

And then I climbed the tree, which was close at hand, a splendid chestnut laden with leaves, where I was so well hidden as to be invisible to the sharpest of eyes. Nevertheless as red is a conspicuous color, I took the precaution to doff my scarlet coat and roll it up with the lining outward.

After effacing with her pocket-handkerchief the marks left by my feet on the bench, a piece of thoughtfulness which I greatly admired, the young lady disappeared.

I had found a hiding-place none too soon. The gendarmes and, as I gathered from the noise they made, a contingent of sans-culottes, were so near that I could hear their exclamations and distinguish their words.

" He cannot be far off," said one.

" It is not five minutes since I saw him," observed another.

" It is impossible for him to escape; this side of the Champs-Elysées is surrounded, and if he shows himself outside he will be knocked on the head," added a third.

" A thousand thunders! Behold a garden wall! Can he have got over it?"

" Out of the question; it is too high."

" But here is a door, and *sacré nom de Dieu*, here is a foot-mark, his footmark!"

" Whose house is it? Run to the front door—this is locked — some of you, and demand admission, while we watch here; surround the garden and guard every exit. We will have him yet, the cursed Swiss! They say he killed twenty patriots with his own hand, and I am afraid he has done for our brigadier."

And then the talk ceased or became inaudible, but presently there was an irruption into the garden from the front. Gendarmes and sans-culottes, of whom I caught occasional glimpses, were all over the place, searching every thicket and looking behind every shrub and bush.

Though I knew I was invisible, I could not help feeling nervous, and when they passed under the chestnut-tree I drew myself into as small a compass as possible and kept as still as a mouse, for the slightest movement would have betrayed me.

When the miscreants failed to find me they vented their disappointment in curses both loud and deep.

"He must be here. Where can he be else?" said one who appeared to be in authority.

"Hiding outside, perhaps. Anyhow, I'll take my oath he isn't here."

"We have sought everywhere, and questioned the servants; and it is easy to see from their manner that they have seen naught of him."

"But how about the footmarks?"

"How do you know they are the footmarks of this Swiss? And footmarks outside do not prove either that he got over the wall or came in at the door. No, my friend, we are on a wrong scent, and the sooner we acknowledge the fact and act on it the better."

After a brief conference, held under the chestnut-tree, it was decided to continue the quest in the Champs-Elysées and post a sentry at every corner of the garden, with orders to keep a sharp lookout, and if I appeared to shoot me at sight.

A pleasant prospect this! It was evident that I could not get away before dark, which meant that I should have to remain where I was for at least eight or nine hours. But that was better than being shot at sight or hanged *à la lanterne*, and when I thought how many of my poor comrades had been maimed or killed on that fatal day I esteemed myself highly fortunate, and with all my heart thanked God for his goodness in delivering me from so many dangers.

And then, so great was my exhaustion, so soothing the gentle breeze which murmured among the leaves, that despite my constrained position, the smarting of my wounds, and the bitterness of my thoughts, I fell into a doze, from which I was awakened by nearly falling from my perch. At the same time I heard a light footstep in the garden, and, looking down, spied my hostess coming leisurely towards the tree. In one hand she carried what appeared to be a large basket, in the other, a slender cane. Now and then she stopped for a moment and looked round, and after, as might appear, having satisfied herself that there were no interlopers in the garden or peeping over the wall, she sat down on the bench, and taking a piece of work out of the basket, began to knit or embroider—in seeming forgetfulness that the fugitive whom she had saved was astride a branch a few feet above her head.

CHAPTER IX

ANGÉLIQUE

AFTER the knitting had gone on for a few minutes, my fair neighbor raised her head and whispered a word which I failed to hear. Then she raised her voice a little, and by listening intently I made out that the word was "Monsieur."

"Yes, mademoiselle," I answered, descending a branch or two, and also whispering.

"Speak low, please. I have sharp ears. They are gone, those wicked people. They were not so bad as they might have been; they contented themselves with searching the garden and the lower rooms; but four are on guard outside, one at each corner of the garden, so we must be very cautious. Are you listening, monsieur?"

"Most attentively, mademoiselle."

"Good! Now listen still more attentively. At the end of this cane, which I am going to give you, is a cord. You must take one end of it in your hand and pull up something which I shall fasten to the other end. Now! Have you got it?"

"Yes."

"Good again! Now, when I say 'Pull,' pull, but gently withal, for I am fastening to the cord a bag which contains half a roast fowl, half a loaf, and half a bottle of Bordeaux."

"O mademoiselle! I thank you a thousand times. How can I repay?"

"By pulling up the bag. Now! Pull!"

I pulled accordingly, and set to work on the contents of
the bag with the appetite of a hungry man, for I had eaten
hardly any breakfast, the exertions and excitement of the
last few hours had tired me out, and I was faint with fatigue and loss of blood.

In little more than ten minutes the wine, the bread, and
the roast fowl were gone, and with them went my weakness
and fatigue. I felt like another man.

"Have you had enough?" asked the young lady as I lowered the bag, into which I had put the empty bottle and
the fragments of my repast.

"Quite, I thank you. And now won't you tell me to
whom I am indebted for all this kindness?"

"My name is Marie Angélique de la Tour; but here in
Paris we call ourselves only Tour, my mother and I. And
you, monsieur?"

"My name is Von Astor, or D'Astor, as we were called in
the regiment, my poor uncle and I. But I think we had
better dispense with the particle for the present."

"You are right. An aristocratic name is dangerous in
these times. You spoke of your poor uncle—I hope no
harm has befallen him."

"My uncle, Captain von Astor, of the regiment, was killed
little more than an hour ago, at the foot of the statue in
the Place Louis XV."

"O *mon Dieu*, how terrible! And my poor father, he
also was killed, though he had fought for France in seven
campaigns and received as many wounds. But your uncle
died for the king; it was a noble death."

"His death did not serve the king, mademoiselle. The
king had already surrendered to the enemy. My uncle
died for honor, and, as you say, it was a noble death."

"May God keep his soul in peace! It is better to die
nobly than to live ignobly. But I must leave you, mon-

sieur. It were imprudent to remain longer. I am afraid you will have to stay where you are until nightfall. I shall make a confidant of Paul Tremblay, my father's old soldier-servant. He is as good as gold, and quite trustworthy. I shall send him to you after a while, perhaps you and he will be able to hit upon a plan. And, as I said before, I expect a visit from my Uncle Claude. He, too, is in danger, and I am always in fear for him. But he is very clever and re-sourceful, and you may count confidently on my help. *Au revoir*, monsieur."

"*Au revoir*, mademoiselle," I returned, and then she gathered up her work, put the bag into her basket, and walked slowly and with pensive mien towards the house, and I was left once more to the companionship of my thoughts.

I had not been in bed for two nights, and fearing that I might again be overcome with sleep and, peradventure, fall out of the tree, I buckled my sword-belt loosely round a stout branch and passed my arm through the loop.

It was a wise precaution, for despite my efforts to keep awake I did fall asleep, dreamed that I was being guillo-tined, and awoke with my neck bending over a bough and my legs dangling in the air. For a few seconds I could not recall where I was nor what had happened.

A man was under the tree, plying a broom. As I opened my eyes he looked up and said in a low, gruff voice :

" Monsieur Astor, are you still there ?"

Evidently the old soldier-servant of whom Mademoiselle de la Tour had spoken. Only from her could he have learned my name.

" I am still here," I answered.

" I called several times, and as you did not answer I be-gan to fear you were gone."

" I was asleep."

"Asleep, when half Paris is thirsting for your blood! I admire your courage, monsieur."

"Half Paris thirsting for my blood! What do you mean?"

"Yours, and the blood of every Swiss guardsman in the city. They are being hunted like mad dogs, the few who survive. The sans-culottes have even killed several Swiss porters. If one has an enemy whom he wishes to destroy it is enough to denounce him as a Swiss."

"That is the talk, I suppose?"

"I am afraid it is the truth, monsieur."

I did not think so. I thought Tremblay was exaggerating, but as nothing was to be gained by arguing the point I changed the subject by inquiring whether the sentinels had been withdrawn.

"I don't know about being withdrawn—those fellows are under no sort of discipline. But they are gone."

"The coast is clear, then?"

"I suppose so," dubiously. "All the same, it would not be safe for monsieur to leave before dark, and even then it would be as much as monsieur's life is worth to wear his uniform."

"Could you lend or sell me some of your clothes?"

"With pleasure. It was what I was going to propose—a blouse and a *pantalon*."

"And an old hat."

"Perfectly, and an old hat. And if you will descend from the tree you can go into my tool-house. It is not precisely a drawing-room, but I think you will find it better than a perch. On the other side, please, and then nobody can see you from the house."

I climbed down with some difficulty, for my legs were stiff and my wound was painful.

"Slip behind the laurels, and then straight on," continued Tremblay.

I limped in the direction indicated, followed by the friendly gardener.

The tool-house, though, as he had observed, not exactly a drawing-room, was a vast improvement on the tree. There was a rough table, also a damaged rustic chair, which, with the help of an empty sack that lay on the floor, could be converted into a comfortable couch.

It was a place one might pass the night in.

From a cupboard in which he kept his seeds Tremblay produced a blouse and a pair of trousers.

"Is there anything else I can get for you?" he asked. "I will bring you a hat presently."

"You are very good. Yes, I should like a pail of water, a towel, soap, and, if possible, something to bind up this wound in my thigh. I don't want it to begin bleeding again."

"I will ask mademoiselle. The maids would wonder what on earth I wanted with a towel and soap, and might ask questions which I should find it hard to answer."

Whereupon the old soldier hurried off, and after a short absence returned with soap, towel, bandages, lint, plaster, a pair of scissors, and a hat.

"Mademoiselle thinks of everything," he said, admiringly. "My faith, she has got an old head on young shoulders, and not without need, for she has all the care."

"But her mother?"

"Her mother is one of her cares, monsieur. Mademoiselle desired me to ask whether you wanted anything more."

"Nothing, thank you, only when you see her say how grateful I am for her kindness."

And then I had a good wash, and with Tremblay's help bound up my wounded thigh and plastered the cut on my head. When I had donned his coat and trousers he took up a part of the floor and placed underneath it my sword and outer garments. He would also have concealed my pistols, but as they could be hidden under my blouse and might be useful, I preferred to keep them.

Before he went away Tremblay advised me on no account to quit my refuge. The visit of the gendarmes had made the servants frantic with fear, and if they caught a glimpse of me they would leave the house at once and, as likely as not, denounce us to the police. At any rate, they would make no secret of what they had seen.

"And then," added Tremblay, "we should all be arrested—or worse."

I told him that he need be under no apprehension, that I should not stir until dark, nor even then unless I had his assurance that I could leave unobserved.

When he was gone I arranged the sack as a cushion and made myself comfortable. The repast, the sleep, the wash, and the dressing of my wounds had made me feel like another man. But mentally I was ill at ease. The events of the day weighed heavily on my mind, and I grieved sorely for my lost comrades and my murdered uncle. I feared that I was the sole survivor of the rear column, and with good reason. But for the horse and the open door and the kindness of Mademoiselle de la Tour I could not have escaped. Was it likely that any of the others had been equally fortunate?

And Von Durler's people! Had any of them succeeded in reaching the Assembly? And then how fared the king and queen and the column commanded by Von Salis? Had the royal family and their escort been destroyed by the treachery of the National Guard and the fury of the populace? The thought made me shudder, yet the possibility was undeniable.

But the most pressing question at the moment—for me—was whither I should go when I left my present refuge. I could not risk compromising the sweet girl who had helped me in my need by staying a moment longer than was needful. Among the few people whom I knew in Paris were none whom I could ask to take me in at the peril of their lives.

After long thought, and pondering various projects, I came to the conclusion that only one was feasible—to return to Courbevoie. True, I had no papers, but disguised as a workman I might pass the barrier unquestioned, and once outside Paris I hoped I should be safe.

We had left at the barracks a corporal's guard and three or four invalids, among the latter Glutz, who was laid up with a badly sprained ankle and had been compelled to stay behind, greatly to his disappointment. But it was well for him that he had stayed behind ; his presence could have made no difference in the result, and he would almost certainly have lost his life.

Yes, I would try to get to Courbevoie. I had two hundred louis d'or there, which would be more than enough to enable Glutz and myself to make our way to England, even though I had to buy horses and a carriage and charter a boat for the passage of the Channel.

This I planned and much else which it is not necessary to relate, and I was still deep in thought when I was roused from my reverie by the sound of approaching footsteps. I had sharp ears in those days and could identify a footfall as unerringly as I could recognize a voice, and these were neither the footsteps of Mlle. de la Tour nor of Paul Tremblay. They were too heavy to be hers, too light to be his. Yet only he and she knew where I was. It might be one of the maids—or an enemy. I could not fasten the door, it possessed neither bolt nor bar, so by way of being prepared for whatever might befall, I cocked my pistols, laid them ready to hand, armed myself with a spade, set my back against the wall, and awaited the issue.

CHAPTER X

A SURPRISE

WHEN the door of the tool-house opened, and there appeared on the threshold a soberly attired, slightly built gentleman, with black whiskers, blue spectacles, and powdered hair, his only weapon a clouded cane, I felt rather foolish, and put the spade down.

"Good-day, Monsieur Astor," he said, doffing his hat and making a courtly bow. Then, observing the pistols, he added, with a smile: "You are prepared for all eventualities, I see. It is well. But I am a man of peace. Don't you recognize me?"

"How should I recognize a gentleman whom I see for the first time?"

"Not for the first time. I had the pleasure of making your acquaintance a few weeks ago."

And with that my visitor removed his spectacles.

"Is it possible?" I asked, regarding him with a bewildered stare. "If whiskers like those grew in a month, I should say you were Monsieur Boulanger."

"They can grow in a moment, and disappear as quickly" (removing the whiskers).

The ex-vicomte, beyond a doubt; and looking much younger than he did on the night when he so narrowly missed being hanged.

"I am delighted to meet you again," said I; "but how did you know I was here?"

"I had the pleasure of learning the fact from my niece, Mademoiselle Tour."

" So! You are Uncle Claude."

" I have that honor; sir, and it is an honor to be the uncle of so brave and good a girl as Angélique."

" If she were not both good and brave, my head would just now be at the end of a pike. She saved my life, Monsieur Boulanger."

" And you saved mine."

" So we are quits."

" Not at all. Angélique could not have acted otherwise, and I count myself still your debtor. . . . Ah, this has been a terrible day, my friend—a day marked by only one redeeming feature: the heroism and devotion of the Swiss Guard. I take shame to myself that I did not fight by your side and share in your danger. But I reached Paris only at noon, and it was then too late. Were you aware of a project for carrying off the king and the royal family ?"

" I have heard rumors without end, but nothing definite."

" Well, there was a scheme, and a very promising one ; but as it has failed, my lips are unsealed, and I can tell you all about it. In point of fact, the attempt was never seriously made, else it had surely succeeded. The plan was for the royal family to leave the Tuileries at night, escorted by the Swiss Guard, and make for Rouen, whither three hundred men of the regiment were sent four days ago, ostensibly to assist in the collection of taxes, really to co-operate in the movement. Moreover, the people of Normandy are well affected to the king, and there is a regiment of regulars at Rouen which would have taken his part, and from thence we might have gone to Dieppe, and from Dieppe to England. His majesty was quite willing, but at the last minute the queen persuaded her husband to withdraw his consent. It was in connection with this project that I left Paris three days ago."

"I suppose the queen thought that resistance would be nobler than flight."

"Partly for that reason, partly because she suspected Monsieur de Lafayette had a hand in the scheme, and Monsieur de Lafayette is a gentleman whom she distrusts. I, too, think that resistance would have been nobler than flight. But we knew that when it came to the point the king would not resist, and we had reason to believe that the National Guard would join the rebels; that, in short, the only means of saving him was to get him away. Now it is too late. But even yet I do not abandon hope, and a few of us, royalists like myself, are resolved to rescue the royal captives at all hazards. And now, my friend, about yourself; for I dare say you know your life hangs by a thread."

"When night comes I shall go to Courbevoie."

"How about the barrier?"

"With this disguise —"

"You think you may slip through. Possibly. But they are very strict at the barriers, and inability to produce a passport, if you are asked for one, will insure your immediate arrest, and probably your immediate execution. You had better lie *perdu* in Paris for a few days; and I engage to find you a hiding-place."

I thanked M. Boulanger for his kindness, but persisted in my idea of returning to the barracks.

"Well, you can try; but I fear it will be a case of out of the frying-pan into the fire. I would lend you my passport, which, by the way, is forged, only as it describes my personal appearance rather minutely, and you are fair and long, and I am dark and short, it would do you more harm than good. You might remain here—"

"That is quite out of the question. Not for the world will I expose these ladies to any further risk. They have done more than enough for me already."

"I was going to say you would not be safe here. You were marked down to the garden door, and there may be a domiciliary visit any moment, and both for their sakes and your own you must get away quickly. And there are other reasons. My sister is an invalid, and already in bad odor with the Jacobins, whose victory to-day will make them more vicious than ever. Twelve months ago my late brother-in-law committed the unpardonable crime of firing on the people — in defence of his life and property — and was shortly afterwards murdered in his wife's presence. She has never recovered from the shock ; her nervous system is quite unstrung, and she seldom stirs from her room. Since that time Angélique has had entire charge of the house — of everything, in fact — and well she manages, and nobly she bears the burden. Though not yet seventeen, she is older in experience and character than many who are twice her age. It is all wrong, of course. According to our French ideas, young girls should be allowed neither initiative nor freedom, much less be placed at the head of a household. But what would you? Need must when the devil drives, as your English proverb has it, and times like these make strong natures stronger, weak natures weaker. After her father's death she and her mother left their country-house and came hither. They live very quietly, both from necessity and choice. The revolution has seriously impaired my sister's fortune."

"Do you live with them ?"

"My faith, no! I am a marked man. I only escape arrest by adopting disguises and continually changing my quarters. Here I am known as Dr. Boulanger, and my visits are strictly professional. By the way, my patient's daughter has invited us to sup with them this evening."

"Do you mean that I am included in the invitation ?"

"Certainly."

" But—"

" Oh, the ladies will excuse your costume. One does not stand on ceremony nowadays."

" But will it be safe — for them ?"

" I think so. The sun is already beginning to set. When it is a little lower you will slip in at one of the ground-floor windows, which I shall point out to you. Tremblay, who can turn his hand to anything, waits at table. None of the other servants will know that you are in the house. You will come, of course ? Good ! Now behold ! In an hour from this time turn into that path, and follow it to the end, when you will find yourself opposite a long window with two wings which will be left ajar. Go in without knocking, sit down and wait. Only — and this is important—if there is a light in the room, remain in the shrubbery until it is removed."

" I must regard the light as a danger signal."

" Precisely. And now I shall say good-bye for the present. I am going outside to see whether the coast is clear, and ascertain, if I can, what these ruffians propose to do with the king and queen, and those of your comrades whom they have not already destroyed. . . . In an hour, remember ; and till then, good-bye."

It seemed a long hour, for my thoughts were not happy, and I was getting weary of inaction and suspense ; but it came to an end, and at the time appointed by M. Boulanger I was at the window which he had described to me. After pausing for a moment to make sure that I was not observed, I pushed the window open and went in, and was about to sit down when I heard the rustling of a gown.

" Monsieur Astor ?" said a voice which I recognized as that of the daughter of the house.

" The same, mademoiselle, at your service."

" Will you give yourself the trouble to come this way,

monsieur?" opening a door which seemed to lead into a dark passage.

I followed her; at the end of the passage she opened another door, and I found myself in a spacious drawing-room, handsomely furnished, but rather dimly lighted. The table was laid for dinner with covers for three, from which I inferred that either Mme. de la Tour or her brother was not to be of the party.

"Isn't Dr. Boulanger coming?" I asked.

"He will be here in a few minutes. But I am sorry to say my mother is not able to dine with us this evening."

Just then I happened to glance at my reflected image in one of the mirrors that adorned the room, and was both amused and annoyed at the figure I cut in my borrowed clothes. I had never worn trousers before, and besides being shabby, Tremblay's nether garments were a world too short for me. Moreover, in addition to being equally shabby, the blouse by no means set off my figure to advantage.

Mlle. de la Tour seemed to guess my thoughts.

"It is a very effectual disguise," she said, with an amused smile. "But hadn't you better dispense with those gaiters before you venture outside? They have a suspiciously military look, and gardeners don't generally wear hair powder, I think."

"You are quite right, and I am very stupid. Yes, white buckskin gaiters and a powdered poll would betray me to the first gendarme I met. I must dispense with both before I set out for Courbevoie. Ah, here comes your uncle."

As he entered the room, followed by Tremblay, M. Boulanger gave me a friendly greeting and spoke a word to his niece; but he looked unusually grave, as though he had bad news.

When we were all seated, he asked Tremblay whether he had taken every precaution.

"I think so," answered the old soldier; "the dogs are on guard, and if anybody approaches the front gate will give the alarm in ample time to enable monsieur (glancing at me) to return to his tree. The maids haven't the least suspicion that you are not the only guest;. I accounted for the third cover by saying that Madame de la Tour would probably come down to dinner."

"Nobody suspects anything, we cannot be taken by surprise. So far good, if anything can be good on this disastrous day."

"What has happened beyond what we know, uncle?" asked Angélique, anxiously. "That is bad enough."

"Worse has happened. Colonel Maillardoz, Major Bachmann, and the other officers and soldiers of the Swiss Guard who escorted the king to the Assembly were arrested on their arrival thither, and are now in prison. When the remnant of Captain von Durler's column reached the same place the king actually gave them a written order to lay down their arms, which they had no sooner done than they, too, were imprisoned. The soldiers who refused to surrender were massacred on the spot."

"If I had been the King of France, I would have died rather than give such an order!" exclaimed Angélique, warmly.

"My poor comrades!" said I, in a broken voice, for my heart was full. "And the regiment so brave and loyal! All save the few who have escaped for the moment, the handful at Courbevoie and the detachment in Normandy, dead or in prison!"

"For which you have to thank his majesty. Uncle Claude, I do believe he is a poltroon."

Dr. Boulanger looked inexpressibly shocked.

"Hush! For Heaven's sake hush, Angélique! You must not defame the king," he said, severely. "Besides, he is not a poltroon. Think what courage he showed when the sans-culottes invaded the Tuileries."

" Yes, the passive courage of a spiritless woman. No man worthy the name would have surrendered to a mob, and ordered his brave defenders to lay down their arms. Oh, I don't pity him at all. But I do with all my heart pity the queen. Poor queen, to be tied to a—"

" Angélique !" interrupted her uncle, warningly.

" Well, I won't call him a poltroon again, though he is one all the same. But you must admit that Louis XVI. is a very poor specimen of a king."

" He is a king no longer, except by divine right."

" How ?"

" They have decreed the dethronement, and the king and the royal family are to be imprisoned in the Temple."

" And afterwards ?"

" Heaven only knows. Probably the block."

" My God ! You surely don't think they will guillotine the queen ?"

" Indeed I do, unless we can rescue her."

" Will that be possible ?"

" Everything is possible for resolute men with a good cause."

And then followed a long silence. The ex-vicomte, though he ate little, drank freely, but the wine seemed only to deepen his gloom. I, too, drank more than my wont; eating was out of the question. Angélique's beautiful face was overcast with the sadness of her thoughts, and a tear trembled on her long eyelashes—in sorrow for her father or pity for the queen—not, I felt sure, for the king. Though so young, she was tall and well grown, and the simplicity of her attire showed her good taste as much as it heightened her charms. Her only ornaments were a diamond mourning-ring on one of her slender fingers, and a red rose at her breast; and her dark eyes and still darker eyebrows, fair skin and peach-like complexion, matched well with her hair, powdered for the evening in the fashion of the day.

After the silence had endured several minutes, it was broken with startling effect by the loud baying of the watch-dogs at the gate.

Angélique gave a little scream.

"Go and see what it is," said Dr. Boulanger to Tremblay, who at this moment entered the room. "And you, Monsieur Astor, had better resume your perch for a few minutes. If it is a false alarm I will whistle."

I obeyed on the instant; but I had no sooner climbed up to my old place than the preconcerted signal recalled me to the house.

"It was a false alarm, then?" I observed to Boulanger.

"In a sense; that is to say, there has been no demand for admission, but Tremblay reports that a suspicious look-ing individual is loitering about the gate—probably a spy."

"In that case, it would probably be as well for me to go at once."

"I almost think so. You are still minded to go to Courbevoie?"

"I am."

"The barracks may be attacked."

"All the more reason I should be there to take a hand in their defence."

"Spoken like a brave man. I shall bear you company as far as the barrier and see how you fare. If you get into a difficulty I may be able to help you out. What name do you propose to give yourself?"

"Let me see! You are a Baker, I will be Butcher."

"Good! Your name for the nonce is Anatole Boucher. Now listen: I shall leave by the front gate, and as Tremblay lets me out he will say, 'Good-night, Monsieur le Docteur,' in a voice loud enough to be heard by the spy, whom I shall accost and keep in conversation for a minute or two. In the meanwhile you will leave by the side door, and take the path to the right which leads into the main road, where I shall presently join you. Go at your ease, and don't look behind you. There may be other spies about, and the best way to throw those fellows off the scent is to appear unconscious of their presence. Are you armed?"

"I have a pair of pistols under my blouse."

"You may need a weapon that can be used without making a noise, and does not require reloading."

As Dr. Boulanger spoke he whipped into the hall and returned with a broad-bladed dagger in a shagreen scabbard.

"Take that; it may serve you in good stead before this time to-morrow," said he.

I thanked him, and put the dagger inside my blouse.

"And now I had better set off," he added. "If you leave by the side door, in three or four minutes we shall meet in the avenue. But be careful neither to loiter, hurry, nor look back."

"And those gaiters and your hair?" observed Angélique, when her uncle was gone.

"Will you allow me?" I asked.

"Of course. This is no time for standing on ceremony, and you have no time to lose."

I doffed the telltale gaiters, and, taking a napkin from the table, rubbed the powder out of my hair, which, fortunately, was short.

This done, I bade Angélique good-bye.

"Heaven only knows whether we shall meet again!" I said, in a voice tremulous with the emotion which I could not conceal. "But while I live I shall never forget this night, and that to your kindness and hospitality I owe my escape from a great danger."

"And it will always be a pleasure to me to think," she answered, "that it has been my good-fortune to render a service to a brave soldier, who not long ago rendered a still greater service to my dear uncle."

Then we shook hands, and three minutes later I was outside the garden.

CHAPTER XI

IT was a beautiful night, calm and windless ; and though there was no light of the moon, the stars were so bright and the air so clear that, save where the trees intercepted the view, I could see a fair distance, both front and rear, for, notwithstanding my mentor's injunctions, I did once look backward, and, as I expected, saw nobody.

Then I went on at an easy pace, and was soon so deeply absorbed in thought that my walk became automatic, and when somebody touched me on the shoulder I did what startled people generally do, obeyed the first impulse, which, in this instance, was to wheel round and seize the intruder by the throat.

"Not so fast," said M. Boulanger, who seemed as much surprised at feeling my hand at his windpipe as I had been at feeling his on my shoulder. "I congratulate you on your alertness, but I would rather you displayed it for the confusion of your enemies than the bewilderment of your friends."

"I was not alert. If I had been I should have heard your footsteps."

"Well, I did step rather softly, with the intention of surprising you. I shall not repeat the experiment, and you were justified in resenting that touch ; it was too suggestive."

"Of what?"

"Handcuffs, a dungeon, the guillotine, according to circumstances. A touch on the shoulder is the usual preliminary to an arrest. Tremblay was right; that fellow was a spy, and unless I am mistaken I caught a glimpse of a second."

" Whom are they after, do you suppose ?"

" One of us; that goes without saying. Either they imagine that the Swiss officer, who so mysteriously evaded the gendarmes, may be hiding in or about the house, or suspect that the *ci-devant* Vicomte de Lancy pays occasional visits to his sister, and, as you are aware, the police are very anxious to lay that gentleman by the heels."

" Did you accost the scoundrel ?"

" Of course, and had a talk with him. He pretended that he had lost his way, asked whose house it was I had just quitted, and when I told him, said he had heard the lady was not well, and made several inquiries, to which I gave suitable answers."

" And you don't suppose he suspected who you were ?"

" If he had I should not be here just now. But it is clear that unless my visits to the Villa de la Tour are few and far between I shall be suspected. And now about Courbevoie. It is a dangerous enterprise on which you are bent, Monsieur Astor. The guards at the barriers have all been doubled since morning; they are very much on the *qui vive*, and eager to catch any fugitive Swiss who may have escaped the massacre, and if you are arrested you will be a lost man."

" Nobody can recognize me in these clothes."

" Perhaps not; but if you are arrested you will be searched, and a *soi-disant* gardener, with a brace of pistols and a dagger under his belt, would find it difficult to convince his captors that he was what he pretended to be. He would be detained, pending further inquiries, and further inquiries might lead to his premature removal from this world to another."

"Shall I throw the pistols away? Or will you take them and the dagger?"

"A thousand thanks. The remedy might be worse than the disease — for me. No, keep them for the present, and when we have reconnoitred the barrier— Hark! What is that?"

I also had heard something, and, after listening for a few seconds, we exclaimed with one voice:

"A mob!"

There was no mistake about it. Once heard, the clamor of a revolutionary mob could never be confounded with aught else. A confused murmur, now dying away, anon rising to a roar, amid which might now and then be distinguished shrill cries, hoarse shouts, and the clash of weapons.

"Coming this way, too, and from the barrier," said Boulanger. "Can we see them, I wonder?"

By this time we had reached the principal avenue, and perceived, coming towards us, a line of torches, which threw a lurid light on the dense mass of howling maniacs behind them, some of whom were singing the " Marseillaise," others the "Carmagnole" and the " Ça Ira."

On my companion's proposal, we stepped under a big beech-tree, whence, by keeping well in the shade, we could see without being observed.

As the procession drew nearer we perceived, between the torch-bearers and the main body, a row of pikes with something at the ends.

"Are those things on the pike-points caps of liberty, or— ?"

"Heads," added Boulanger. " I fear they are heads."

"God forbid! One, two, three, four—why, there are ten of them!"

"Yes, ten, and they are not caps. Caps of liberty are

red. Those things are— And doesn't that which is turned this way look like a bearded face streaked with blood?"

When the hideous procession came over against our tree a halt was called, and the demoniacs chanted the "Marseillaise" to the accompaniment of kettle-drums and cymbals. The torch-bearers and a horde of dishevelled furies formed a circle round the ten pikemen and danced.

"It is like hell broke loose," muttered Boulanger.

As the torch-bearers in their wild whirlings uplifted their torches, I got a better view of the ghastly trophies carried by the pikemen, and my soul froze with horror when, in the bearded face streaked with blood, I recognized the features of the corporal of the barrack-guard, and in another those of my friend Glutz.

I had gone through the day's fighting and alarms without losing courage or presence of mind, but at that terrible moment my nerve failed me. For the first time in my life I knew fear--downright bodily fear. My knees knocked together, and I closed my eyes to shut out the dreadful sight. So completely did I become unmanned that I was on the point of running away, which had been to court death. But at this moment my companion spoke to me. His voice broke the spell and recalled me to my senses.

"What is it, Astor? What is the matter? Are you ill?" he asked, anxiously.

"The heads!" I gasped. "I know them. The corporal of the guard—my comrade, Glutz. We left ten men at the barracks, nearly all invalids."

"And these are their heads. No wonder you are so overcome. "Oh, the fiends! I would give all that is left to me of life for a couple of field-guns and a few whiffs of grape-shot."

At these words my mood changed. My fear turned to blind rage. I drew my pistols, and but for Boulanger's restraining band I should have attacked the mob single-handed.

"Why throw your life away?" he said. "How would that avenge your slaughtered comrades? Restrain your-self. Revenge is for those who know how to wait. See, they are going, and those hateful trophies will soon be out of sight."

There was reason in my friend's remonstrance, and as the savages marched away I grew calmer, though my heart was full to bursting of rage and grief.

Not all went. The line of march was strewn with pros-trate men and women, who looked as though they were dead, but were simply dead-drunk.

"They have plundered somebody's cellar," observed Boulanger, grimly. "I wish they had all drunk to suffo-cation. You cannot go to Courbevoie after this. It were sheer suicide."

"It is the last place I want to go to—now; and I should probably find the barracks in ruins. But whither shall I go?"

"With me, if you will; I think I can find you a refuge for the night."

"At your lodgings?"

"No; that were to compromise us both. I think they will take you in at the house of the late General de Bésen-val, who was a dear friend of mine. It now belongs to his widow. The family is from home, but the porter, a coun-tryman of yours and a very decent fellow, is in sole charge."

"You mean he is a Swiss?"

"Yes, like yourself."

"I am an Englishman." And then I explained how I had come to join the Swiss Guard.

"Well, I think you would have done better to join one of the guard regiments of King George," said Boulanger, dryly.

" So do I; but that is not to the point. I want to let
my father know that I have survived the massacre. Can
it be done?"

" Why not? There is the post."

" The name might be recognized and my letter opened."

" There is no reason why you should give your address.
and if I post your letter in the Rue de Coquillere it will afford no clew to your hiding-place in the Place de l'Hôtel
des Invalides."

" Is that where we are going?"

" Hard by. Let us go while the road is clear."

At the end of the Champs-Elysées we turned onto the
Quai de la Conference, and crossed the Seine by the bridge
Louis XVI., which at that time was under repair or not
quite finished—I forget which. Then by the Palais Bourbon, and down the Rue de Bourgogne, as far as the Rue de
Varennes. On the way we met several patrols, who, fortunately, gave us no trouble.

Mme. de Bésenval's house was in the regular style of
architecture of that aristocratic quarter, a carriage gateway
opening into a court which you had to cross in order to
gain the front door. The porter's lodge was inside the
gateway.

The large doors were closed, and as Boulanger knocked
at the wicket he informed me that the porter's name was
Schlessinger, and suggested that it might be as well to
avoid mentioning that I was not a born Switzer. The
wicket opened a few inches, and at the opening appeared
an elderly man, who eyed us suspiciously by the light of a
lantern, which he held on a level with his head.

" Who are you, and what do you want?" he demanded.

" The last time I had the pleasure of dining here, Monsieur Schlessinger, I was the Vicomte de Lancy."

" You don't look much like him."

"It would be a serious reflection on my disguise if I did. Perhaps I look more like him now" (taking off his spectacles).

"Yes, now I recognize you. Pray excuse my doubts, but these are times when one has to be cautious, and I am quite alone. The house is unoccupied. Will you give yourselves the trouble to enter, gentlemen?"

Schlessinger opened the wicket, and so soon as we were inside carefully bolted it; then led the way to his lodge, a snug little room principally furnished with a huge arm-chair.

"What can I do for you, Monsieur le Vicomte?" he asked, after inviting us to be seated.

"Dr. Boulanger, if you please, Monsieur Schlessinger. Vicomtes are not popular in Paris at present. I want you, out of the goodness of your heart, to give this gentleman a lodging for a few days in some remote part of the house. He is one of the few officers of the Swiss Guard who escaped the massacre—"

"*Gott in Himmel!* you were in the fight at the Tuileries and are still alive!" (turning to me).

"Yes." And then I had to tell him all about it, and answer many questions; after which we came to the crucial point: would he take me in?

Schlessinger was obviously kind-hearted and sympathetic; but the times were dangerous, and he naturally reflected before answering.

"You see this is not my house, and I don't know whether Madame de Bésenval would like it," quoth he; "and they have killed several Swiss porters already, and are continually making domiciliary visits; and spies simply swarm. All the same, being a Switzer and having bowels, I cannot turn a countryman away, and if you will consent to occupy a little chamber right at the top, under the tiles, you may stay there a day or two, or until you find safer quarters; for I really don't think you will be safe here. This is an aristocratic quarter, remember."

I gratefully accepted M. Schlessinger's offer. "Put me where you will," quoth I, "a soldier should always be ready to rough it, and I am not fastidious. All I ask is some place to put my head in, and as I should be sorry to expose you to danger, I shall be ready to quit whenever you think there is any likelihood of a domiciliary visit."

And then I asked him for writing materials, and wrote a few lines to my father:

"I am alive and only slightly wounded. Uncle Daniel died a soldier's death. With his dying breath he sent you his love. The regiment did its duty.   Fritz."

I folded and sealed the letter, and gave it to Boulanger to post.

"I shall call to-morrow or the next day to see how you are going on," he said.

On which we shook hands, and, after seeing him out, Schlessinger showed me to my bedroom. It was, as he said, quite at the top of the house—a mere hole, little larger than a cupboard, and might well pass unobserved in the event of an unexpected intrusion.

"I shall bring you your breakfast in the morning," said he; "but as you value your life, don't show your nose outside until I come. Domiciliary visits are often made early in the day. *Schlafen sie wohl!*" (sleep you well).

And then he left me to myself.

CHAPTER XII

HIDE - AND - SEEK

My head aches, my wound smarts, and, worse still, my mind is on the rack. My thoughts are as dark as the night; and when, overcome by bodily weariness, I sleep, my dreams are nightmares, hideous and grotesque. I see again, with additions and distortions, the deadly march through the palace gardens, the fight at the swinging bridge, and bend over my dying uncle at the foot of the statue. I race for my life across the great square, pursued by fiery steeds and fiends with flaming swords, and as their weapons are descending on my head waken with a cry of terror.

After a long interval spent in disordered musings, I sleep again, and dream of severed heads and headless bodies. I am surrounded by a horde of decapitated sans-culottes, each of whom holds in one hand a sword, in the other a torch. I feel like one paralyzed, I can neither stir nor speak; but as they close in on me and raise their weapons to strike, the scene changes, the sans-culottes vanish, and their places are taken by a circle of head-crowned pikes. One is Glutz, another the corporal of the guard. I know them all. They dance round me as though they were alive, but their eyes are fixed and expressionless, their mouths wide open, and their white blood-streaked faces are the faces of the dead.

Presently the ten are joined by two others — Angélique and the vicomte. He looks as ghastly as the others, yet her face is life-like and her eyes speak, and as they meet mine, she smiles, then bends forward as though to kiss me. But when her lips are close to mine, her jaws drop, her face

6

takes the hue of death, and I waken with a cry of horror, trembling like a leaf.

After this I slept no more, and when the first gleam of dawn shone through the little dormer-window that lighted my garret I felt truly thankful and intensely relieved.

After looking through the window, which commanded an extensive view of the steep roofs and long chimneys, I lay down again and closed my eyes, and might have fallen asleep had I not been disturbed and roused to full wakefulness by the clash of bells. At first I thought it was the tocsin again, but the next moment I remembered that it was Sunday morning, and that the same bells that had called the people to arms and rebellion thirty hours previously were now calling them to prayer.

I was not much given to moralizing in those days, but it seemed a strange world, and I thought that of all the people it contained the French were surely the strangest. They were celebrating the advent of what they called freedom by the slaughter of the innocent, and replacing the mild rule of a feeble king with the ferocious tyranny of mob-law. Like the frogs in the fable, they had deposed King Log in favor of King Stork. So much was obvious even to my inexperienced understanding.

It was growing late, and Schlessinger was long in coming with my breakfast. Not that I felt hungry, but I was sick of solitude and dying for news. If I could have foreseen how much longer and drearier a solitude I was destined to endure I should doubtless have borne the infliction more patiently.

In the end Schlessinger came with coffee and rolls, which greatly refreshed me. He had been out making inquiries; this it was that had made him so late. From an acquaintance who belonged to the National Guard he had heard news that surpassed my worst anticipations, and showed that the account given by Tremblay, which I thought exaggerated, was less terrible than the truth.

The regiment, as a military force, was utterly destroyed, and the few survivors were either prisoners or fugitives. All the wounded officers, except M. Reding, who was afterwards foully murdered in the Abbaye prison, had been killed. On the other hand, several officers of the first column, including Captain von Durler, had escaped from durance and so far avoided recapture. But Major Bachmann and ten other officers were under arrest, and had been, or would be, transferred to the Abbaye. As to the men, it was hardly possible that, except a few who had contrived to change their uniforms for plain clothes, any could have escaped. All of them who outlived the combat at the palace and the fight in the garden and at the bridge had been hunted down and slain.

I greatly feared that among these were Sternberg and Waldteufel, and that I should never see them again.

Schlessinger, as I could see, sorrowed sincerely for his slaughtered countrymen, many of whom he had known; but what seemed most to concern him at the moment was that, as he had been informed, strenuous efforts were being made to take the five or six officers of the regiment who were still at large. Their names were known; the police had been furnished with full descriptions of their persons, my own among the number, and ordered to spare no pains to discover their whereabouts and hale them to prison. It had, moreover, been given out that whosoever sheltered the fugitives would be held equally guilty.

"Which means that if you are found here we shall both lose our heads," added Schlessinger; and the prospect did not seem to give him much pleasure.

Though just then so overwhelmed with grief that I cared little what became of me, I could neither ignore the old man's apprehensions nor appear indifferent to his safety. I told him that I should take whatever precautions he deemed necessary, or, if he liked, depart forthwith.

But this he would not hear of; for albeit nervous (and no wonder), he was no dastard.

"No, no," he said; "to let you go now were to send you to your death."

"I don't see that. You forget my blouse."

"The blouse might do after dark; but in the daytime it is less a disguise than a telltale. I saw at once when you came into my lodge last night that you were no workman."

"How so?"

"Your hands are clean and soft, your nails nicely trimmed; you don't slouch in your gait, you are well set up, your hair is short, and your bearing military. A spy or a detective would spot you at once. He would say to himself: 'That fellow is no laborer; I must follow him and find out what he is.'"

"You are a keen observer, Monsieur Schlessinger."

"A *concierge* must be an observer; it is part of his business. I have been at the job nearly forty years, and I can tell a gentleman, let him disguise himself as he may."

"So you think I should have a better chance of escaping detection dressed as a gentleman than posing as a gardener."

"Unquestionably. If you want to avoid detection, do nothing to attract attention."

"In that case, I had better buy myself another suit of clothes."

"I should certainly advise you to do so. Get yourself up as a bourgeois, a government employé, or a student—anything but a workman. But the wisest thing you can do for the present is to stay where you are."

" In this room?"

" Where else? It is the only place the police might over-look in the event of a domiciliary visit, and you must not show yourself down-stairs on any account. If they were to get wind that I had a visitor, the police would be on us at once. Besides, you look quite worn out; two or three days' rest will do you all the good in the world."

This was quite true, though I would rather have had a better resting-place than a cupboard. However, as I could not gainsay a host who was entertaining me at the risk of his life, I said I should abide by his advice, and he on his part was good enough to say that he would pay me an occa-sional visit during the day, and the next time he came bring me some books.

After he was gone I had a spell of sound sleep, and on awaking felt much better in body and more composed in mind. I could now think consecutively and calmly, and the first result of my reflections were a vivid sense of the diffi-culty of escaping from the dangers by which I was menaced, and a decided conviction that I could only escape them by getting out of Paris as quickly as might be.

On the other hand, it was madness to make the attempt for the present, and neither then nor later would it be possi-ble to leave without a regular passport. And where and how was I to get a passport?

Moreover, I had very little money. The gold pieces left at Courbevoie were either gone, stolen by the sans-culottes, or unavailable. Without money I could neither travel nor pay my way in Paris; and as neither gendarmes nor patriots were incorruptible, a few louis, discreetly dispensed, might remove many obstacles, and even be instrumental in saving my life. True, I could draw on my father; but where was the banker who would purchase my draft and keep my se-cret?

And there was something else. I did not mean to leave Paris without taking leave of Mademoiselle de la Tour, and seeing whether I could be of any use to her. She had laid me under an obligation which it behooved me to make an effort to redeem. Moreover, I was very anxious about her. All her male relatives had run the country—save De Lancy, and he was under a ban—she bore a hated name, and now that the Jacobins had got the upper hand, it was likely to go ill with the class to which she belonged.

Yes, I must see Angélique again. It were base to quit Paris without repeating my thanks and offering my services. What service, in my then predicament, I could render her, or any other body, I did not stop to inquire. If I had been quite frank with myself, I should probably have said I must see her because I wanted to see her.

Schlessinger was as good as his word. Between twelve and one he brought me a substantial second breakfast, to which, having recovered my appetite, I did full justice. A healthy organism demands its due, even when the mind is oppressed with care; and I was young in ninety-two.

He also brought me some books, and reported that all was quiet in the street.

Recalling his strictures on my workman's costume, I inquired whether he could obtain me something less likely to attract attention.

"A suit of bourgeois?" he asked.

"Yes, a suit of bourgeois," said I.

"New, or second-hand?"

Having regard for the slenderness of my purse, I decided for second-hand, and requested Schlessinger to get me at the same time a hat to match, and a pair of common spectacles.

"Good! I will try to manage it either to-day or to-morrow. What are your dimensions? (measuring me with his eye). Height, six feet; chest measurement, forty inches; girth, thirty two or three; square shoulders, longish arms, medium legs. That is about it, I think. But men of the bourgeois class don't wear mustaches. I am afraid you will have to shave yours." Then, seeing that I hesitated, he added: "You can grow another pair of mustaches, but you would find it difficult to grow another head."

The argument was unanswerable. I consented—albeit, not without a pang—to make the sacrifice, and made it within the hour, using for the purpose one of my host's razors. He visited me again in the evening, and on the day following brought the clothes. They were of the shabby-genteel order, which Schlessinger held to be a decided advantage, also the fashion and fit, which were simply deplorable.

"Well-fitting clothes are the exception," he observed, gravely. "To be well-dressed is to be conspicuous; the more like the crowd you are the better."

When I had put them on, and donned the horn-rimmed spectacles and the unobtrusive hat, which he had been good enough to buy for me, I hardly knew myself.

"This is capital!" I exclaimed. "Now I can go anywhere without risk of detection."

"I am not so sure of that," said Schlessinger, grimly. "You must have been seen by thousands when you were on guard at the palace and marching about Paris, and the police don't go entirely by clothes; they go by height, complexion, and other physical peculiarities. Read that!"

"That" was a hand-bill containing a minute description of my person, and of the persons of my brother-officers, who were being hunted like myself. It even made mention of a too conspicuous mole on my left cheek, and a slight scar over my right eyebrow, and suggested that I had probably shaved off my mustache.

"Where did you get it?" I asked, in dismay.

".A gendarme left it an hour ago, and intimated that if I saw anybody answering to any of these descriptions and failed to give information to the police, it would go hard with me. He was leaving a bill with every *concierge* in the quarter. I am not popular with the police," added Schlessinger; "most Paris *concierges* act as spies for them; I won't. And as my late master commanded the Swiss regiments of the Guard, and after the taking of the Bastile was tried for his life on a charge of high-treason against the nation, and I also am a Switzer—"

" I understand. The house is 'suspect.' You regard the call as a warning, and expect a perquisition. Not for the world would I get you into trouble. I must go at once."

"Well, I think you had better, and quite as much in your own interest as mine. You would be the first victim. But don't go before dark, if you please. Were it reported to the police that a stranger was seen leaving the house, I might have to answer some awkward questions, and if you are wise you will shun daylight."

"As you think best, Monsieur Schlessinger; and if the Vicomte calls—I mean Monsieur Boulanger—"

" He is not going to call. Here is a note from him, addressed to me, but meant for you. It came half an hour ago."

The note ran as follows:

" I am hindered by unforeseen circumstances from making my promised visit. But if your friend, M. Anatole Boucher, wants another situation, he cannot do better than apply to M. de Castellan, whose house is in the Rue Cléry."

"This is opportune," said I. " It means that Monsieur de Castellan will find me quarters."

"Without a doubt. Monsieur de Castellan is a good man. His house is over against the Hôtel de Chatule. You can find it without asking questions?"

"Yes, I know the Rue Cléry. I wonder what the unforeseen circumstances are. I hope Dr. Boulanger has not been laid by the heels."

"I don't think so. If he had we should not have got that note. He has either heard what a hue-and-cry there is after you, and thinks that calling here by daylight might endanger all concerned, or he is playing hide-and-seek on his own account. I hope you will fall into no danger by the way. If you meet a patrol, turn into a by-street or step into a blind-alley. Prevention is better than cure."

CHAPTER XIII

MADAME DUFOUR

SCHLESSINGER put his head out of the wicket, and after looking up the street and down the street, and listening intently, turned to me and reported that all was quiet.

"You may go now," said he. "Over against the Hôtel de Chatule, remember! The *concierge* is a Switzer and a friend of mine. Use my name and tell him who you are, and he will be yours also. I wish you good-night, and good-luck to you, *meinherr*."

I wrung the old man's hand, thanked him warmly for his hospitality, and passed through the wicket.

Night was settling over the city; and so quiet were the streets, and the few wayfarers whom I met took so little notice of each other and of me, that I jumped somewhat hastily to the conclusion that Schlessinger's apprehensions were either baseless or exaggerated. It did not occur to me that people might be staying at home because they were afraid to venture abroad, and that those whom I met were probably no less anxious to escape observation than I was myself.

There were two ways of reaching my destination: by the Pont Royal and the Galerie du Louvre, and then by one of the streets leading into the Rue St. Honoré, or by the Pont Neuf and the Rue de la Monnaie. I had intended to take the latter route; but when I got to the end of the Rue du Bac, I felt a strong desire to revisit the scene of Sunday's tragedy. At first I resisted the impulse — it seemed sheer madness, but reflecting that the neighborhood of the Tuile-

ries was the very last place in Paris where the most suspicious of detectives would be likely to look for an officer
of the Swiss Guard, I crossed the Pont Royal, and entered
the Carrousel from the Louvre Gallery.

Here, at least, was no lack of life and movement. The
place was thronged with sans-culottes, and worse than sans-
culottes—the abandoned of both sexes, creatures of the night,
drawn from the lowest dregs of the population, who had taken
part in the plunder of the palace and the murder and muti-
lation of my wounded comrades, and were now celebrating
their victory.

In the middle of the square blazed a huge fire, round
which danced a horde of half-naked harpies, howling the
"Carmagnole." They wore Phrygian caps, their bare arms
were red with blood, and from time to time they fed the fire
with what at a distance appeared to be billets of wood, but
were really, as I too soon perceived, the butchered remains
of their victims.

When the women whirled round, raising their reddened
arms and throwing back their heads, and the glare of the
bonfire lighted up their fiendish faces, the scene could be lik-
ened only to a witches' sabbath or a dance of the damned.

Horror held me enchained. For a moment or two I
stood still, as though fascinated, unwilling to witness the
dreadful scene, yet unable to avert my gaze. Then I
thought to turn back ; but quickly realizing that any show
of disgust or even disapproval on my part would entail my
destruction, I went deliberately forward, threading and
shouldering my way through the press, and when the mob
shouted "Vive la Nation !" I shouted with them. For
God knows I had nothing against the nation ; but as for
those brigands and cutthroats, I would have shot them
down with as little remorse as I would have killed so many
wolves.

With some difficulty, and slowly—any appearance of haste might have attracted unpleasant attentions—I made my way to the Rue St. Honoré. Here the crowd, though less dense, was of the same stamp. Not until I reached the obscurity of the Rue de la Touelerie did I feel myself safe. Several times had I been roughly addressed and threatened by those whom I had thrust aside; yet by dint of apologies and soft answers, and, once, by standing the price of a drink, I got through, unsuspected and unscathed. But just as I was rejoicing over my good-luck (better than my rashness deserved), and thinking that I should reach my destination without further trouble, I heard a cry of distress and a call for help.

Looking forward with eyes now accustomed to the semi-darkness of the summer night, I perceived at the corner of the Rue Artois the dimly-defined figures of two men and a woman.

"Help! Unhand me! Let me go!" cried the last. "Robbers! Help!"

I had no desire to court an adventure or run gratuitous risks; but as it was impossible to turn a deaf ear to a woman's appeal for help (though, considering the place and the hour, the woman might be no better than she should be), I hurried to the spot.

The two men, both sans-culottes, had hold of the woman (who was veiled, and, so far as I could see, well dressed) by the wrists, and were dragging her along.

"Oh, monsieur, deliver me from these villains! They have insulted me. They are hurting me, they wanted—"

"Hold your noise, or I'll hit you in the mouth!" growled one of the brutes. "Come along!"

"Why have you arrested this lady? What has she done?" I asked.

"You mind your own business. Come along, I say!"

" My business is to know why you have arrested this lady."

" She is a *ci-devant*" (ex-aristocrat), "and we are taking her to the police-station."

" It is not true," said the woman, excitedly. " I was going quietly along. They stopped me and demanded money, and because I could give them none, not having brought my purse, they arrested me."

" Let her go," I said, quietly.

" We will let daylight into you, if you don't stand aside."

I had already decided what to do. To use my pistols would be dangerous, hardly less so to use my dagger, for unless I killed both the fellows at a stroke the survivor would make a noise and bring a police patrol on the scene before I could get out of the way. On the other hand, as both were in liquor and undersized I did not regard them as formidable antagonists, despite the pikes and sabres with which they were weaponed.

" Let her go," I repeated.

" Out of the way, or *pardieu* I'll—" lowering his pike.

Retreating a step as though yielding to the threat, I put myself in boxing attitude and, quick as thought, gave the fellow a blow between the eyes, delivered straight from the shoulder and with a will. Down he went like a felled ox, and before his companion could recover from his surprise I served him in like fashion. " They are both *hors de combat* for a few minutes," quoth I to the lady. " Do you live far from here? Shall I have the pleasure of seeing you home?" offering my arm.

" Thanks, monsieur, a thousand thanks! I live in the Rue St. Denis. Let us go quickly, please," she said, excitedly and half sobbing. " It may seem strange that I am out so late and without an escort. But I have been to see a dear friend who is sick and like to die. My husband could not come with me, and my maid was afraid. Besides, she is such a timid creature that she would have been of no use. Those horrid men! But for you I should have been locked up, in what company Heaven only knows."

A short walk brought us to the Rue St. Denis, where the lady presently pointed out as her home a house with closed shutters which looked like a shop.

" In that case, madame, you will permit me to wish you good-evening," said I.

"Oh, you will surely come in and let my husband thank you for the great service you have rendered me."

I hesitated for a moment, but, curiosity getting the better of discretion, I bowed assent, whereupon the lady opened a side-door with a latch-key, and I followed her into the house and up a narrow, dimly lighted staircase, which, rather to my surprise, terminated in a spacious, well-lighted gallery adorned with paintings and bright with flowers.

The lady drew aside a portière and opened a door.

"*Allons,*" she said softly, and the next moment we were in a handsomely furnished room, where sat a gentleman in a gorgeous dressing-gown and an easy-chair, with his foot on a rest. His features were Hebraic, his eyes dark and shrewd, and he was probably some thirty years old.

At the sight of me he looked more than surprised and glanced inquiringly at his wife, a fair young woman with violet eyes and brown hair.

" This gentleman has done me a great service, Adolphe," said she. " Rescued me from two half-tipsy sans-culottes, who, as I had no money to give them, charged me with being a *ci-devant*, and in spite of my cries and protests were dragging me off to the police-station when this gentleman was good enough to knock them down with his fist, one after the other. He must have arms like sledge-hammers. And then he kindly escorted me hither, and I have asked him in to be thanked by you."

"In rendering Madame Dufour this service you have made me your debtor, and I thank you warmly," said the man of the house, politely. "Excuse me for not rising; for the moment I am a cripple," glancing at his leg. "These sans-culottes are triple brutes. Did you tell them who you were, Berthe?"

"Of course I did. But it was of no use. They protested that I was a *ci-devant*, and if this gentleman had not come so promptly to the rescue—"

"You would have been locked up all night in a filthy cell. I shudder at the mere thought. But I beg you a thousand pardons, monsieur—I have not introduced myself : Adolphe Dufour, goldsmith and money-changer, at your service."

"My name is Anatole Boucher," said I.

"It gives me great pleasure to make your acquaintance, Monsieur Boucher. I have also the honor of being a captain in the National Guard and president of my section, and another honor with which I would have gladly dispensed— that of a wound, happily not very serious, received during the attack on the Tuileries. The last volley fired by those infernal Swiss."

This was bad hearing. I was in the enemy's camp, and though I had nothing to fear from the lame gentleman in the easy-chair, prudence suggested that it were well to take my leave.

"You will surely stop and take supper with us," exclaimed M. Dufour as I rose from my chair.

"Impossible, monsieur, I have an engagement."

"At least you will drink a glass of wine with my husband," put in the lady. "I shall take it very unkindly if you don't."

Fearing that to refuse the invitation might provoke suspicion. I resumed my seat, and Mme. Dufour brought a decanter and glasses from the cupboard.

"I hope we shall have the pleasure of seeing you again," said my host, raising his glass and eying me keenly. "And if you will favor me with your address I shall do myself the honor of calling upon you."

Not being prepared with an answer, I merely bowed.

"I beg your pardon, I fear I have asked an indiscreet question," continued M. Dufour after a short pause. "These are strange times—and I don't think you are what you seem."

"Pray what do you take me for, monsieur?" I demanded angrily, for the remark was an impertinence.

"Judging by your attire, a notary's clerk or shopkeeper's assistant; but judging by your face and bearing and the vigorous way in which you dealt with those two ruffians, I should say you have served—"

"And if I have, what—"

"Precisely. What is it to me? This. Though a patriot, I am no fanatic. I am for universal brotherhood, and have absolutely no prejudices. I make a specialty of toleration, and war only against opinion."

"Were you acting in this spirit when you got your wound?"

"Perfectly. The Swiss Guard were of opinion that the monarchy should be upheld, we patriots were of opinion that it should be overthrown. But now that the fight is over, we can afford to be magnanimous."

"And you show your magnanimity by murdering and mutilating your prisoners," I broke in impulsively and, as I thought the next moment, with more frankness than wisdom.

"Yes, that is deplorable, I admit. But there are always exceptions, and though the people, when left to themselves, are good, they sometimes yield to impulse when they should be guided by reason. What is that, Berthe—a knock at the door? My faith, suppose it is Serin!"

" I am afraid it is Serin.   He often calls about this time."

" Serin, Monsieur Boucher, is a passionate patriot and a
member of the National Assembly and the Jacobin Club,
also very sharp and curious ; and if he were to suspect,
what we suspect, it might be very unpleasant for all of us.
Would you mind—?   There! he is knocking again.   Jeannette must let him in.   Berthe, take Monsieur Boucher into
the other passage.   If it prove to be Serin I shall sneeze,
and you can let monsieur out at the back.   Another time,
I hope—"

" Quick !   This way!" interrupted Mme. Dufour, anxiously, opening a door at the other end of the room.

I followed her, in some amusement at the bold captain's
trepidation, and we stood at attention in the passage.

Presently the danger signal went off.   Defour sneezed
loudly enough to be heard in the next street.

" I am afraid you must go," whispered Mme. Dufour.
" *Allons !*"

We went to the end of the passage, then down a flight of
stairs, next along another passage until we came to a door,
which she unbolted, and, holding it ajar, observed in an
emphatic undertone that Serin was a *misérable.*

" But," she added, " he is powerful, and when crossed,
dangerous.   Otherwise I would not let him darken my
door.   My husband, though he has taken the revolutionary
fever rather badly and is too much disposed to swim with
the stream, is good, and will serve you if he can.   In fact,
I shall make him—for at heart I am a royalist—like yourself."

" How—what ?"

" I am sure you are, also that Boucher is an *alias.*   I
think, from Adolphe's manner, that he has seen you before.
I shall make him tell me.   If you are in need of a temporary asylum, don't fail to come hither.   One good turn de-

7

serves another.   And now you must permit me to return to
the salon, or that *misérable* will be curious.   He is simply
made up of curiosity and suspicion.   This is a back street.
Take the first turn to the right, and you will find yourself
once more in the Rue St. Denis.   Be sure you come again.
Au revoir."

CHAPTER XIV

THE VICOMTE'S PROPOSAL

"So much for my disguise," I thought while wending towards the Rue Cléry. "Detected at the first inspection! I do believe that this confounded Dufour recognized me as an officer of the regiment. What a fool I was to go in! I am glad I gave him no inkling whither I was going, for though he spoke fairly, a patriot who consorts with members of the Jacobin Club is not to be trusted. Madame is a nice woman, good-looking, too, and I dare say would be as good as her word. . . . I must clear out of Paris before anybody else recognizes me—after I have seen Angélique. I hope no harm has befallen her. I dare say the vicomte knows. But where is he? . . . Hello! What is that? Another police patrol."

And as the police were gentlemen whom I had no desire to meet, I stepped into a dark entry until they were out of sight and hearing.

I had no difficulty in finding M. de Castellan's house, and the Swiss *concierge*, to whom I made myself known and delivered Schlessinger's message, showed me into a salon where I was presently joined by his master, a fine-looking middle-aged gentleman with a kindly face and a winning manner.

After congratulating me on my escape, of which he had heard from the vicomte, M. de Castellan asked me divers questions as touching what had befallen me during the previous twenty-four hours. When I told him of my latest adventure and my call at the house of M. Dufour, he looked very grave, saying that I had run a terrible risk. Of Du-

four he knew nothing, but of Serin too much.   He was one
of the most violent and truculent members of the Jacobin
Club and the "insurrectionary Commune."

"If he had come in before you left he would almost certainly have had you arrested, and probably the Dufours
also," observed M. de Castellan.

"I should not have surrendered without a struggle, sir,"
said I.   "I am armed as you see," opening my coat and
showing my pistols and dagger.

"You would have been quite right.   If they try to arrest
you resist to the death, for if you are taken they will have
your life.   But I hope you will not be arrested, and I shall
do my best to prevent any such misfortune.   I will find you
a hiding-place, and you must stay there until the storm has
blown over."

After heartily thanking M. de Castellan for his friendly
reception, I suggested that my wisest course would be to
quit Paris without delay.   It was terrible to think that I
could not accept a friend's hospitality without hazarding
his liberty, possibly his life.

To which he answered that quitting Paris was an impos-
sibility.   All the barriers were closed, and nobody was allowed to pass out on any pretext whatever.   Moreover, the
National Assembly had just made a law authorizing gendarmes and "active citizens" to arrest, on their own responsibility, whomsoever they might suspect of "*incivisme*,"
which meant sympathy with the nation's enemies or disaffection to the new government.

"Only members of the National Assembly, the Paris
Commune, and the Jacobin Club are safe," added M. de
Castellan.   "I thought a revolution necessary, and at the
outset gave it my support; but the present government is
more tyrannical than that of Louis XVI., and I know not
what will be the end."

He feared that I was the sole survivor of the second column, though a rumor had reached his ears that two or three of the fugitives had found a refuge in the cellars of the Ministry of Marine, and, with the connivance of friends, who supplied them with plain clothes, got safely away. But being private soldiers and unidentified they were less eagerly sought after than I was. Moreover, my escape and the way in which I had served their brigadier had greatly incensed the gendarmes, and they were moving heaven and earth to effect my capture.

"I shall give you a little room at the top of the house," said M. de Castellan, "and there you must stay for a few days, perhaps for a few weeks. It will be wearisome, no doubt, yet better than the Conciergerie and the scaffold."

This there was no gainsaying. My latest experience showed me that how cunningly soever I might disguise myself I could not appear outside without risk, and, having no desire to lose either my liberty or my head, I made up my mind to lie *perdu* in my host's little room until it should be safe for me to shift my quarters and quit the country.

I should probably see the vicomte in a few days, said M. de Castellan, in answer to my inquiries about him. He was keeping quiet, rather to avoid being suspected than because he was in any immediate danger. The police believed that he had left the city, and it was a belief which he was desirous not to disturb.

At this point our conversation was interrupted by Langbein, the Swiss porter, who informed his master that M. Monval wished to see him.

"Show Monsieur Monval in," said M. de Castellan. Then, turning to me, "I think you had better slip behind that screen."

I bowed and obeyed. The visitor stayed half an hour. I tried not to listen to their conversation, and succeeded so well (having much on my mind) that only a few disjointed scraps of it reached my understanding.

When the gentleman was gone my host called me forth.

" Monval is trustworthy and discreet, and would not have betrayed us," said he. " But he is also old and timid, and I thought you had better not meet. For if it should ever come out that he had met, and not denounced, a fugitive officer of the Swiss Guard, he would get into trouble."

" And yet you receive me as your guest ?"

" Deliberately, and with my eyes open to the possible consequences. But that is no reason why I should let a third person compromise himself unwittingly. Besides, I am Swiss by origin and connection, which Monval is not, and I regard it as the duty and privilege of a Christian gentleman to do to others as he would that they should do to him, even at the peril of his life. Who knows that before long I may not have to ask from some kind soul the same help I am now giving you ?"

And then M. de Castellan himself took me to my room. Like the chamber I had occupied at Mme. de Bésenval's house, it was under the tiles, though larger and more commodious, and outside was a corridor where I could take walking exercise when the servants were having their meals, only my host and Langbein being in the secret.

In the morning Langbein brought my breakfast, also some books and papers wherewith to beguile my seclusion. Among the papers, to my great delight, was a copy of the *Times* not more than a fortnight old.

Before Langbein went away he called my attention to an overhead trap-door which gave access to the roof, and suggested that, in the event of a sudden intrusion of the police, the surest hiding-place would be among the chimney-stacks on the side farthest from the front entrance.

I remained in my quarters several days, whiling away the

time as best I could. When I grew tired of reading and lying in bed (and I did a good deal of the latter, *faute de mieux*), I would look through the window, which, as it was little bigger than my head and over against the opening into the Rue de Bourbon and very high up, I could do without being observed.

Towards the end of the week came the vicomte, to my great satisfaction. I was dying both for news and company, especially news of Angélique. He said she was in fair health and of good courage, but her mother's health did not improve, and so long as they remained in Paris was not likely to improve; but as Mme. de la Tour was too much of an invalid to travel, leaving it was, as yet, out of the question, even though they could obtain passports, which was doubtful.

Then he explained that although he had been in hiding he had not been inactive, and that the plot for the rescue of the royal family was making good progress, and he invited me to lend him a helping hand—in other words, to join in the conspiracy. On which I laughed and asked him how I could help to rescue anybody. I needed rescuing myself.

"You can do nothing in Paris, of course, while there is this hue-and-cry after you," said he. "But once you are out of Paris—"

"That is precisely where I want to be, but how am I to get out?"

"I think you may—in a few days. The barriers are again open, and though the new regulations about passports are very stringent—none being granted except on a personal application, supported by two well-known citizens of approved patriotism—I hope to get you one. Not on your personal application, of course."

"Whose then?"

"We shall see. Even patriots have their price, and with money everything is possible."

"Unfortunately I have no money, or next to none. Save five louis, of which I have spent three, I left all my cash at the barracks, and you cannot do much bribing with two louis."

"I have some, but I shall need it all. It will take many golden keys to open the Temple. Is there no way?"

"If I could only sell a draft on my father—"

And then I bethought me of Dufour, "jeweller and money-changer," and told Boulanger of my adventure of the previous week and my encounter with the gentleman in question.

"The very thing," he exclaimed, delightedly. "From what you say I take it that Monsieur Dufour is a decent fellow. You have placed him under an obligation. He will certainly buy your draft on monsieur, your father."

"But I should have to put myself in his power by telling him my name, and I am not sure—"

"You would not need to give him your address, and as I shall act as intermediary he will know little more than he knows already."

"You would see him then?"

"Yes."

"When?"

"At once. He lives in the Rue St. Denis, you say?"

"Yes, hard by St. Sauveur. But I should advise you to have a word with Madame Dufour before you speak to her husband. She is a royalist at heart, and, unless I am much mistaken, rules the roost."

"Is she good-looking?"

"Decidedly, and, I think, well disposed towards me."

"Of course. How much can you draw for?"

"Anything in reason. Say, two hundred and fifty pounds

sterling, and you may tell Monsieur Dufour that the firm of
Frederic Astor & Co. is of high repute, both in Manchester
and London, and their paper second to none.   I suppose I
am to understand that the passport is conditional on my
participation in your enterprise."

" Not so far as I am concerned.   I should be only too
glad to get you a passport in any case—if I could.   But
circumstances over which I have no control compel me to
work through friends who, though royalists at heart, like
your friend Madame Dufour, pose as patriots, and would
naturally do more for a fellow-conspirator than for a mere
friend. You understand ?"

" Perfectly," I said, though I had a shrewd suspicion
that my friend was stretching a point in order to gain his
own ends.   " And now tell me what part I am expected to
play in the plot."

On this the vicomte went minutely into the details, which
I need not repeat here any further than to say that the idea
was to smuggle the royal family out of the Temple (with
the connivance of friends inside) some evening after dark,
then out of Paris in a market-cart driven by one of the
conspirators. As the fugitives were to be hidden under
litter and empty sacks, passports would be unnecessary, and
recognition, barring accidents, impossible.

At St. Denis, or some other place near Paris, the royal fugitives were to be transferred to carriages drawn by swift horses,
and once at Rouen they would be in comparative safety.

My share in the business was to proceed thither when
the time came, and arrange with the king's friends for his
reception; also for his further journey to Dieppe and England, whither I was to accompany him.

This done, it would be my duty to return to St. Denis and
take command of a party of ardent young royalists who had
volunteered to escort the royal family to the coast.

I told the vicomte frankly that I did not augur well of his scheme. It seemed to me altogether too hazardous and complicated.

"Oh, don't think I have any illusions," he answered. "It is the curse of conspiracies that if you are few you can do nothing, whereas if you are many you risk betrayal, either by indiscretion or intention. But I see no other way. It is impossible to get their majesties out of the Temple and land them in England without risk of a miscarriage. Nevertheless the attempt is worth making. At the worst, they can only die, and if they stay where they are their days will not be long. I suppose we can count on you?"

"Certainly. I have no great regard for the king, and he is not my king, but I would do anything for the queen and those poor children."

"Good! As you promise me your help I shall not quarrel with your motives. Now I must go and do my errand. Expect me back when you see me. The Dufours may not be at home. But I shall return as soon as possible."

He returned in little over an hour, with a face that proclaimed success.

"It is a thing done, thanks to Madame Dufour," he said. "You were quite right in believing that you had made a favorable impression. She thinks you are a hero *sans peur et sans tache*, and, my faith, I am disposed to agree with her."

"Don't talk nonsense, if you please, vicomte."

"Nonsense! I was never more serious in my life. Without the lady's help my mission would have proved a failure, and if I had not invoked your name — however, to the point. Thanks to his wife's insistence, Monsieur Dufour will buy your draft on the highly respectable house of Frederic Astor & Co. But he is a true bourgeois, timid and grasping. Business was business, he said, and, considering the risk, he could only give for a draft of two hundred and fifty pounds the equivalent of two hundred and twenty-five pounds, half in coin, half in assignats " (depreciated paper money) " at a discount of fifty per cent."

" Well, I don't think I can object to that, considering that if he were found out the penalty would be death."

" No fear! Monsieur Dufour is far too wide awake to be found out. Here are the drafts in duplicate. All you have to do is to sign the draft, and write a line of advice to Frederic Astor & Co."

" But won't that be dangerous? The post-office—"

" Will know nothing about it. The letter, as also the draft, will be sent under cover to Monsieur Dufour's correspondents in London. Moreover, to make assurance doubly sure, the packet will be posted by a trusty messenger at some place outside Paris. And I must do Monsieur Dufour the justice to say that he is a good paymaster. The moment you have signed the draft the money will be at your disposal. Shall I fetch it for you?"

" Thank you. By all means."

And then I set my name to the documents, and wrote the letter of advice, adding by way of postscript a few words informing my father that I was still at liberty, though in hiding, and that I hoped, with the help of the proceeds of the draft, to escape from Paris and make my way to London in the course of a few days or weeks, as fortune might favor me. This done, the vicomte put the papers in his pocket and departed on his second errand, promising to return as quickly as might be.

By this time it was nearly night, to my great content, for I feared these continual comings and goings might provoke suspicion and lead to trouble.

When the vicomte was gone I went to the window and watched the people below, as they moved about silent and ghost-like in the fast-deepening twilight, amusing myself by noting the peculiarities of their gait, and the differences in their stature and appearance, and weaving vagrant fancies as to whence they came, whither they were going, and what they did.

Suddenly, as by common consent, these wayfarers disappear. Some go one way, some another, and the end of the Rue de Bourbon, which is all I can see, becomes a lonesome waste. At the same moment there falls on my ear the tramp of an approaching patrol. In those days people were nearly as much afraid of a patrol as of a mob.

When the detachment came opposite the house I heard a shout, followed by the word "Halt!" Then I thought I could distinguish the grounding of arms and a ring of steel, as when soldiers fix bayonets.

I was wondering what all this might portend — for short of putting my head completely out of the window (which would have been dangerous) I could not see what was passing directly beneath it—when my door suddenly opened and Langbein appeared at the threshold.

"A domiciliary visit, Herr Astor!" he exclaimed, excitedly. "Quick! Out on the roof as you value your life."

CHAPTER XV

THE INCIDENT OF THE FLOWER-POT

LANGBEIN departed as abruptly as he had come, and before the sound of his retreating footsteps had died away I was on the house-top, making for the chimney-stacks. The roof being long and steep, and slippery with recent rain, this was no easy task. I had to crawl, slowly and painfully, on my hands and knees. Though night was falling, and the street so narrow and the house so high that I ran little risk of being seen from below, it was possible that some gendarme of exceptionally keen vision might catch a glimpse of me; wherefore I clung closely to the tiles. and effaced myself as much as might be.

At length I reached the ridge, and sat down on it. under the shadow of a big chimney-stack.

After resting a few minutes, I shifted my position with a view to taking post on the other side of the ridge. In doing so I slipped (Heaven only knows how), and before I realized my danger was sliding down the high-pitched roof.

In vain I clutch at the tiles with my hands and try to stop myself with my heels. I go on with ever increasing momentum. A few seconds, and I shall be shot from the roof and dashed to pieces on the pavement.

A thought of my father, England, and Angélique flashes through my brain. I shut my eyes and commend my soul to God; and then, with a shock that bends my knees, wrenches my loins, and shakes every bone in my body, I stop.

The heels of my shoes have struck the stone gutter that runs along the edge of the roof, stopping my *glissade.*

My feeling of relief was so intense, and the fear that if I stirred I might fall so great, that for several minutes I lay quite still, neither desiring nor daring to move.

I think, too, that I must have been slightly stunned.

The first thing I did so soon as I recovered my scattered wits was to doff my shoes one after the other, yet gingerly and carefully withal; for I was at the edge of the slope, and a single false step had been fatal.

This done, I recommenced the ascent, and had not gone far when I heard Langbein's voice in the region of the trap-door.

"Are you there, Herr Astor?" he asked.

"Yes."

"It is all right; you can come in."

I returned to my room with a thankful heart. My brief experience of roof-climbing had confirmed me in my preference for inside quarters, and here were two more dangers narrowly escaped.

Langbein had lighted my lamp.

"*Gott im Himmel!* where have you been?" he exclaimed as I dropped through the trap. "Your hands are bleeding, your head is bleeding, and your coat is in rags."

This was true. The back of my head, which had come in contact with the tiles, was bruised and cut, and in trying to stop myself, I had wounded my hands and torn off two or three of my finger-nails.

I told Langbein what had happened.

"Well for you the gutter was there," he said. "Well for us also. If you had come tumbling off the roof among the Blues it would have been worse than the flower-pot."

Had Langbein looked less painfully serious I should have thought he was laughing at my misadventure.

"Worse than the flower-pot! What on earth do you mean?" I asked.

"A flower-pot caused all the mischief, *meinherr*. It fell from a window-sill as the patrol was passing, and narrowly missed giving one of the ruffians his quietus. Thinking it had been done on purpose, they smashed the door in, threatened to search the house from top to bottom, and lock us all up. It was all Monsieur de Castellan could do to pacify them, and they went away growling, and saying they would report the incident at the Hôtel de Ville. That means the house will be 'suspect' and watched, and is no longer a safe asylum for you. Monsieur de Castellan is of opinion that you had better change your quarters before worse befall."

"But whither shall I go?" I asked in dismay, since, even though Mme. Dufour's invitation were serious, it had not been seconded by her husband, and I doubted whether I should be safe in a house belonging to a patriot and frequented by Jacobins.

"Monsieur de Castellan knows of a place. He is always taking thought for others. He will be here shortly, and tell you about it. Meanwhile, I must fetch plaster and water and dress your wounds."

Whereupon Langbein went, and in a few minutes returned and began operations. While he was acting the part of Good Samaritan his master appeared, looking very grave, and after hearing how I had come by my hurts, said that, to his great regret, he was compelled to urge my immediate departure. The departure was imperative. He quite expected, as the first result of the unfortunate incident of the flower-pot, that a sentinel would be posted at the door, probably within the hour, and if he escaped a domiciliary visit he should esteem himself fortunate, adding that a good friend of his, who lived in a more tranquil part of Paris than himself, would put me up for a few days, and that he should accompany me thither himself.

I answered that he had already done more than enough

for one who had no claim on him, and was beseeching him to let me shift for myself when he silenced me with an imperative gesture, saying that, though he could no longer keep me in his house, I was still his guest, that he considered it his duty to find me another asylum, and wherever I was he should continue to watch over my safety—if I would allow him.

My eyes filled with tears, and I was so deeply moved that I could do no more than take both my dear friend's hands in mine and murmur incoherent thanks.

Then he found me a coat, my own being all in tatters. Our destination was the Rue des Trois Pavillons; but as it would not have been well for us to leave the house together, I started first, and M. de Castellan agreed to join me ten or fifteen minutes later at the corner of the Rue Mauconseil. Before setting out I mentioned Boulanger's expected visit, and Langbein was instructed to tell him that if he called again on the morrow he would learn whither I was gone, and that I was very desirous to see him.

I wanted the proceeds of my draft. My "cash in hand" had diminished almost to nothingness. I needed a change of clothes, under and over, and I might at any moment find myself in a predicament from which the judicious application of money would be the sole means of deliverance.

M. de Castellan joined me at the corner of the Rue Mauconseil, according to arrangement. I proposed that we should take a fiacre, but he thought we had better not; most of the drivers thereabouts knew him, and we could not be too cautious. And then he told me that the Assembly had just decreed the establishment of a new tribunal for dealing with "offences against the nation" (which might mean pretty nearly anything). This tribunal could inflict only one punishment—death; and against its judgments there was to be no appeal. As M. de Castellan said, it was well to be cautious.

The house to which he took me was lofty and spacious, and belonged to a tailor called Verner, who turned an honest penny by letting furnished rooms and taking lodgers. One of his tenants was a member of the Assembly.   In one sense this would be an advantage, a house where dwelt a deputy being less likely to become "suspect" than one not so fortunate.   On the other hand, I should need to lie closely *perdu*, both for my own sake and that of my new host. Verner, as M. de Castellan informed me, was an excellent fellow, in whom I might place implicit confidence, and albeit solicitude for his wife and family, and a natural desire to keep his head on his shoulders, constrained him to swim with the revolutionary stream, he compounded for his pliancy by giving aid and comfort to the revolution's victims.

He was a dapper, fussy little man with a round belly, a rotund, smiling face, and a fluent tongue.   He received us with great cordiality, and gave me a room on the first floor, with a window looking towards an inner court.   It had also the advantage of communicating with the kitchen by a back staircase, which might be useful in certain eventualities, and the room was so placed that unless I was very demonstrative I could neither be seen nor heard either by insiders or outsiders ; and as only Verner and his wife were aware of my presence in the house, I might consider myself tolerably safe.   At any rate, he said so ; and I was, of course, bound to believe him.

When M. de Castellan was gone I had a pleasant talk with M. Verner, in the course of which I took occasion to inquire the name of his tenant, the deputy.

"Monsieur Serin, or, as he prefers to be called, Citizen Deputy, and his room is next to yours," answered the tailor.

"Serin!   Why, he is a fanatical Jacobin."

s

"Exactly, and I wish he had his deserts. Only the night before last he made a speech at the Jacobin Club, in which he denounced the poor king as an enemy of the human race, and in the name of an outraged people demanded the tyrant's head. Yes, Serin is a monster, and I was very sorry when he proposed to become my tenant; but I could not say him nay, and you must remember that his presence here constitutes a sort of guarantee of the soundness of my political principles, which in these days is an immense advantage."

"I dare say. But suppose he and I were to meet, by some untoward accident? Being a deputy, he has probably seen me on parade at the palace or strolling in the gardens, where I used often to walk; and though I look very different in these clothes, and have shaved my mustache and abandoned powder, he might recognize me."

Verner turned pale at the mere idea.

"But you must not meet him!" he exclaimed. "Serin is as sharp as a needle, and as suspicious as his friend Murat. When he is in you must not show your nose outside your room door on any pretext whatever, nor make the slightest noise. Only this wall divides your room from his. Thank goodness, he is not here much. He is away all day, sometimes all night, and the only meal he takes in the house is breakfast. And now I think I had better leave you."

What Verner had imparted caused me considerable apprehension; but I retired soon after his departure, and fell into a troubled sleep.

CHAPTER XVI

CITIZEN SERIN FIRES A PISTOL

I HAD slept I don't know how long—perhaps two hours—when I was awakened by a violent scratching at my door, followed by several gentle, yet emphatic, knocks.

"What is it?" said I, getting up and going to the door.

"For God's sake, let me in!" whispered Verner.

I let him in.

"Put something on and come out," he said. "We are betrayed; the Blues and a lot of sans-culottes are coming to search the house. A good friend of mine heard them say so, and ran on to warn me. He left them in the Rue Franc Bourgeois. They will be here in two minutes. Quick!"

"Impossible!" I answered, as I got into my breeches and threw on my coat. "Nobody but Monsieur de Castellan knows I am here."

"You may have been tracked. Anyhow, they are coming, and if they find you here we shall all be ruined—all! all!"

"Is there a way out?"

"None. You would meet them; you would be seen. The house is beset. But there is a place in the kitchen, and, fortunately, the servants have gone to bed, and Serin hasn't come home. Come along! Quick! To the kitchen!"

I followed my host softly down the back stairs. As he stood at the bottom, holding above his head, for my benefit, a long, thin candle with an untrimmed wick, its flickering light fell on a pale and frightened face. For this, however,

I thought none the worse of him; every decent father of a family in Paris was in a chronic condition of fear just then, and, for my own part, I frankly confess that I would rather have been somewhere else.

"This is the place," said Verner, when we were in the kitchen, motioning with his candle to a sort of black hole close to the hearth. "It is bigger than it looks, and roomy inside; but when closed, looks so small that nobody would think it could hold a man. Fortunately, the fire has been out some time, or you might be roasted. But there are holes for the admission of air at the farther end. Hark! The ruffians are thundering at the door. They will break it in. I must run and open it for them. That is it! Now you are in, and be sure you stop there until I tell you to come out."

I had to creep in on my hands and knees. Once inside, however, I could stand half upright; but as the position left a good deal to be desired in the way of ease, I sought for something whereon I might sit or recline; and after groping about, found a heap of refuse that answered my purpose indifferently well, and from which I inferred that the place was what Lancashire folk call a "cinder hoyle."

It was also hot—very hot; and there was so sulphurous a reek from the still warm cinders that I breathed with difficulty, and the sweat rolled down my face and fell on the ground like drops of rain.

Yet after a few minutes these discomforts were forgotten in a new excitement. Through the air-holes mentioned by my host I could see lights moving about the court-yard. They were carried by gendarmes and sans-culottes. I could likewise hear the officer in command of the detachment giving directions for the quest, and ordering poor Verner to make a general illumination by putting lights in every window.

The men were bidden to look everywhere—search every cupboard and closet, sound the walls and floors, and even to probe the mattresses with their pikes and bayonets.

Little they thought that the man they wanted was watching them, with a pistol in either hand and a dagger in his belt.

For the heat at length grew so oppressive, the air so stifling, that I debated in my mind whether it were not wiser to sally forth and die fighting than tarry in the cinder-hole at the risk of being smothered.

I had almost decided that the former was the better and more manly course, when a gleam of light shone through the chinks of the door, or rather, manhole, on the kitchen side of the recess. As the door fitted loosely, the chinks were wide, and it occurred to me that by kneeling down and putting my mouth to them I should be able to breathe more freely.

The experiment succeeded. A current of cool air came in through the chinks which refreshed my body and revived my spirits. I found, also, that I could see into the kitchen, albeit, as the light vanished as soon as it appeared, I was unable to make out by whom, or for what purpose, it had been brought in.

In the meantime the searchers went on with their work. I could hear them above me, and through the air-holes observe their movements in the rooms on the opposite side of the court-yard ; and soon the sound of voices and the tramp of approaching feet warned me that they were making for the kitchen.

First came poor Verner with a candle, and though obviously doing his best to put a bold face on it, looking like a doomed man. I felt sorry beyond measure that I had been the means, however unintentionally, of involving him in so terrible a misfortune, for as he was accompanied by six

gendarmes, and there were only three places in the kitchen
that could hold a man—a closet, the chimney, and the cinder-hole—discovery seemed inevitable.　It was inconceiva-
ble that the searchers, who had been told to seek everywhere, and even to probe the mattresses, should overlook
the cinder-hole.

Nevertheless, I resolved to make an effort to escape, and,
failing that, to sell my life dearly.　My plan was this: When
the gendarmes were stooping to open the door, I would
kick it aside, and give them two pistol shots point-blank;
then, drawing my dagger, burst out, and try to gain the
street before they recovered from the bewilderment into
which so sudden an attack would be sure to throw them.

At the worst I could but die, and if I let myself be taken
I should perish on the scaffold.　I preferred a soldier's
death, and the fortune that had already so often befriended
me might befriend me again.

But, to my surprise, the gendarmes, each of whom carried
a light, instead of examining the closet and the cinder-hole,
began to overhaul the drawers, presses, and cupboards,
which, though they might have held a child, could not possibly have contained a well-grown boy.　They tumbled all
the contents on the floor—without, of course, finding what
they wanted — and were beginning to search the closet
when the kitchen door opened, and a harsh and peremptory
voice demanded what the devil they were doing.

The new-comer was a tall, spare man, with deep-sunken
eyes, and a sallow and sinister, yet not altogether ill-favored
face, and, as touching his person, got up like a glorified
sans-culotte.　He wore a blouse, Phrygian cap, and very
roomy trousers.　Round his waist was a three-colored tie,
round his throat a red handkerchief, and a murderous-look-
ing sabre dangled from his belt.

"What the devil are you doing?" he repeated, with an

air which showed that he was a man in authority and fully aware of his own importance.

"Searching for arms, Citizen Deputy," answered the brigadier in command of the party.

"By whose order, may I ask?"

"By order of the Committee of the Section, Rights of Man, Citizen Deputy."

"Don't you know that the law disapproves of domiciliary visits after sunset, and that the law is the voice of the nation, and the voice of the nation the voice of God?"

"We are simply doing as we were told, Citizen Deputy. The responsibility rests with the Committee of the Section, not with us."

"True! All the same, this is an irregularity that must be reported. On whose denunciation was the search ordered?"

"On the denunciation of Joseph Foucroy, master white-smith, Rue Brac."

"What say you to this, Citizen Verner?" asked the deputy, turning to the gentleman in question, whose face, I was glad to observe, had undergone a change for the better. Erstwhile anxious and despairing, it was now radiant and smiling.

"What do I say?" he answered, indignantly. "I say that it is a foul slander. This Foucroy is a poltroon and a rogue, Citizen Serin. He owes me five hundred francs for work done, honest work. I press him for payment, and he revenges himself by denouncing me as a concealer of arms."

"Ah, this also must be seen to," making a note on his tablets; "it is a crime to use the law as an engine for the gratification of private vengeance, and I shall take care that this sneak gets his deserts. Citizen Verner is a true patriot and an honest man, Citizen Brigadier. Aristides

Serin answers for him. He is my landlord and my tailor. Before France became free he made breeches for aristocrats, now he makes trousers for sans-culottes. He made these I am now wearing," glancing admiringly at his nether garments. "Aristocrats despise tailors. We patriots despise aristocrats and honor tailors. They clothe our persons; they are as useful and indispensable as butchers, bakers, and candlestick-makers, and, like them, belong to the vast army of workers which is one of the glories of France."

"It is true, it is true," murmured the gendarmes, admiringly.

"My father was a tailor. It is my pride to spring from the people, my privilege to spend my days and nights in their service. Our brave soldiers who are defending the sacred soil of France against the coalesced kings of Europe are in sore need of arms, and if those who possess arms do not voluntarily lay them on the altar of the country the country takes them. Therefore, searches must be made. But before this search was ordered, I think that I, who live in this house, ought to have been consulted. Have you found any arms, brigadier?"

"Only this pistol, Citizen Deputy," handing it to Serin.

"Ah, well, a citizen must be allowed at least one weapon for his personal use. It looks valuable—double-barrelled and silver mounted."

"I had forgotten its existence," put in Verner, eagerly. "I took it from a customer who had no other means of settling my little bill. He said it was worth all he owed me."

"The customer was a *ci-devant*, I suppose?"

"You are right, Citizen Deputy. It belonged to a *ci-devant* noble."

"It looks like the pistol of a *ci-devant*. Furbished up, it would make a handsome weapon."

"And look well in your belt, Citizen Deputy. Do me the favor to accept it as a gift—friendship's tribute to high-souled patriotism."

"You do me too much honor, dear Citizen Verner," said Serin, with a smile of serene self-satisfaction. "I am proud to own you as my friend, and I am at least a sincere patriot —whether high-souled, it will be for France and posterity to decide. I cannot refuse a gift so graciously offered, and I shall ever cherish it as a souvenir of our friendship and your merits. Is it loaded?"

"I cannot say. It is just as I got it. I never either loaded or discharged a fire-arm in my life."

"I shall soon see," priming the pistol.

"Had you not better try it with the ramrod?" suggested the brigadier.

"No, I am going to fire it."

And then, to my consternation, Serin pointed the pistol straight at my head, which I promptly removed from the line of his fire.

"Shoot up the chimney, and then you cannot hurt any-body," said the tailor, thoughtfully.

"Unless there is a *ci-devant* or a Swiss hiding there," said Serin, grimly. "Good! I will act on your sugges-tion, Citizen Verner," cocking the pistol.

Then followed a loud explosion and a cry of dismay, and the next moment the Citizen Deputy was dancing round the kitchen as black as a sweep, and with his fingers in his mouth. One of the barrels had burst, damaging his hand, and the concussion had brought down an avalanche of soot.

"Oh, oh, oh!" he cried, "a thousand thunders! *Sacré nom!* To the devil with your pistol, Citizen Verner! It has broken my forefinger. To the devil with it, I say! And that cursed soot has got into my eyes and throat," coughing violently. "Your chimney has not been swept for ages, Citizen Verner."

Here some of the gendarmes tittered audibly, whereupon Serin, completely losing his temper, turned on them fiercely.

"You dare to laugh at me!" he screamed. "Get you gone this instant, riff-raff! Who are you to violate an honest citizen's domicile at dead of night? I'll report you to the commune; I'll bring your conduct before the Assembly; I'll have your blood. *Sacré nom!* You shall be tried by the Revolutionary Tribunal and beheaded. Get you gone, I say. March!"

The gendarmes marched.

CHAPTER XVII

BAD NEWS

"I AM afraid my finger is broken, Citizen Verner," observed Serin, ruefully. "It hurts dreadfully, and I cannot move it."

"I don't think so," examining the injured digit. "Bruised and cut, but not fractured. I have a liniment which will reduce the inflammation and relieve the pain. Shall I?—"

"Thank you. By all means."

Verner produced a bottle, poured some of the contents on the wounded finger, and rubbed it vigorously in.

"It will smart a little at first," said he, "but afterwards—"

"Smart!" exclaimed the deputy, snatching his hand away and resuming his dance. "Smart! It burns! To the devil with your liniment! It is *aqua-fortis!*"

"Only have a little patience," quoth Verner, soothingly— "only have a little patience, and you will experience great relief. Just one more application."

"I'll see you guillotined first, Citizen Verner. . . . It does begin to feel a little better, though. Should it be bound up?"

"Yes, with a wet rag. Allow me."

When the bandage had been applied, Serin gave a sigh of satisfaction.

"That is good," he said. "Why didn't you do it before? Now I shall go to my room. Don't think I shall sleep much, though, and my clothes are ruined. To the devil with your pistol, Citizen Verner! I wish I had never seen it."

Notwithstanding this abuse of his gift, Verner accompanied the deputy obsequiously to the door and across the court-yard, then returned to the kitchen.

"They are all gone; you can emerge," he said, at the same time opening the cinder-hole door.

As I crawled out, Verner began to laugh—laughed till the tears rolled down his cheeks, and went on laughing so long that I thought he would never stop.

"Excuse me," he gasped at length. "But I really could not restrain myself any longer. I was nearly bursting. What a comedy! Did you see him dance? I wish the pistol had blown his head off. It had been loaded a twelvemonth. To think that you were saved by Serin! I told you it was an advantage to have a deputy as tenant. How he gave it those Blues!"

"They were searching for arms, not for me?"

"So it seems; and that sneak, Foucroy, was the cause. But all I knew in the first instance was that they were going to make me a domiciliary visit, whence I naturally concluded that we had been betrayed, and that they had heard you were here. All the same, if they had found you it would have been just as bad; and had not Serin appeared in the nick of time, they would have done so. I know I was in mortal terror, and you must have passed a bad quarter of an hour."

"Indeed I did. I was nearly smothered."

"Are you thirsty?"

"I am dying of thirst."

"You shall have something to drink that will do you good." Whereupon Verner went into the cellar, and presently returned with a bottle under each arm.

"Champagne wine," quoth he, smacking his lips. "I don't often indulge in it, but this is an occasion that ought to be celebrated: the discomfiture of the Blues and your rescue by Serin. What a sight he was! I knew the liniment would make him dance. It contains turpentine and acetic acid, and his finger is gashed as well as bruised."

" Isn't your deputy somewhat of a fool ?" I asked.

" No. Serin talks nonsense, like his kind, and is eaten up with vanity ; but he is shrewd and clever withal, and an implacable enemy. If he only knew. But he must neither know nor suspect," added Verner, gravely; "that were fatal."

And then we clinked our glasses and drank the king's health and to the confusion of his enemies; and the little man grew so hilarious that it was all I could do to keep him from breaking into song. But before we separated he sobered down, and again cautioned me to go to bed quietly and stay there until he scratched at my door.

This injunction I obeyed to the letter, falling asleep the moment I turned in, and so remaining until I was roused by the preconcerted signal.

On letting Verner in I learned that Serin was gone for the day. He had slept ill and left in an evil temper, vowing vengeance against the brigadier and his men, and carrying his arm in a sling.

Verner looked anxious, from which I opined that the champagne (of which he took the lion's share) had made his head ache, or reflection had damped his overnight's elation.

" When I think what a narrow escape we had I cannot help trembling," said he. " If Serin were to find out that he had prevented the arrest of an officer of the Swiss Guard, or that, while posing as a patriot, I was harboring you, his rage would be boundless."

" How can he find out ?"

" Accidents happen sometimes, and his manner this morning was not reassuring. It would not take much to

rouse his suspicions. You will need to keep very quiet,
Monsieur Boucher. I know it will be irksome, but the
consequence of discovery would be—decapitation."

I assured M. Verner that both for his sake and mine—
more, even, for his sake than mine—I should keep very
quiet, and obey his behests to the letter. This seemed to
relieve the good man greatly, and he went away comforted.

Later in the day came the vicomte, ostensibly to order a
coat from Verner, and was introduced into my rooms with
infinite precautions. He brought the proceeds of the draft,
but no news. He had heard nothing more of Angélique
and her mother, and did not propose to do aught further in
the matter of the plot and my passport until the storm had
blown over, and the hue-and-cry after me become less
strenuous.

"We must wait : but it won't be for long," he said, cheerfully. "Only keep out of their hands—and sight—for another week or two, and the police will conclude that you have
left Paris, and cease looking for you. By that time, too, I
dare say, the mob will have forgotten what they call the
treason, we the treacherous massacre, of the Swiss Guard
in some new excitement."

The money he had received from Dufour amounted to
some three thousand francs in coin (chiefly silver), and
six thousand in assignats (paper), but as these were worth
less than half their face value, I was not so rich as might
appear.

When I had given Boulanger a thousand francs in paper
and five hundred in silver for the purchase of a passport,
and was putting the balance in my pocket, he suggested
that, considering my precarious position and the possibility
of further changes of quarters, I might do well to make
Dufour my banker.

"Add the possibility of my being captured and my money

confiscated," quoth I. "Yes; it were a wise thing to do, if
Dufour be trustworthy."

The vicomte thought that Dufour, though politically a
malignant, was financially a man of honor. Moreover, by
cashing my draft he had put himself in our power as much
as I had put myself in his, and would not dare to play any
tricks.

So, with the exception of two thousand francs (the equivalent of about fifty pounds), mostly in assignats, which I kept
for present use and possible emergencies, I returned the
money to my friend, and it was agreed that he should place
it on deposit with Dufour.

One of the first uses I made of my accession of fortune
was to bespeak a suit of clothes from my landlord, and
commission him to buy me some undergarments, of which I
stood sorely in need. And then followed several tranquil
days—days which, albeit they travelled with leaden wings,
were free from excitement and alarms. I kept my room
religiously, seeing only Verner and his wife, except once,
when the vicomte made me a second visit.

Emboldened by this impunity and the fact that Serin was
so engrossed with politics that he departed early and
returned late, occasionally not at all, Verner now and then
allowed me to slip out of the house after dark, and stretch
my legs in the neighboring streets—but only when he had
first ascertained that they were quiet, and on condition that
my absence did not exceed one hour.

Twice was he good enough to bear me company. The
second time something happened.

We had finished our walk and were nearing Verner's
dwelling, when he touched my arm and whispered, "That
man just ahead is Serin. If he sees us he will want to know
all about you. Let us turn back."

"And if he were to turn round and catch sight of us! He

is looking round now. Put a bold face on it, and introduce me as a gentleman from the country who is looking for lodgings."

The night not being very dark, and ourselves under a lamp, Serin recognized my companion at once and greeted him, at the same time eying me curiously.

" Here is a gentleman who wants apartments," said Verner. "Citizen Boucher, Citizen Serin. I doubt, though, whether I can accommodate him."

" From the country?" And then, without waiting for an answer, " Have you been in Paris long?"

" Only a few days?"

" You are from the North, if I may judge from your accent."

This was an awkward question, and I had to deal with an awkward customer, likewise a sharp one; none other could have detected any accent in the three words I had spoken: " *Seulement quelques jours.*" But a happy thought came to my aid, and I answered without hesitation:

"From Alsace, Citizen Deputy."

" That accounts for the accent. Rather a strange time to visit Paris on pleasure, though, is it not?"

" I am not on a pleasure visit. My father is a dyer and calico printer, and my visit has to do with his business."

" A stalwart young fellow of your inches should have a nobler occupation than buying dyestuffs or selling calicoes. Don't you know that the country is in danger? If you are a true patriot you will at once enroll yourself in a regiment of volunteers and march to the frontier."

" I should like nothing better, Citizen Deputy, for, to tell the truth, I detest business."

" Enroll yourself, then, and I shall do myself the honor of writing to your father, if you will give me his address, applauding your resolution and accepting the responsibility of my advice. And if he is a good patriot he will be highly gratified."

"My father is an ardent patriot, Citizen Deputy, and I am sure your letter would be a great satisfaction to him."

I gave Serin, as the address of Citizen Frédéric Boucher, the name of the place at which my father had formerly lived in Elsass, and it was duly recorded in the deputy's tablets.

"I am delighted to have secured so promising a recruit for the army of the republic," said he, blandly. "If you come to me at the Hôtel de Ville, between ten and eleven to-morrow, you shall be duly enrolled. Where have you been staying?"

"At the Hôtel des Princes, Rue de Grenelle; but as I find it expensive, I am looking for lodgings in a cheaper quarter."

"The nation will provide you with lodgings for the future—occasionally, I dare say, *à la belle étoile*" (under the stars). "The Assembly took an important resolution to-night, Citizen Verner, of which I am sure you, like all other patriots, will approve. On the motion of Danton it has been decreed that on Wednesday night every house in Paris shall be searched for counter-revolutionists and arms. The municipal officers who conduct the visits will be empowered to arrest all whom they may suspect of disaffection to the republic, or who cannot give a satisfactory account of themselves. Meanwhile the barriers are to be closed, so that none of these aristocrats, who are plotting against the country, may escape. And now I must leave you; I have had a hard day's work, and am dying for a good night's rest. You won't forget to come to me in the morning, Citizen Boucher—not later than eleven, if you please. Good-night."

9

"*Mon Dieu! mon Dieu!* what a misfortune!" said Verner, in an agonized whisper.   "All Paris to be visited the
second night from this, and you under engagement to meet
Serin to-morrow!   What will become of us?   What shall
we do?"

CHAPTER XVIII

IN PERIL

"What shall we do? What will become of us?" repeated Verner, turning into his work-room, where at that hour we could count on immunity from eavesdroppers and busy-bodies.

"What shall we do? You will stay where you are, of course, and I must find a fresh billet. That is all," said I.

"You don't propose to keep your appointment with Serin, then?"

"Go to the Hôtel de Ville, you mean? Not I, faith."

"But what will he say?"

"That is his affair."

"What will he say to me, I mean."

"What can he say? You are in no way responsible for my conduct. We met accidentally at a cabaret in the Rue St. Honoré. I inquired about lodgings, and when we fell in with Serin you were bringing me here to view your only vacant room. Considering that I am going to be enrolled to-morrow morning, I decide not to take the room, and return, as you suppose, to the Hôtel des Princes. What can be simpler? If Serin wants me, let him find me."

"It is so. That is the line I must take. I shall feign ignorance, and sympathize with Serin in his anger and disappointment. Deception is a virtue when you have to do with such a fellow. But you, my poor Monsieur Astor, what will you do?"

"Throw myself on the hospitality of Monsieur de Castellan."

"But on Wednesday night, when every house in Paris is to be searched from top to bottom?"

"Oh, I shall find some corner to hide in, or I might walk the streets, or sleep under a bush in the Champs-Elysées or Parc Monceau. And a great deal may happen before Wednesday night."

The end of it was that, after a cordial leave-taking with Verner, I set out for the Rue Cléry, saw Langbein, and had an interview with M. de Castellan, who kindly offered me my old room under the tiles, provided I would share it with a wounded soldier of the regiment, whom he had taken in.

With this proposal I gladly closed. A fellow-soldier is none the less a comrade because when you carried the colors he carried a musket; and misfortune, which is said to make strange bedfellows, effaces social distinctions.

Nevertheless, M. de Castellan left me under no illusion as to the dangers that confronted me. Two nights at the utmost could he keep us—the wounded Switzer and myself—in his house. No corner of it was likely to remain unsearched, and he feared that my plan of walking the streets or lurking in the Champs-Elysées was impracticable; but he would make inquiry, and do his best to find me a shelter from the storm elsewhere.

When we were done talking, my great-hearted host accompanied me to the garret, and, after introducing me to my bedfellow, left us to ourselves. His name was Morgen. He had served in Von Durler's company, and marched with the second column through the gardens to the Assembly. When the king ordered the remnant of the regiment to lay down their arms, a few, of whom Morgen was one, refused to surrender, yet contrived to escape. Chased by the mob, they found an asylum in the Hôtel Dieu, where the chief physician made them strip and go to bed, so that when their pursuers came to look for them they were unable to distinguish the fugitives from the patients. The former were afterwards provided with plain clothes and dismissed, and, being private soldiers, and not especially singled out for pursuit, had no great difficulty in losing themselves in the crowd. Morgen's wounds, though not serious, rendered it necessary for him to lie *perdu* for a while, and he found a hiding-place with his sweetheart, who lived in the Faubourg St. Antoine. But the house becoming "suspect," he had to seek fresh quarters, and was finally harbored by Langbein (who came from the same canton) in the garret—of course, by leave of its owner.

Morgen's hurts, though not disabling, were obvious. His right ear had been shot off, and one side of his head and face ploughed with a bullet, and the plasters and bandages which he was forced to wear were apt to attract attention and suggest inquiry as to how he had come by his wounds, else had he tried to obtain employment until such time as he could get away from Paris.

I was delighted to learn from Morgen that there was good reason to believe that Sternberg and Waldteufel had survived the slaughter of the 10th. According to the account he had heard they were run to ground in the cellars of the Ministry of Marine, where some kind soul concealed them and reclothed them. As to how they fared afterwards Morgen had no information. Yet he hoped for the best. No news was good news. If they had been taken, he should have heard.

Shortly before noon next morning M. de Castellan came to us with a deeply troubled face. The municipality had made known in what manner they proposed to execute the Assembly's decree for a general domiciliary visit. It was to begin that day, and the nets were being so widely spread and their meshes so tightly drawn that, as the Jacobins believed, no royalist, aristocrat or fugitive could avoid capture.

With the tocsin sounding and drummers of the National Guard beating the *rappel*, every citizen was to betake himself to his domicile, the streets were to be cleared, traffic stopped, and all shops and public institutions closed. The sittings of the Assembly and the courts were to be suspended. A line of posts was to be established beyond the barriers, in order to catch anybody who might pass them. Armed boats were to traverse the river, and the public buildings on its banks to be garrisoned. Armed sans-culottes were to be stationed at street corners, with orders to arrest whosoever might appear in the streets after a certain hour. Battues were to be made in all the woods, parks, and walks, and every individual found in them haled off to prison. Every man or woman found in a friend's house was to be treated in like fashion, and citizens were ordered to facilitate the search by a general illumination of their dwellings. The visits, conducted by several hundred groups of inquisitors armed to the teeth, were to begin at ten o'clock that night and continue forty-eight hours.

The government counted on taking ten thousand weapons and bagging ten thousand royalists.

"I expected that the search would be rigorous," observed M. de Castellan, when he had told us these things, "but this exceeds my worst anticipations."

We looked at each other in consternation. It seemed as though escape were impossible. Nevertheless, I refused to abandon hope. There was surely a corner somewhere into which we could disappear for a couple of days.

"The roof!" I exclaimed. "Why cannot we go on the roof and hide behind the chimney-stacks?"

"Because we are not sure that the visitors will come during the night, and after sunrise detection would be inevitable."

"Couldn't we get inside a church?"

" No; the churches will be shut up, and even the floating wash-houses on the Seine are to be occupied by sans-culottes."

" But surely there is a hay-loft or a cellar, or some such place. I am not without money; I could make it worth a man's while."

" It would take a good deal of money to tempt a man to risk his liberty, probably his life. Besides, he who took money to shelter you might take money to betray you; and hay-lofts and cellars will be more rigorously explored than less likely hiding-places. The safest place is where nobody would think of hiding, therefore of seeking. The main difficulty is that it will not be safe for you to go out before dark, and that by ten o'clock we must all be in-doors. However, I shall do my best."

With that M. de Castellan went on his errand, and he had so many friends and so much influence, and my confidence in him was so great, that I entertained little doubt that he would succeed in finding a haven where we might hope to weather the storm.

Yet we had an anxious time after his departure, being continually on the alert and in a fever of suspense. I was also concerned about Angélique and the vicomte, of whom I had not heard for several days, and M. de Castellan could tell me nothing.

Twice during the day Langbein came with food. The second time he reported that Paris appeared to be paralyzed with fear. Sans-culottes, gendarmes, and National Guards were marching about in all directions, no women and few civilians were to be seen in the streets, and though the order for closing business establishments and suspending traffic had not yet been enforced, people were putting up their shutters, and neither fiacre nor cabriolet was to be obtained for love or money.

Between eight and nine Langbein came for the third time, and announced that M. de Castellan was below, and would be pleased to see us at once.

We ran down-stairs with an indescribable sense of relief, for we had just come to the conclusion that we should have to turn out and find a refuge for ourselves or face the alternative ; and we were resolved not to be taken alive.

"Come along ; we have not a moment to lose !" exclaimed M. de Castellan, as soon as he saw me.

"You have found a place, then ?" I asked.

"I think so. We shall see. And now silence in the ranks, if you please. *Allons !* Step out !"

The streets were thronged with armed emissaries of the Commune, guards were at every corner, drums beating, bugles blowing, aides-de-camp and orderlies hurrying to and fro, every door closed, all windows alight. It seemed as though Paris had been taken by assault and the foe were in full possession.

Fearing we should be arrested, I kept my hand on my pistol, and whispered to Morgen, who was also armed, to be ready for whatever might befall. But nobody troubled us, probably because we went on, looking neither to the right nor left, and in part, no doubt, because M. de Castellan, who had an imposing presence and wore his sword, looked like a man in authority.

We made straight for the river, down the Rue du Mail and the Rue des Bons Enfants and across the Carrousel, that place of terrible memories. When we reached the Pont Royal our conductor, pointing to a spot near the water, deep in shade, bade us wait there until he returned.

We waited a long time, and, as sans-culottes were continually passing and repassing, at times almost touching us, were in imminent danger ; and I was suggesting that we had better get under the thwarts of a small boat which was moored to the bank when M. de Castellan reappeared.

"Rue du Bac, third gateway, right," he whispered, and then hurried away.

The clocks were striking the last quarter before ten, and he had said all that was necessary.

CHAPTER XIX

THE RAVEN

WE crossed the bridge and were entering the Rue du Bac when me met three sans-culottes, who motioned us to stop, and barred the way.

" Whither are you going ?" demanded one of them.

" To our lodgings, a little farther on," quoth I, civilly.

" No, you are not. You are going with us. Consider yourselves under arrest."

" Why, it is not ten o'clock."

" All but ; and our business is to act, not to argue. Will you go quietly, or shall we make you ?"

It was all I could do to refrain from chastising the fellow for his insolence as he deserved ; but knowing that violence just then would be highly impolitic, I put a restraint on myself, and, showing my pistol, answered even more courteously than before :

" As our arrest before ten o'clock would be illegal, we shall deem it our duty to resist. But we are quiet citizens on our way home, and I think it will be worth your while to let us go in peace. A hundred francs are not to be picked up at every street corner," slipping paper money of that value into his hand.

" My faith, I believe you. I believe, too, that you are good patriots ; so depart in peace, according to your desire, and get home quickly, lest you fall in with a less complaisant patrol."

Five minutes later I knocked at the wicket of the third gateway, and before I took my hand from the knocker the gate was cautiously opened by a stout man in porter's livery.

" From ?" he asked.

" Monsieur de Castellan," said I.

" Enter quickly and follow me, but ask no questions. There is no time for talk.   Hark !"

The clocks were going ten, and at the last stroke a great din broke out all over Paris—a din of clanging bells, resounding drums, and far-reaching bugle-calls, the measured tread of marching battalions, and the hoarse murmur of many voices.

" Hark !" repeated the porter.   " This is going to be a dreadful night."

He took us across the court-yard into a garden, where was a detached flat-roofed building, which might be a billiard-room, summer-house, or conservatory, or all three.   The porter unhooked a ladder from the garden-wall, and reared it against the building ; then bade us mount and lie down on the roof.   It did not seem a very promising hiding-place ; but remembering that beggars cannot be choosers, we mounted, without more ado.

When we were on the top, the porter wished us good-night and went his way, carrying off the ladder.   The roof was of lead, and surrounded by a ledge or cornice barely high enough to hide us when we lay prone, and, as we soon found, it made a cruelly hard bed.

But I did not see any immediate necessity to lie down, and was saying to Morgen that I hoped the *concierge* would return and throw us up a few sacks, or what not, that might serve as bedclothes, when we were startled by a series of knocks at the entrance-gate that sounded like so many pistol-shots.

" They are come," said I ; and down we went with one accord, and began the longest spell of star-gazing in which either of us had ever indulged.

A minute or two later we heard voices and the clash of arms, and half a dozen men, as I judged by the noise they made, entered the garden and surveyed our refuge.

"I don't think there is anybody hidden hereabouts," said one of them, probably the "municipal" in command of the search-party. "But I must obey orders; so you, Cornichon, will remain here until you are relieved, and see that nobody either enters or leaves the garden. If anybody who cannot give the password should make the attempt, and, on being summoned, refuse to surrender, you will shoot. You understand?"

"Perfectly."

"It is well. I shall post another sentry in the court-yard and a third at the gate, so you will have plenty of help within call, and the firing of your pistol will inform the patrol outside that a fugitive is on the run."

When the "municipal" had given these instructions, he left the garden, and the sentry began his monotonous march, which never took him more than twenty or thirty paces from the summer-house, and whenever he intermitted his walk with a halt, leaned against the wall two yards from where we lay. I could hear him breathe and mutter to himself—occasionally laugh and swear, as the humor took him; from which I inferred that Cornichon was a man of imagination—possibly a poet.

My first idea was that the house would be searched either at once or shortly; but as time went on, and Cornichon remained at his post—albeit with waning patience, and swearing much oftener than he laughed—I concluded that the inquisitors were gone elsewhere, and had set a guard about the premises to prevent ingress or egress during their absence, which I fervently hoped would be brief; for as the night wore on the air grew chilly, and we were thinly clad and the lead desperately cold. To make matters worse, we dared neither move not converse lest we should attract the sentry's attention. Yet all these perils and discomforts did not suffice to prevent Morgen from falling into an occasional snooze and showing an alarming tendency to snore, which I had to repress by kicks and pinches.

Meanwhile the discordant noises with which the night had begun went on—now rising, now falling, yet never ceasing—mingled at intervals with fitful musket-shots, fired, as we imagined, at suspected royalists who refused to surrender or were trying to escape.

So the night wore on, yet slowly withal, as though it would never end, and, as if to increase our wretchedness, there fell shortly before dawn a smart shower of rain which wet us to the skin, and, owing to some obstruction in the gutters, did not run off the roof, so that we had water both under and over us.

About this time the sentry was relieved, which we took as a sign that our vigil was drawing to a close.

Two men came into the garden, and in the voice of one of them I recognized the "municipal" who had given Cornichon his instructions.

"My poor Cornichon, I am very sorry," said he. "I gave orders for you to be relieved at two o'clock, but, owing to some misunderstanding—"

Here Cornichon, who was much more sans-culotte than soldier, broke in with angry exclamations and swore with great energy, only desisting when the officer bade him go into the house and get something to eat and drink. He added that the search was just beginning, and that as the owners and occupiers were ladies, it would be strange if they did not find a man "hidden away somewhere."

The two quitted the garden in company, leaving the new sentry at his post, and soon the kindly sun arose and cheered us with his rays. But the light brought with it fresh alarms. The ledge round the roof was so low that the inadvertent raising of a hand might be fatal, and we presently discovered that we could be seen from the dormer-window of a neighboring house. And then, as though this were not bad enough, a tame raven, coming from I know not where, must needs alight on the summer-house and begin croaking and hopping and circling over our heads, as if it were bent on betraying us to the enemy.

Fortunately, the sentry was too dense to take a hint or understand aught save plain French. Nevertheless, the raven persevered, and so angered me that I risked my life in a vain attempt to wring his neck.

After a while the searchers came into the garden, and, as we gathered from their exclamations, thoroughly explored it, without, however, finding anything. Neither had they found aught compromising in the house.

When they reached our billet the "municipal" told his men to look inside, which they did, and presently reported that it contained only plants, a few chairs, and an old billiard-table. The walls and floors seemed to be solid, and there were no receptacles where weapons or persons could be stowed away.

"I didn't suppose there were. Nobody would be such a fool as to hide there, much less on the roof," said the "municipal," carelessly. "However, we may as well look; and then we can take our oath that we have left no corner unsearched."

Seeing that the supreme moment was at hand, Morgen and I cocked our pistols, and agreed, in a suppressed whisper, that I should fire first.

Meanwhile the raven was perched on the cornice, with his head on one side, quietly observant of the scene below.

"Is there a ladder anywhere about?" continued the "municipal." "Ask the *concierge*. But no! We can do without. You are a tall fellow, Simon. Plant yourself against the wall, and let Cornichon get on your shoulders. A glance will be enough."

On this the raven, to our unspeakable amazement, flapped his wings, and at the top of his queer voice croaked, " *Vive le roi! Vive le roi! Vive le roi!*"

The sans-culottes laughed boisterously, and their chief, after an exclamation of surprise, shouted excitedly:

"'That confounded bird belongs to some royalist. Shoot it!" Whereupon the men blazed away unanimously, and a dozen bullets whizzed over our heads, all wide of the mark, while the cause of the commotion flew away croaking, defiantly, "*Vive le roi!*"

"Idiots! Triple brutes! I did not mean you were all to shoot," exclaimed the now exasperated "municipal." "We shall have all the Blues and sans-culottes in the quarter here. And what will they think of us? Bird-shooting when the country is in danger!"

" And nothing bagged !" put in Cornichon.

"And nothing bagged. It is simply disgraceful. Twelve shots, and the raven not a feather the worse. I am ashamed of you. Run into the Rue du Bac, Cornichon, and tell the people there it was all a mistake—a false alarm ; they need not come, and— We will go ; let us clear out."

And, to our great contentment, they did clear out. But whether the raven's opportune diversion had saved our lives or merely secured us a short respite remained to be seen. The too conscientious "municipal" and his sans-culottes might return and complete their work, and we had to consider whether it were better to stay where we were a while longer, or make an effort to escape while the coast was clear.

CHAPTER XX

A NEW ACQUAINTANCE

" How can we get away while so many of these cutthroats are about?" asked Morgen. "The streets are swarming with them. We should be pounced upon at once; whereas if we stay here—"

" And how if the 'municipal' and his men come back and have a look up here?" said I.

" Let us hope they won't."

" By all means. Let us get down — it isn't much of a drop; let us get down and hide in the billiard-room, which they have explored, and then if they return and try the roof, they will draw blank. Anyhow, I am going. You can please yourself."

But I was so stiff with the cold and the rain and the long lying on my leaden couch that I could hardly move. My limbs were benumbed, my back ached horribly, and it was all I could do to get up. Morgen was even worse. The cold had got into his bones. He groaned audibly, and was so stiff withal that I had to help him to rise.

I dropped first, and alighted safely. Morgen came down clumsily and fell on his back, so that I had to set him on his legs and help him into the billiard-room, which we no sooner entered than the sound of approaching footsteps again fell on our ears, sharpened by apprehension and anxiety. Not daring to show my face at the window, I looked through the keyhole, and to my great gladness spied the *concierge* — alone. He came opposite the door, and, raising his head, said, in a loud whisper :

"Are you still there, gentlemen?"

"No, we are here," I answered, in a voice hoarse and hollow with cold and exhaustion, whereupon the *concierge* jumped like a shot man, and looked as scared as if he had seen something uncanny.

"A thousand thunders! How the devil did you get there?" he exclaimed.

I opened the door and told him.

"You did quite right to get down, although I don't think the brigands are likely to return," said he. "Why should they? They have not left a corner unsearched. They even tapped the walls, looked under the beds, and over-hauled the water-butts. And as I have double-bolted the front gate, they cannot take us by surprise, so come in and have something warm; you look as though you needed it."

Our looks did not belie our feelings. We accepted the proposal with heartfelt thanks, and followed our conductor to his lodge, where he presently set before us a breakfast of coffee and rolls. But we were not to enjoy it undisturbed, for even as I raised the cup to my lips there came a great knocking at the outer gate.

"A thousand thunders! I do believe the beggars are back again," said the porter. "Get onto my bed in the alcove, and draw the curtains."

Which we did quickly, and the porter went to open the gate.

"What now? You are surely not going to make another search?" we heard him say.

"Only the roof of the billiard-room, or summer-house, or whatever you call it," replied the intruder. "It is all non-sense. There is nobody there: we know that well enough. But Citizen Blaize, our 'municipal,' you know, is so confoundedly particular, and that cursed raven put it out of his head for a moment. So he has sent me back, the devil take him, as though I were not tired to death already. Is there a ladder anywhere about?"

"Oh dear, yes: I can accommodate you with a ladder. Come along." The two went off together, to return in five minutes laughing and joking.

"I hope Citizen Blaize will be satisfied now," said the *concierge*.

"At any rate, he ought to be," returned the gendarme. "He may safely take his oath that there isn't a *ci-devant* on these premises—except your mistress, and she doesn't count. The republic is not afraid of old women. While as for arms, we haven't found so much as a pistol. We shall trouble you no more, Citizen Concierge."

And then the wicket went to with a bang, the bolts were shot, and as Morgen and myself emerged from the alcove the porter returned to his lodge.

"Now you may finish your breakfast with easy minds," said he. "A narrow shave, though. But for that blessed raven we should all three have been walked off to the Abbaye, or some such infernal place. I never thought they would want to search the roof, and I put you there partly for that reason, but mainly because if you had been lagged the marchioness would not have been compromised."

"The marchioness! Who is she?"

"Madame la Marquise de Malartic is the owner of this house and my mistress, and I, Auguste Rod, have the honor to be her *concierge* and major-domo."

"Does she know we are here?"

"Not yet. There was no time to tell her last night. Monsieur de Castellan was so pressed that I had to act on my own responsibility, and as he got me this place many years ago, and is, besides, a friend of the family, I could not refuse him."

"And for your kindness we are very grateful, Monsieur

Rod. You have rendered us a service that we shall never forget. But what will Madame la Marquise say?"

"I have no fear on that score. I should have, though, if I turned you away. She is a brave old lady, and, though past eighty, as high spirited as a young girl. Her sons and grandsons emigrated two years ago, but Madame la Marquise declined either to accompany or follow them. She says that in Paris she was born and in Paris she will die. You should have heard her talk to the Blues. She told them that if they wanted what of life remained to her they might take it. She had had more than her share."

We went on talking for an hour or more. Rod was a genial old man, and mentioned, among other things, that we need be under no apprehension as to his fellow-servants ; they were both trustworthy and discreet. Moreover, the household was small, and the marchioness neither visited nor received, save two or three old friends, whose calls were few and far between.

This was satisfactory—in a sense. We were safe for the moment ; but Rod said nothing as to the duration of our stay, and if we had to turn out while the streets were still thronged with sans-culottes and gendarmes, we should sure-ly fall into their hands. On the other hand, as he had kept his promise to M. de Castellan, and given us quarters at great risk and on his own responsibility, I felt that it would not be right to trespass further on M. Rod's hospitality, and so said.

"No, no ; that would not do at all," he answered, smiling. "You would be lagged before you got to the end of the Rue du Bac. And how could I look Monsieur de Castellan in the face ? No ; you must remain with us until the visits are over, and the brigand who was here just now said they would go on for at least twenty-four hours longer; and until they are over it won't be safe for anybody who isn't either a sans-culotte or a Blue to show his nose outside."

After a while the *concierge* left us to ourselves, and. presently returning, said that he had informed Madame la Marquise of all that had befallen, and that she would be pleased to see me in her room and hear an account of my adventures from my own lips.

So to her room we went.

Rod announced me in my own name, which I had confided to him, and the marchioness received me with the high-bred courtesy of the old *régime*. She was wonderfully well preserved, and had no doubt once been eminently handsome— was, indeed, handsome still. For though her hair was white and her face wrinkled, her cheeks had a richer color than those of many a young girl, her eyebrows. like her eyes, were black, and her teeth seemed perfect; but she was fourscore and four, and appearances are sometimes deceptive. Only her hearing was defective, and during our long talk she made me draw my chair close to the fauteuil on which she reclined.

Madame de Malartic was the most curious lady, young or old, I ever encountered. After relating my recent adventures, I had to give her a full account of my birth, parentage and education, and answer many searching questions in relation thereto. When she had, so to speak. pumped me dry, she took a pinch of snuff from a richly jewelled snuff-box, and reciprocated my confidences by telling me much about her family and herself, the which, as I am relating my story, not hers, I need not repeat.

Then she tapped me playfully on the cheek, and said that she once knew somebody whom I greatly resembled, and inquired whether Colonel Balthazar von Astor, who was killed at Rosbach, was of my family.

" He was my grandfather, madame," said I.

"You—you Colonel von Astor's grandson ! *Mon Dieu, mon dieu,* how time flies ! I knew him well. We danced a minuet together the day Louis XV. was married—I dare not say how many years ago. Yes, we were good friends, your grandfather and I. He was a fine young fellow in those days, and I rather think he admired me."

"And no wonder. His grandson admires you now, madame," quoth I.

"So you can pay compliments," said she, with a smile which showed that mine had not displeased her. "Well, I dare say you have met worse-looking women of my years. But tell me, now; is there not some young girl whom you really admire—in your heart you know? How about this Mademoiselle de la Tour, of whom you were speaking? Ah, I can read in your eyes that I have guessed aright. And you blush! Oh, what an innocent youth! In my time a gentleman of your age could no more blush than a bronze statue. I must make the young lady's acquaintance. I am sure she is charming, or your eyes would not brighten at the mere mention of her name. I shall call on her—trust me to find a pretext—and bring her here. I am sure she is dying to see you again. I know that if, when I was sixteen, it had been my good-fortune to save the life of a handsome young soldier, I should have lost my heart to him."

"But you don't know Mademoiselle de la Tour," I stammered, in confusion, being quite taken aback by the marchioness's badinage; yet I had wit enough to refrain from saying what was on my lips: "She is not that sort of girl."

"I know what you mean," she said, laughing, as I thought, rather maliciously. "You mean that this demoiselle is perfection and not as other demoiselles are. It is well for you to think so, my dear sir. But I, who was once a young girl myself, may perhaps know more of the female heart than you; and I would wager my best fan against your epaulettes that the beautiful Angélique is this very moment thinking of her handsome soldier. Why, I was half in love with

Colonel Balthazar, and he and I were never the hero and heroine of a romantic adventure. And you are very like him. We shall see. . . . Now remember that you are my guest so long as you like to stay. You are safer here than anywhere else in Paris. Those Jacobins won't trouble us any more—for the present; they have a certain respect for me because I did not emigrate with the others, and I dare say they think I am too old to conspire against their precious republic. Rod will find you a room; there are entertaining books in the library, you may walk in the garden without being observed, and for further distraction you will have my company."

I protested that this was the distraction I should most prefer; and after I had ascertained that Morgen might also have quarters in the house until it was safe for him to leave, the interview came to an end.

CHAPTER XXI

QUITE OUT OF THE QUESTION

On the night of September 2d began the massacre of the captives who had been marked for slaughter. The domiciliary visits resulted in the arrest of ten thousand persons, mostly men, of whom twelve hundred were killed in cold blood by a band of murderers appointed for the purpose and paid by the municipality. Among the victims were fifty-four of my comrades of the regiment. They met their fate as became men who had done their duty and feared death less than dishonor.

Captains von Durler and Ghibelin, and a few others, who had evaded capture or escaped from custody on the 10th, were still at large, and eventually succeeded in reaching England. But, so far as I know, not one of those who were put in prison after the fall of the Tuileries was left alive.

With my own eyes I saw several carts pass down the Rue du Bac laden with mutilated and uncoffined corpses—a sight which grieved me so bitterly and roused in my mind such a tempest of impotent rage that I became quite sick, and had to keep my room for two days.

To my grief and pain were added the tortures of suspense. I knew not what was become of the vicomte, nor how it fared with Angélique and her mother; and while Paris was under the heel of martial law I could inquire neither by deputy nor in person.

The massacres ceased on the 6th; people breathed again; and on the following day I received, through M. de Cas-

tellan, a note from De Lancy, asking me to meet him an
hour after sunset, near the statue of Louis XV., the spot
where my uncle had died, and where the scaffold was afterwards erected on which Louis XVI. and so many other victims of the Terror perished. A strange rendezvous! Yet,
being the last place in Paris where the police would look for
fugitives, and only a short walk from the Rue du Bac, well
chosen.

We had no difficulty in finding each other, and my friend,
putting his arm silently within mine, led me into one of the
darkest alleys of the Champs-Elysées.

"Why didn't you come to the house?" was the first question I asked him.

"What house?"

"The Marchioness de Malartie's."

"I knew not you were there, or where else, so wrote under cover to Monsieur de Castellan, for I felt sure that the
good-fortune which has served you so well in the past would
not desert you now."

"You, too, have been fortunate. How did you evade
capture?"

"By doing as you did: hiding in the chestnut-tree."

"And Mademoiselle de la Tour; have you seen her
lately? Is she well?"

"Poor Angélique!"

"Poor Angélique! Good heavens! you surely don't mean
that they took her—and—and—" I exclaimed, in dismay.

"Softly, my friend, softly! Somebody might hear—and
let us speak English. Angélique has not been taken by the
sans-culottes, but her mother has been taken from her by
death. I told you that my sister had never recovered from
the shock of her husband's murder. The shock of the domiciliary visit the other night killed her outright. She is to
be buried to-morrow, and I am going to the funeral."

" Are you mad ? They will take you."

" I don't think so. I shall go as one of the undertaker's assistants. Yet, whether I be taken or not, I am going; and we are not nearly in so much danger as we were a few days ago. The police, like other folk, are too full of the domiciliary visits and the massacres to think of you and me. For the moment, at least, we are out of their minds. Do you know that at every crisis of the revolution the thieves of Paris reap a rich harvest ? The police are too much occupied and preoccupied to look after them. No, I am not afraid of being arrested. My chief concern is for my niece. Her parents had never many friends in Paris, and the few they had are either dispersed or in prison. I know of nobody to whom I should like to confide her, and yet she cannot remain in that house alone."

To this I made no answer, but it suggested an idea; and after a short silence I asked De Lancy—rather, I think, to his surprise, for the question seemed absurdly irrelevant— whether he knew the Marquise de Malartie.

" I never met her," said he; " but I have heard of her In her early days she was a celebrated beauty, and a prominent figure at the court of Louis XV."

" She belongs to a good family, I suppose ?"

" Well, I am afraid some of them were not quite as good as they might have been. But it is an ancient and distinguished family—sixteen quarterings, at the least—and I believe the marchioness is a fine old lady. Why do you ask?"

" As she is my hostess, and has been very kind to me, I naturally want to know something about her."

" Of course. Well, you may take my word for it that your hostess is of the highest respectability. I wish I could find somebody like her to take charge of my niece. But it was not to discuss my family affairs that I brought you here. I want to talk to you about the project."

" You are still resolved to carry it out, then ?"

" More so than ever, because, see you, we shall never have so favorable a time. These horrible massacres are sure to produce a reaction ; public opinion condemns them ; the police will be less vigilant ; the Jacobins, believing that they have struck terror into their opponents, less virulent ; moreover, the approaching election of a second National Convention will keep them busy with their own affairs for some months to come. Unfortunately, several of the friends on whose help I was counting are either dead or in prison. But there are enough good men and true left to enable us to make the attempt with a fair chance of success, and in the course of a few days, when our preparations are further advanced and I have got your passport, I shall ask you to proceed to Rouen, possibly to Dieppe."

And then De Lancy went into details — but as, except so far as will shortly appear, they did not concern me personally, I need not set them down here—and unfolded an ingenious device for keeping out of difficulties during the remainder of our stay in Paris.

In the meantimes we were to keep in-doors, but after dark it would be quite possible to traverse Paris from end to end without danger, simply by steering clear of patrols and police-stations. To this end the vicomte had marked on a map of the town, or got somebody to mark for him, the parts to be shunned ; for only the principal thoroughfares were patrolled, and the number of police-stations being limited and their whereabouts known, these points of peril might, with a little contrivance and forethought, be generally avoided. As for casual rencounters with mobs and sansculottes, we should have to take our chance like everybody else, and, if necessary, use our arms.

De Lancy gave me the map and advised me to con it carefully. He had got it off by heart.

Then we separated; and while he went to the Villa de la Tour, which was hard by, I hied me to my quarters, wishing he had asked me to accompany him, and pondering a scheme suggested by Angélique's bereavement.

The next day I had the honor of dining with my hostess, and set it going. When she began, as usual, to rally me about Mlle. de la Tour, I mentioned her mother's death, dwelling, as I thought at the time, rather eloquently on her desolate condition and De Lancy's dilemma.

Mme. de Malartie rose nobly to the occasion.

"Poor girl! I shall call on her to-morrow. Her mother was a De Lancy, you say," she said. "And her father—wasn't he colonel of the regiment of Anjou?"

"Very likely. I know he was a soldier and fought in several campaigns."

"The same. I felt sure I was right. And the colonel's mother was a De Launai. I remember her well. I shall introduce myself to Mademoiselle de la Tour as an old friend of her grandmother's, and ask her to make my house her home until "—regarding me significantly—" she is otherwise provided for."

Albeit it suited my purpose to feign ignorance of the marchioness's meaning, I saw what she was driving at, and began to suspect that the old lady was an inveterate matchmaker. But she was going too fast, since, though Angélique was a charming girl, to whom I was greatly obliged and whom I greatly admired, I refused to admit, even to myself, that I had fallen in love with her.

So soon as I got back to England I meant to enter the British army. After what I had gone through, my father would surely waive his objection to buying me a commission—I might even obtain one without purchase. Soldiering was my passion, and Colonel Maillardoz had said, one day at mess, that a young soldier had no business to weaken his nerve by taking a wife. My uncle went even further: he held that a soldier ought not to marry until he was good for nothing else—that is to say, until he was either invalided or retired on half-pay.

With these opinions I fully agreed at the time, and tried to persuade myself that I held them still. I liked Angélique immensely; and had we been a little older, and my position less perilous— But no, that was quite out of the question. A young soldier with his way to make had no business to think of love and marriage. Besides, what would my father and mother say? "Quite out of the question," I repeated, resolutely. yet somewhat ruefully withal. But there was no reason why I should not try to console Angélique by being a brother to her—a devoted brother. Yes, that was it; we would be brother and sister. Nothing less, nothing more.

CHAPTER XXII

KNIGHTS OF THE DAGGER

MME. DE MALARTIE's mission met with the success which it deserved. Mlle. de la Tour and the Vicomte de Lancy accepted her proposal with many expressions of gratitude and pleasure, and on the following day Angélique took up her abode in the Rue du Bac. But she was greatly changed, poor girl, and the sadness of her looks cut me to the heart. Her face was pale and worn, her eyes bespoke deep sorrow, and every now and then tears filled them and trembled on her long lashes like dewdrops on blades of grass. The old brightness and alertness which had captivated my fancy were under a cloud, and she looked as quiet and subdued as a nun who has just taken the veil.

Yet her face was still lovely; to me its pathetic expression seemed a charm the more, and roused a tumult in my breast which, had Angélique been less reserved and circumstances more propitious, might have been immediately fatal to my soldierly resolve.

I pitied her now as much as I admired her before, and pity, they say, is akin to love. But she chilled my ardor with short answers, spoken with averted eyes, and behaved so like a typical young girl that I began to think I had either made a wrong estimate of her character or that my society was disagreeable to her, and ended by becoming as cold and distant as herself. It was evident that she did not care for me, and I said to myself that I did not care for her. Nevertheless, I was continually thinking about her

and watching her—when she was not looking; the mere rus-
tle of her gown made my heart flutter, to my great annoyance
and despite strenuous efforts to be as indifferent to her as
she seemed to me.

Disappointed with Angélique and vexed with myself, I
yearned for change and excitement, and when, after a much
longer delay than I expected, the vicomte looked in one
evening and asked me to go out for a walk, I knew there
was something in the wind, and assented gladly.

On this Angélique, who was present, threw off her apathy
and became again the Angélique of the Villa de la Tour.

"Whither are you going?" she asked, anxiously.

"For a walk."

"And for something more. What is afoot? You are
going into some fresh danger. Oh, uncle, haven't you
done enough, you and Monsieur Astor? Why risk your
lives in a hopeless enterprise?"

"We are not going to risk our lives. All the young
Jacobin bloods and a vast number of sans-culottes have
marched to the frontier. Paris is tranquil and the streets
are safe. We are merely going out for a walk, and to meet
some friends to whom I want to introduce Monsieur Astor.
He will be back by eleven."

" From seven to eleven! That will be a long walk, my
uncle."

" Well, I don't think we shall be walking all the time.
One doesn't make a call in five minutes."

" True; and these friends—who are they?"

" You never met them; their names are unknown to
you."

" You mean they are political friends?"

"And what then? You are too curious, my dear Angélique. Young ladies cannot expect to know everything.
. . . But we must go, so good-bye for the present."

"Better bring your arms," he whispered to me, when we were out of the room. "Paris is quiet, but to be defence-less invites aggression. I will wait for you at the gate."

I ran for my pistols and dagger, and joined De Lancy at the point he had mentioned.

"Angélique is not only too curious, she is too sharp," he observed, as we turned into the Rue du Bac. "She has evidently a shrewd suspicion as to the object of this walk of ours."

"Why not tell her, then? You say she is discreet."

"Because I am not alone. Others are concerned in this affair, and the secret is not mine. And even though it were, it would not be right to confide it to Angélique. Let her rest in ignorance, and then if there should be a fiasco and a betrayal, which Heaven forefend, and she is questioned, she can truthfully say she knows nothing. So don't you let her worm aught out of you when you return. . . . Were you growing impatient?"

"A little; also anxious. It is ten days since we met in the Place Louis XV., and delays are dangerous."

"You are right; so is undue haste. And it were folly to make the attempt before our plans are fully matured, and in enterprises of this sort the slowest marchers mark the time; but now everything is in order, and to-night the final dispositions will be made."

"The friends to whom you are going to introduce me are conspirators, then?"

"Yes, I think it is well for you to make their acquaintance, and one of them will be your companion."

"My companion?"

"On your journey to Rouen and Dieppe. It is always well to have a companion, and the highways are not safe for a solitary horseman."

After a walk of some forty minutes, in the course of which

we neither encountered a patrol nor passed a police post, we reached a street which I did not recognize—a street of gloomy houses, half hidden among trees and begirt with high walls. Here we paused, and after listening for a minute and looking carefully all round, the vicomte knocked thrice at the side door opening into one of the gardens, and then gave a low whistle.

" Who goes there ?" demanded a voice from inside.

" Friends from afar."

" How many ?"

" A knight and a new-comer. Two out of thirteen."

" Be pleased to enter."

The door opened, and we went in.

" Good-evening, gentlemen," said the janitor.

" Good-evening," answered De Lancy. " So you are the guardian of the door to-night, Deville. Any of the others arrived ?"

" You and your friend make twelve."

" So there is only one late. That is well. Let us go on."

The vicomte put his arm within mine, and led me towards the house which, as I presumed, was our goal.

" Why did you describe yourself as a knight and me as a new-comer ?" I asked.

" Because I am a sworn member of the society and you are not. Some time ago a number of gentlemen, mostly members of the old Monarchical Club, entered into a compact to defend the king from his enemies; and when the palace was invaded by the mob, in February, 1791, several of them on being arrested were found to be armed with daggers, whereupon the people dubbed them 'Knights of the Dagger.' The appellation bestowed on these gentlemen in derision we have adopted in earnest, as signifying that we war against the revolution to the knife."

Before the door we found another guard, armed with pistols and a pike. To him De Lancy whispered a word which I failed to catch, and then we passed inside and entered a large dining-room, where the Knights of the Dagger were assembled. It was more like a drinking-party than a gathering of plotters. Mostly young men, they laughed and joked and rallied each other and helped themselves to wine as though they had not a care. There was nothing to show that they were engaged in an enterprise which might cost every one of them his life, and as yet not a mention was made either of the cause or the king.

This went on until we were joined by a new arrival—doubtless the laggard of whom the guardian of the gate had spoken to De Lancy.

Then somebody bolted the door, and the vicomte, taking the head of the table, raised his hand, and the clamor ceased.

"Gentlemen, the council is complete," said he. "Let us to business."

"Has your friend taken the oath, Monsieur le President?" demanded one of the knights.

"No; but, as you are aware, he has given his proofs, and I will answer for his loyalty with my life. Nevertheless, if it be your pleasure—"

"It is one of the rules that nobody shall be present at our proceedings who has not taken the oath, and in my opinion the rule ought to be obeyed."

The murmurs of assent that followed this observation showed that it was also the opinion of the meeting.

"May I say you will take the oath?" inquired De Lancy, turning to me.

I answered that I should like to hear it read first, and, on the president's request, the knight who acted as secretary read it. I forget the words of the oath, but, generally, it consisted of a solemn and comprehensive promise of secrecy, "on your honor and by all that you hold most sacred," touching whatever concerned the Knights of the Dagger and their doings, of fealty to the King of France, and an undertaking to execute justice, at the bidding of an Executive Committee, on whomsoever should disobey its orders or betray its secrets.

"You will take it, of course!" observed De Lancy.

"The first part of it, with pleasure," said I. "But not being a Frenchman, I cannot promise blind obedience to the King of France. Neither can I undertake to 'execute justice.' That may mean committing murder, and I am a soldier, not an assassin."

Whereupon angry exclamations, and so great an uproar that De Lancy had much ado to restore order. I proposed to withdraw, but he would not hear of it, and made a short yet vigorous speech which reconciled the meeting to my conditions, and I took the oath—with the exceptions I have named.

Then followed a long conversation, from which I gathered, among other things, that the flight of the royal family was to take place during the following week, when several of the knights, who were also members of the municipality and the National Guard, would be on duty at the Temple. But with this I had nothing to do, my part in the business only beginning when the fugitives were out of Paris, as I have already explained.

In the meanwhile I was to make an excursion into Normandy, accompanied by M. Candolle, one of the knights and a very fine young fellow, to whom I had the pleasure of being introduced. At Rouen it would be my duty to arrange with the king's friends for his reception and safeguarding. At Dieppe I was to see the officer in command of the detachment of the Swiss Guard, which had been sent thither at the beginning of August, and arrange with him, if I could, to meet the royal party on the Rouen road, and protect their embarkation for England. This done, or left undone, as the case might be, I was to return as far as Flins, a village some twenty-three miles from Paris, where I should be met with the latest news and my final instructions.

Two passports had been obtained, one in the name of "Lebrun" for me, the other in the name of "Larrey" for Candolle. In these documents we were described as commercial travellers. My "line" was woollens; Candolle's jewelry. And in order to keep up the characters assigned to us we were to carry in our saddle-bags a few samples of our respective specialties.

Our credentials consisted of certain passwords and letters, the latter so worded that they could be understood only by the initiated.

It was further arranged that Candolle and I were to meet on the following evening, equipped for the journey, at a house in the Rue de Lille, where we should find two good horses waiting for us, also arms and ammunition.

As our papers were quite in order, it was not supposed that we would have any difficulty in passing the barrier.

This concluded the business of the evening, so far as I was concerned, and as it was past ten and the vicomte had promised that I should be in my quarters before eleven, I took my leave. De Lancy walked with me to the garden gate.

"You know your way home," he said; "past the king's garden, and then as we came. It is rather roundabout, yet safe withal, which the direct road is not."

"I shall return the way we came, of course. I can find it easily. I know Paris, and I have studied your map."

"Good! And now I have a last counsel to give you. We are not likely to meet again before the affair comes off.

I hope we shall succeed, and, in any event, I trust no harm will befall you. But a wise general always reckons with the possibility of failure, and if you should by any mischance fall into the toils, answer no questions. Don't admit that your true name is not Lebrun, don't admit that you were ever in the regiment; in short, give no information whatever about anybody or anything. Also, be careful what you say to my niece and the marchioness. As you wend homeward you will have ample time to invent some excuse for your abrupt departure. And now, my dear friend, good-night and a safe journey."

And then we parted, and I set my face towards the Rue du Bac.

Invent some excuse for my abrupt departure! It would have been much more to the purpose if De Lancy had provided me with an excuse. It were easy to satisfy Mme. de Malartie. I might say that as I had obtained a passport it behooved me to quit Paris at once, where, as she knew, I was in continual danger. But this story would not satisfy Angélique, who was already suspicious, and, as her uncle had said, too sharp to be easily deceived. On the other hand, I could not tell her the truth without breaking the oath which was fresh on my lips, while if I refused to answer her questions we should probably part bad friends, and as we might never meet again (for I had no illusions as to the desperate character of the adventure in which I had embarked) this was not a pleasant prospect.

It was a hard problem to solve, and I was so intent on its solution that I did not give sufficient heed to my course, with the result that I presently found myself opposite a police-post, in front of which a gendarme, armed to the teeth, was pacing. He had also his eye on me, for I no sooner caught sight of him than he cried out, "Who goes there? Halt!"

I went on unconcernedly, as though the words had been addressed to somebody else; on which he called out to his comrades inside:

" Here is a fellow passing who disregards my challenge."

" *Allons !* Let us lag him," was the answer, and the next moment three or four gendarmes rushed out of the house, shouting : " Who goes there? Halt, or it will be the worse for you."

As I knew that it would be a vast deal worse for me if I did halt, and fighting a whole police-station was not to be thought of, I tightened my belt, drew a deep breath, and put my best foot foremost.

CHAPTER XXIII

TILL WE MEET AGAIN

I HAD little to fear from the gendarmes. I knew that, barring accidents, I could shake them off in a few minutes. My sole danger, as I thought, was meeting a patrol or coming to another police-post, and so getting between two fires. To avoid this peril I tried to regain the route from which I had so stupidly wandered. The streets were almost deserted, and if it had not been nearly full moon I should have slipped into a doorway or dark entry, and so given my pursuers the slip.

But the light that enabled them to see me enabled me to see them, and I presently perceived, to my great satisfaction, that they were losing ground, and would soon be lost to sight—all save one, who kept well ahead of his companions, and was evidently a fair runner and in good wind. He went resolutely, too, as though he had a mind to run me to ground or be in at the death. So I made a spurt, thinking to shake him off as I had shaken off the others. But he also made a spurt, and it was a better one than mine. The in-door life of the last six weeks had impaired my wind, and I found, to my dismay, that I could run no faster and very little farther.

The gendarme gained on me; in a few seconds his hand would be on my shoulder, and I was so blown that in a rough-and-tumble I should probably come off second best. On the other hand, I did not want to shoot the man—he was only doing his duty. Moreover, a pistol-shot would rouse the neighborhood and put the other gendarmes on my track.

What should I do?

A look forward answered the question. The street we were in was straight and gloomy, narrowing at the end almost to a point, and shutting out the moonlight.

For this narrow point I made, and when I reached it put my back against the wall and my hand on my dagger.

The gendarme, a big man, followed panting, with lowered head, like a charging bull, his arms hanging loosely by his side. When he caught sight of me he stopped short.

"At last I have you! Surrender, you scoundrel, or—"

He said no more, for even as he spoke I dashed the hilt of my dagger in his face with all the strength I could muster. With a hoarse cry he staggered backward, then fell in a heap on the pavement; and I went my way.

Half an hour afterwards I knocked at Mme. de Malartie's gate.

"You are late, monsieur," said Rod, as he let me in.

"Only a little past eleven, I think. The ladies are gone to bed, I suppose?"

"It is nearly twelve. The ladies retired at eleven. Mademoiselle de la Tour's maid was here a little while ago, inquiring whether you had arrived. Is monsieur aware that his right hand is covered with blood?"

"God bless me! So it is."

"I hope you are not hurt?"

"Only a scratch; I must have knocked it against something. Good-night, Monsieur Rod."

And with that I also retired, and, after washing my hand of the gendarme's blood, went to bed, and lay awake half the night thinking over the events of the evening, and trying to invent a plausible excuse for my impending departure. After inventing a dozen, each less likely to find acceptance than the other, I decided to be perfectly straightforward, and answer whatever questions Angélique asked me, save such as were barred by the tenor of my oath.

I did not see the ladies until we met at second breakfast. Mlle. de la Tour looked pensive and anxious, yet alert and collected withal. Madame la Marquise was curious and querulous, from which I concluded that Angélique had made her the confidante of her misgivings.

After we had exchanged the usual greetings, I opened the ball by telling the marchioness, point-blank, that having at length succeeded in obtaining a passport, I proposed to quit Paris.

"You are going to leave us!" she exclaimed, with a start of surprise and a look of displeasure. "Why? Are you not happy with us?"

"Thanks to your kindness and hospitality, Madame la Marquise, I have been almost too happy here," I replied. "But, as you know, I am under a ban, and were I arrested here not only would my life be forfeit, but you and your household gravely compromised."

"Why should you be arrested? Do you suppose any of my people are capable of denouncing you?"

"Not at all; and, if it depended on them— But I may be recognized the next time I show my face at the window or pass out at your gate; and it behooves me to get away while I have the chance. The police are in an indulgent mood just now, but there is no telling how long it will last, and the passport which is good to-day may to-morrow be rendered useless by some new regulation."

"Well, I cannot ask you to stay here at the risk of your life. Yet we shall be sorry to lose you," glancing at Angélique. "You are going to England?"

"I hope so."

"You only hope so," said Angélique, joining for the first time in the conversation.

"I intend to go to England, mademoiselle, as soon as possible. But one cannot be sure. I may meet with un-expected difficulties."

"Now tell me, Monsieur Astor, has not my Uncle Claude's call here last night, and what happened afterwards, some-thing to do with your proposed departure for—England?"

"What happened afterwards?"

"Yes. You did not return till midnight, and one of your hands was covered with blood. . . . I beg your pardon; it is no business of mine. I have no right to question you, only—"

(This in a low voice, obviously inaudible to the marchion-ess, whose hearing was dulled by age.)

"Pray continue, mademoiselle. I fully admit your right to question me," quoth I. "Don't I owe you my life? And it is pleasant to think that you take an interest in my wel-fare. You were saying—"

Angélique blushed, lowered her eyes, and seemed uncer-tain whether to yield to my request or not. But instantly regaining her self-possession, she looked me frankly in the face, and observed, quietly:

"I will be plain with you, Monsieur Astor; yet I cannot admit that because I was so fortunate as to render you a service, you are in any way accountable to me for your con-duct. But I know my uncle—know him and love him. He is a brave and chivalrous gentleman, also an ardent loyal-ist and a fanatical hater of the revolution. To rescue the king he would stop at nothing, neither sparing himself nor anybody else. He thinks that if his majesty could be got out of the country the revolution would collapse. I don't. However, that is nothing; I am only a girl, and my uncle is quite within his right. But you are not a Frenchman, and considering what you have already done and suffered, and that, as you say, you are under a ban, I don't think you should be asked to take part in a second plot for the king's rescue—especially when success is almost past praying for. There is a plot, is there not?"

"That is a question I am not at liberty to answer, mademoiselle. You will understand me when I say that it concerns not myself alone."

"There is a plot, then, and you are engaged in it. I thought so; and this supposed journey to England is merely a pretext."

"I beg your pardon, mademoiselle, I do really propose to go to England."

"You propose! Well, I have no more to say, only I am very sorry. Seeing that you saved my uncle's life, I don't think he ought to let you risk yours in one of his hopeless enterprises."

"Don't say hopeless, mademoiselle."

"Yes, hopeless. The king was born under an evil star. He brings misfortune to all who try to serve him. Besides, how can you get him out of the Temple, guarded as he is? And if you do get him out he will commit some stupidity, as he did at Varennes, and be retaken. The mere attempt will make the Jacobins more furious than ever, and Heaven only knows where it will end."

Angélique sighed deeply, and her eyes filled with tears.

"Well?" said the marchioness, looking at us.

"We were talking about my journey," said I. "Mademoiselle de la Tour thinks I may not reach the end, but I am more hopeful; and the risk of going away is at least no greater than the risk of remaining in Paris."

"You know best about that, monsieur; and though I shall be sorry for you to go, it would be a pity for you to stay and fall into the toils. But you will return? We shall meet again?"

"I hope so—when these troubles are over."

"And they will be over soon. The great powers of Europe cannot suffer anarchy to prevail in France. They will overthrow the republic and restore the monarchy, and then we shall settle accounts with these wretches who imprison their king and put ladies and gentlemen to death in cold blood," said the old lady, fiercely, her eyes flashing in anticipation of victory and revenge.

Later in the day I waited on the ladies to take my leave. The marchioness gave me her hand to kiss, saying, kindly, she would not bid me farewell, only "good-bye till we meet again" (*au revoir*), adding: "You may be back sooner than you expect."

"Perhaps," quoth I; yet my heart did not echo the wish which the words implied. If I returned to Paris sooner than I expected it could only be as a prisoner.

Angélique seemed very subdued; her face was pale and her eyes avoided mine, but her hand lingered in my grasp.

"Good-bye till we meet again," said I.

"*Au revoir*, monsieur," she murmured. And then I hurried away, for the hour of my departure had struck, and my heart was heavy with the thought that we might never meet again.

I found Candolle at the rendezvous in the Rue de Lille. The horses were ready, and, after transferring my scanty kit to the saddle-bags, loading and priming my pistols, and buckling on the sword which my companion had brought me, we set out on our journey.

I had withdrawn my deposit from M. Dufour a few days previously, and sewn the greater part of the money in the lining of my vest.

As we crossed the Place Louis XV. in the deepening twilight, I saw that the king's statue had been removed, and in its room loomed a scaffold, gaunt and hideous, with two skeleton-like arms painted red and pointing skyward.

" The new guillotine," observed Candolle; "and they have renamed the square Place de la Révolution."

When we sighted the barrier my companion made the obvious remark that once through we should be all right.

" Is there any doubt about our getting through ?" I asked.

" Well, our passports are in order; but if the brigadier in charge is a pedant, a martinet, or a fool, he may make difficulties and turn us back or detain us, pending inquiry."

" Which would probably mean making the acquaintance of the new guillotine. Anything were better than that. I don't intend either to be detained or turned back. If the people at the barrier make any objection, let us brush them aside and ride on. Our horses are fresh, we are well armed, and night is nigh. What say you, Monsieur Candolle ?"

" Yes, with all my heart. With liberty before, and that thing behind us, there can be no two opinions. Better wait till those market-carts are out of the way, though."

CHAPTER XXIV

AT THE GOLDEN PIG

CANDOLLE's passport passed muster, but to mine the brigadier demurred.

"Blue eyes!" said he. "How can one tell the color of your eyes through those big spectacles? Six feet high! How can one measure the height of a man on horseback? I should like to have a closer look at you, Citizen Commercial Traveller. Be good enough to dismount and step into the bureau."

This proposal did not suit me, and I was going to bid the fellow get out of my way or I would ride him down, when Candolle whispered, "Try backsheesh"—a hint on which I promptly acted.

"Nothing would please me better than to step into the bureau, Citizen Brigadier, if I were not pressed for time," I returned. "I have a business appointment at St. Germain for nine o'clock, which it were as much as my place is worth to miss. Here is another credential which, I trust, will satisfy you as touching my eyes and inches."

And with that I leaned over my saddle-bow, and tipped him a hundred-franc assignat, worth about thirty.

"It is well," crumpling up the assignat in his hand and returning the passport. "You can pass on, Citizen Commercial Traveller, but I advise you to keep a sharp lookout; there are robbers on the Rouen road."

"Also at the barrier of the Champs-Elysées," thought I.

"That was a happy thought of yours, Monsieur Candolle," I remarked, as soon as we were under way again.

" All the same, I should have liked to ride over that rascal-ly black-mailer."

" So should I, and we could have got away. But the guard would have fired, and one of their bullets might have found a billet. Anyhow, there would have been a great to do, and inquiries made concerning Auguste Lebrun and Théophile Larrey, which might have led to discoveries and ruined the plot."

This observation naturally led to a talk touching our own part in the plot, and the details of our itinerary. Our instructions were to wait at St. Germaine-en-Laye and sleep at Flins, a village some three-and-twenty miles from Paris. On the following day, which would be Tuesday, we were to push on to Rouen, a march of more than fifty miles ; but as our horses were fit, they would be able to do it without distress. Moreover, they would have two days' rest at Rouen, where I should hire another horse, or post-chaise, to take me to Dieppe, going thither one day and returning the next.

This would bring us to Thursday night, and by sunset on Friday we meant to be back at Flins, or, rather, at La Soli-tude, a manor-house hard by belonging to one of the con-spirators, where we expected to find a dozen or more of the Knights of the Dagger, who were to proceed thither mean-while in twos and threes, so as to avoid attracting atten-tion.

Now the chief, indeed the sole, danger which threatened the royal party after leaving Paris was recapture, either by pursuing gendarmes, or the populace or authorities of any of the villages through which they might pass.

Hence the necessity of an escort.

Once beyond the barrier, the king and queen, their two children, and Mme. Elizabeth, the king's sister, were to be transferred from the market-cart, their first conveyance, to two carriages, and driven to St. Germaine-en-Laye, where fifteen knights would be on the lookout for them, and thenceforward ride with them. But as this was to be at dead of night, the fugitives were not likely to be recognized, and, in any case, the fifteen defenders might be trusted to clear a way for them.

At the manor-house of La Solitude there was to be a short halt for rest and refreshment. The escort, reinforced by our party, would then be placed under my command, and as all the regular troops were at the front, and the local authorities *en route* would be unprepared for resistance, we should be able to requisition horses for the journey to Rouen, which we hoped to accomplish in seven or eight hours.

A two-mile covert trot brought us to St. Germaine, where we had proposed to halt for an hour; but as there were several gendarmes hanging about, and the inn where we pulled up was crowded with revellers, we rode on till we came to the Golden Pig, a lonely hostelry at the edge of the forest. Its aspect was not inviting, but our wants being modest — a bite and sup for ourselves, and a feed for our horses—we thought it might serve, so led them into the tumble-down old stable, inhabited at the moment by four other horses and a very dirty old groom, who met us at the door with a lantern.

When we had seen our beasts watered and fed we went into the hostelry—an ancient, low-roofed, timbered building, dilapidated and picturesque. The landlord, a beetle-browed, obsequious ruffian, whose countenance did not inspire confidence, ushered us into the travellers'-room, where we found four men playing cards. Being booted and spurred, they were doubtless the owners of the horses we had seen in the stable.

On entering, we gave them the usual greeting, which

they duly returned, and, after taking a look at us, went on with their card-playing. While we were waiting for the frugal supper—a pottage, an omelet, and a bottle of wine—which the innkeeper had promised to serve in "some minutes," I observed that Candolle was closely watching the four gamblers, and that, though they seemed to be intent on their play, they were closely watching us.

After this had gone on for a while, Candolle, exclaiming something about dying of hunger, abruptly left the room, as I supposed, to look after the supper.

" Is it ready ?" I asked when he returned.

" Nearly. It will be served in a few minutes," he said; and then, lowering his voice to a whisper, "I have been doing what we should have done at the outset — securing our pistols. You heard the brigadier's warning about robbers on the Rouen road. Well, regard those fellows. Have they the air of honest travellers ?"

"They don't look like gentlemen, if that's what you mean."

" They look like highwaymen, in my opinion ; though, look you, they may be police-agents in the pay of the Foreign Office."

" In that guise, and in this place ? What can they want here ?"

"To rob a courier. An ambassador's courier is as sacred as his master—neither gendarme nor soldier dare lay hands on him. So when the government wants to overhaul the British ambassador's despatches, for instance, they arrange to have his courier robbed *en route* to the coast, either by gendarmes got up as highwaymen, or robbers with whom the police have an understanding. That is a common diplomatic dodge nowadays. But as couriers don't often travel to England *via* Dieppe, these fellows are probably *bona fide* brigands, wherefore I thought it just as well to secure our pistols."

"You surely don't think they would fall on us here?"

"That would not suit the landlord's purpose. But if, as I suspect, he is an accomplice, he or his hostler might tamper with our arms. One has heard of such things being done."

"You are quite right, and I cannot sufficiently applaud De Lancy's foresight in providing me with a comrade so much more familiar with the ways of the road than myself. Here comes the supper."

When the viands came in the card-players went out, each man as he passed our table saluting, and politely wishing us good-night.

A few minutes afterwards we heard their horses clatter out of the inn yard.

"From the way in which that tall, red-haired chap is set up I fancy he has served," said I.

"He is probably a deserter; there are lots of them about —possibly a gendarme in disguise."

When we had finished our supper and paid the score we went round to the stable for our horses.

To my consternation my horse came out dead lame.

"What can be the matter?" I exclaimed. "He was quite sound on the road."

"Lame horses always go worse after a rest," said the hostler, who was standing by with a lantern.

Candolle ran his hand down my horse's near fore-leg, dwelling for an instant on the fetlock-joint. Then, springing up, he seized the hostler by the throat and pinned him against the wall.

"You scoundrel!" he hissed. "I know what you have done, and I have a great mind to run you through. Bring your lantern here."

The fellow, who trembled like a leaf, held the light, while Candolle, with his penknife, severed a piece of packthread which had been tied so tightly round the fetlock-joint that it cut into the flesh.

"Now the horse is sound again. If this villain were not an old man I would kick him into fits. *Allons*, Monsieur Lebrun! Let us mount and be gone."

"You were right, Monsieur Candolle," I began, when we were out of the inn yard.

"Drop the Candolle, if you please, my dear sir. Do let us be careful. I nearly called you Astor just now."

"I beg your pardon, Monsieur Larrey. I was going to observe that this incident confirms your suspicions. The card-players are certainly highwaymen, and the hostler is in league with them, probably the landlord also. Are they lying in wait for us? That is the question."

"Here are your pistols. They are all right. I have primed them afresh. They probably are lying in wait for us, though I don't think the villains will attack us openly unless the odds are vastly in their favor. Plunder, not fighting, is their game."

"You mean that they may be in ambush and fire at us from behind the trees. If so, we had better hurry on; the faster we go the less likely we are to be hit."

"And the more likely to be entangled in the cords which they may stretch across the road."

"The devil they may! You seem to know the ways of these gentry, Monsieur Larrey."

"So I ought, seeing that I served four years in the gendarmerie."

"I am delighted to hear it. You are the right man in the right place. I gladly place myself under your orders, and if we can have a brush with the rogues and give them a lesson I shall be all the better pleased, always provided that our journey is not delayed."

"I will try to meet your wishes, and I have bethought

me of a plan. As for the brush, we shall see. Now the four men are ahead. I heard them leave the inn yard, and know by the sound of their horses' hoofs that they turned in this direction. They may have joined forces with another body, and consider themselves strong enough to bar our way and bid us stand and deliver. But that makes no difference to my plan, which is this: to ride on at full speed, keeping a sharp lookout for the possible cord, pausing now and then to listen until we hear the tramp of their horses, or, it may be, catch a glimpse of them in the distance. It is a clear night."

"And then charge them?"

"No; turn back."

"What?"

"I said turn back, making as much noise as we can. If they are what we take them for, they will think we are afraid and ride after us, and we, when we get to a suitable place, will pull up and back our horses among the trees."

"I see; and as the brigands pass, charge them on the flank."

"If there are not more than four."

"Say six. They will be taken by surprise, remember, and you and I are good for half a dozen highwaymen any day. We shall have two of them down before they can draw, and the others will bolt."

"Very well. But if there are more than six we had better let them alone and go on our way. Our mission is important, and we have no right to run unnecessary risks."

"True. It is a thing agreed, then. We fight six and run from seven. And now, shall we trot?"

"No; rather let us go at a hunting gallop" (canter). "The more noise we make and the sooner we sight them the better."

CHAPTER XXV

DOGGED

It was a clear night—one of those still autumnal nights when unnumbered millions of stars, shining in a purple sky, give nearly as much light as the moon; so that where the road was straight we could discern, vaguely, objects two or three score yards ahead of us. Owing to the absence of distracting noises and the lightness of the wind, which blew caressingly in our faces, it was also a good night for hearing. As we pulled up after our preliminary canter we could hear the melancholy howling of a hound which must have been at least a mile away, and the patter of leaves as they fluttered softly to the ground.

But nothing more.

" Forward again !" said Candolle ; and on we went.

Then a second pull up.

" Hark ! Wasn't that the neigh of a horse ?"

" Yes. They must be going at a walk, or we should hear the tramp of their horses. Another *galop de chasse !*"

We rode, bending forward in our saddles, listening intently and straining our eyes for a first sight of the supposed brigands.

" Halt !" exclaimed Candolle. "Don't you see something ?"

" Yes, but I cannot make out what. It moves, though."

" From us or towards us ?"

" From— No ; towards us."

" So I think. Anyhow, they must have heard us, and if they don't see us— They do see us, and are turning hitherward. Right-about face and full gallop !"

A spin of ten minutes brought us to a bend where the road was fringed with trees and bushes. Here we drew rein, and took post among the timber in such fashion that though our view backward was unimpeded, we were well hidden.

Soon we heard the galloping of our pursuers' horses, and presently we perceived them, at first as a dark, moving mass, soon more distinctly. At their head rode one whom, from his build and height, I took to be the supposed deserter.

"One, two, three, four, five," muttered my colleague. "No more. Good. The odd ruffian has been on the lookout down the road. They are riding like the devil. So much the better."

"Steel or fire?" I asked.

"Fire first, then at 'em with the steel."

We let the red-haired man go by (which, in my opinion, was a mistake), and so soon as the main body came over against us, emptied our pistols into the thick of them; then drew and charged. Two of the rascals went down like nine-pins, one was unhorsed, the third galloped away, and the riderless steed turned tail and ran back the way he had come.

"Enough!" said Candolle, sheathing his sword. "Those fellows will trouble us no more. Let us go."

We went on steadily, now and then trotting, yet mostly at a walk, and reached the neighborhood of Flins shortly before midnight ; but not liking to disturb the inmates of the manor-house at so late an hour, we put up at the village inn, where the accommodations were quite as good as we had expected, and the fare vastly better than that of the Golden Pig. The innkeeper made curious inquiries as to the condition of the road, and seemed surprised that nobody had meddled with us ; for we deemed it unadvisable to tell him of our encounter with the highwaymen. It would not have suited our purpose to be interviewed and cross-questioned by the local brigadier of gendarmerie, and perhaps invited to pay a visit to the local justice of the peace.

After sleeping six hours we started for Rouen, travelled by easy stages, baiting or gruelling the horses at the end of every ten miles, and reached our destination at nine o'clock, post-meridian, feeling very fit, and our horses looking none the worse for their journey. "Fair and easy go long in a day," as old Wiggin used to say when I set out for Manchester. Lancashire and Wiggin and my father and the print-shop seemed a long way off now.

The first thing I did after supper was to write home. I thought I might have an opportunity of despatching a letter from Dieppe. As my missive might fall into unfriendly hands, I could say no more than that I was safe and sound, and so soon as I was quit of a business which it concerned my honor to see through I should make for England.

Leaving Candolle to arrange matters at Rouen, I set out early next morning in a two-horse post-chaise for Dieppe, whither I arrived shortly before noon, and presented my passport to the guard of the city gate, hoping that, as at Rouen, I should be admitted without further trouble. But the brigadier said I should have to accompany one of his men to the police-office in order that the document might be *viséd*. To my dismay, for I had once been stationed a month at Dieppe, it was on the cards that I might be recognized. And the inspector, or commissionnaire, or whatever might be his rank, into whose room I was shown, stared at me so hard, and read and reread the passport so diligently, and asked me so many questions, as to render it evident that he either suspected something or wanted something. Putting the more favorable construction on his proceedings, I let a hundred-franc assignat flutter unobtrusively on his table. He seemed not to see it, yet became wondrously affable withal, endorsed and returned my passport, saying it was quite in order, and bowed me politely into the street.

So far good. I was free of Dieppe, and made my way with an easier mind to the barracks, where I found Von Affry, Rusca, Karrer, and other old comrades. The dear fellows put their arms round me and welcomed me as one from the grave, for they thought I was among the dead. Rusca was affected to tears, and endless were the questions they asked me about the events of the fatal 10th and what had befallen me since.

It was a meeting darkened by sorrowful memories; yet I felt an inexpressible pleasure in meeting again, probably for the last time, these true friends and brave brother-soldiers, and they, though grieving sorely for fallen comrades, were consoled by the glory which their heroic deaths had won for themselves, the regiment, and their native land.

"I think there is none here who would not say, 'Let my last end be like theirs,'" said Karl von Affry, solemnly; and all murmured assent.

When I told them of my errand my friends looked grave.

"Do you know, boy, that you are asking us for our lives?" exclaimed Von Affry. "If we connived at the escape of the king we should be massacred to the last man. Not that this consideration would hinder us from doing our duty; but what you want us to do is not our duty. The monarch whom we served is deposed and a captive. Nor is that all. The regiment has been disbanded by the *de facto* government of France, the cantons have ordered us to return to our homes, and so soon as we get our back pay and safe-conducts—which may be to-morrow—we shall quit the country."

This was unanswerable. I had nothing to urge against it, and could only ask Von Affry whether he thought, if the king came to Havre, he could find a craft to carry him to

England, and what force would be needed to protect his em-barkation.

"Finding a craft is a mere matter of money. At the moment there is no military force here, but Louis is not popular at Dieppe, and you would need at least a hundred resolute well-armed men to insure his safety."

Thus Von Affry, a man of ripe experience and many years my senior, answered my query, and next inquired why, seeing that the regiment had ceased to exist, I did not return straightway to England, instead of mixing myself up in matters which concerned Frenchmen only, adding that I should never have such a chance, and that he could introduce me to a smuggler who, for a thousand francs in gold, would undertake to land me at Newhaven.

On this I told him of the condition on which I had obtained my passport, and of my great desire to lend a hand in the rescue of the queen.

Von Affry said that he, too, would risk his life to rescue Marie Antoinette. "But has it occurred to you," he went on, "that if this attempt fails her captivity will be made all the harder, and that the Jacobins will have a plausible pretext for further measures of repression? And the chances are about a thousand to one that it will fail. You must see that yourself. It is conceivable that one of the prisoners might be smuggled out of the Temple — but five, and two of them children! As for De Lancy, I have no doubt he is a man of honor: any more than that he is a fanatic. And fanatics, whether they call themselves royalists or religionists, stick at nothing, and to serve cause or creed will sacrifice their friends with as little scruple as they would sacrifice themselves. As for this passport, for which you have to pay so high a price, don't you think that if Jacques Lebrun were to become 'suspect' it would be a danger rather than a safeguard? And it will be very strange if among all these conspirators there is not at least one babbler or traitor."

All this was so obvious that I wondered that it had not occurred to me. Yet as touching De Lancy, I called Von Affry's attention to the fact that the vicomte had twice found me a hiding-place when I was in imminent danger, and that though he might have acted disingenuously in the matter of the passport, I could not honorably withdraw from the engagement I had made with him. On the other hand, if the fugitives did not appear at Flins at the time appointed for their arrival I should feel myself at liberty to abandon the enterprise and leave the country.

" You need not put it in that way," said Von Affry, dryly. " The enterprise will have abandoned you. You are quite right, though, to prefer honor to safety. Having given your word, you must keep it ; and as we may not be here when you return, I shall introduce you to a trustworthy man, one Blondin, smack-owner and smuggler, who for a fair consideration will run you across the Channel."

I accepted the offer and saw the man, and on the morrow bade my friends a sorrowful farewell and posted back to Rouen, disconsolate and unhappy, for the thought suggested by Von Affry that the detection of the conspiracy might make it worse for the queen, and perchance lead to a renewed persecution of the royalists, weighed heavily on my mind.

Candolle was greatly disappointed with the result of my mission. So far as promises and predictions went he had been more fortunate. The royalists whom he had seen were of opinion that the king would be well received at Rouen, and undertook that a contingent of them should join his escort and go with him to Dieppe, albeit there was a difficulty about arms which suggested grave doubts as to its fighting efficiency.

This was no more than De Lancy knew already. The main object of our expedition was to secure the co-operation of the remnant of the regiment at Dieppe (for which purpose, now that my eyes were opened, I saw that the vicomte had inveigled me into his plot). Failing therein, we had failed in all. But we could do no more, and started early next morning (Friday) on our return journey. The horses being fresh, we made good progress, and nothing worth mentioning happened until between two and three o'clock in the afternoon, when we were some fifteen miles from our destination. At this point we began to think that we were being shadowed. We never looked backward where the road was straight without seeing a solitary horseman, who always adapted his speed to ours: if we went slow, he went slow; if we went fast, so did he; yet he never came near enough to allow us to distinguish his features.

This was disquieting, and might mean danger; so in order to shake the fellow off we stopped at a road-side inn, put up our horses, and remained there until after dark. After this we saw the solitary horseman no more, but every now and then we heard the sound of hoofs in our rear which warned us that he was still on our track.

The position of the manor-house of La Solitude had been so minutely described to us that we were able to find it without asking questions. It lay half a league from the main road, and to get there we were to take the first lane to the right beyond Flins; and unless we wanted our follower to dog us to the door, it was absolutely necessary to throw him out; to which end I proposed that we should turn into the fields, which were divided from the road by a narrow ditch. My companion assenting, we put our horses at it, and, though not exactly steeple-chasers, they got over —mine with a stride, Candolle's with a scramble. Then we sent them on at a hand-gallop, trusting to their instinct and superior eyesight to keep us out of difficulties. Our confidence was not misplaced. The sagacious creatures pulled up short at the brink of an unjumpable chasm, whereupon we took once more to the road, and presently reached the lane leading to La Solitude.

So far as we could tell, the stratagem had succeeded; since, though we listened intently, we heard no more pursuing footsteps. Candolle thought the fellow was a police spy, and had followed me from Dieppe. I thought the same; also that he was none other than our friend with the red hair, and that he and his pals had been more or less on our track ever since we left St. Germain-en-Laye.

To this Candolle demurred; but he could not deny that it was an ominous incident, and might mean danger—possibly disaster.

CHAPTER XXVI

BETRAYED

THE mansion-house of La Solitude was an ancient ivy-clad mansion of many rooms, with an inner court, large gardens, and extensive stabling. To the rear was a farmstead surrounded by high walls, and the remains of a moat and other indications showed that once upon a time La Solitude had been a strong place. It was probably still strong enough to withstand any engines of war less formidable than battering-rams and cannon.

The owner and occupier of the place was a *ci-devant* noble, one Count Agénor de Veridet, now plain Monsieur or Citizen Veridet, yet still addressed in the old style by his household and his friends.

It need hardly be said that he was an ardent royalist; none other would have risked life and property by receiving, or agreeing to receive, the fallen monarch in his house, and conniving at his escape; for this constituted treason to the nation, and its penalty was confiscation and death.

The count, a stately middle-aged gentleman, received us with exquisite courtesy, and introduced us to his wife and daughters, two charming young ladies whom I was rather surprised to find there, as in the event of things going wrong they would probably be involved in their father's ruin.

Several of our party had already arrived—gallant young fellows, full of life and energy, and sanguine as to the result of our enterprise. They reported that everything was going on well at Paris; the "evasion," as they called it, would take place on the following night, and there was no reason to suppose that the police had the least inkling of what was going on.

We should know more in the morning when the others came, and De Lancy, who foresaw everything, had organized a reciprocal service of homing pigeons; that is to say, there were pigeons at La Solitude which, when released, would fly to a certain house at Paris, and pigeons there whose home was La Solitude. They could go from one place to the other under the hour. This necessarily implied a code of signals. A white ribbon or thread round a pigeon's neck would signify "all right;" a green one, that the flight was deferred until the next night; red would mean danger; black, disaster.

Neither M. de Veridet nor the Knights of the Dagger attached so much importance to the failure of our mission and the appearance of the supposed spy as did Candolle and myself. They thought that the twenty-five or thirty men of the escort, reinforced by the promised Rouen contingent, would be quite strong enough to protect the king from mob violence, while as for spies, they were everywhere and dogged everybody. Moreover, the man who had followed us might be a highwayman or a highwayman's tout.

In any case, the incident was not sufficiently grave to justify the despatch of a danger signal, which would mean in effect the abandonment of the enterprise, and, short of that, nothing could be done.

This was not my opinion; but being an outsider and in a minority of one, I deemed it expedient to hold my peace.

During the morning came the remainder of the party. The last-comers, who arrived a little before noon, brought satisfactory news. All was going on well. According to the latest arrangements, the royal family would arrive at St. Germain-en-Laye about midnight, and we might look for them and the first division of the escort towards two o'clock on Saturday morning. They would stop at La Solitude only just long enough to change horses and breakfast—probably not more than half an hour.

It was regarded as a good augury that the gentlemen of the escort had all passed the barriers without difficulty, and that the few gendarmes whom they encountered on the way neither questioned nor seemed to note them.

So far good ; and when our host announced at second breakfast that a white-ribboned pigeon had just "homed," confidence became certainty, and the king's health was drunk with great enthusiasm.

The day was spent in playing tennis and raquette, and strolling in the grounds. A few of us visited the stables and inspected the count's stud. After remarking that the horse I had ridden seemed to be somewhat under my weight, M. de Veridet kindly offered to place at my disposal an animal of greater power and substance, yet well-bred withal, which had already attracted my attention. He was a big horse every way, and so high (nearly seventeen hands) as to deserve his name of Goliath. His only fault was a "bit of a temper," to which, knowing that temper often indicates quality, I did not object.

"As you are to command the escort, you should have a horse of commanding presence," said the count, with a smile.

It was an offer not to be refused, and I accepted it with gratitude.

At the edge of dark, Candolle and I took a walk down the lane as far as the high-road.

It was a narrow, tortuous old lane, winding for the most part through a wood, but dipped as it neared the main road, forming a hollow way bordered by high banks, making at this point, as I pointed out to Candolle, a fine defensive position.

"A handful protected by a breastwork of fallen trees, or an overturned cart, might hold this lane against a host," I remarked.

" Provided the host had no field-guns."

"Of course. I assume equality of weapons. And now tell me frankly, Candolle, what you think of the outlook."

" I regard it as fair—very fair, indeed; almost too much so, indeed."

" You mean disaster is still possible."

"That is obvious. There may be a breakdown at the last moment, though our young friends at the manor-house don't seem to think so. I mean it looks as though the police were asleep, and somehow I don't think they are. Anyhow, I shall be greatly relieved when I hear the clatter of the king's escort and the sound of his carriage wheels."

And then we retraced our steps, thinking anxiously of the morrow.

Nobody went to bed; but knowing that they would probably get no rest till the next night but one, the more sensible of the party had stolen a few hours' sleep during the day.

We supped at midnight, and between one and two o'clock went to the stable and saddled our horses, and saw them watered and fed.

These preparations made, we betook ourselves to the front of the house and listened in excited silence for the ring of hoofs, the rattle of wheels, or what sound might herald the king's coming.

Two o'clock went, then half-past two, then three.

An hour's delay ; that was nothing. The fugitives might easily have been delayed an hour in Paris or on the road. But as the night sped and the great clock struck quarter after quarter, and four o'clock came and went, and the stillness of the night remained unbroken, hope waned, and the most sanguine began to think something had gone wrong.

Yet as no danger signal had appeared, there was still room for hope.

At length the count proposed that some of us should ride a few miles towards Paris, and see whether his expected guests were on the way; to which I agreed, albeit the proceeding seemed rather absurd; for if they were actually *en route* they had every reason for pushing on, and naught we might do could hasten their arrival.

All wanted to go; but thinking a large party unnecessary, I took with me only Candolle and one other, M. St. Jean, who, in the event of our meeting the king's party, would gallop back with the tidings to La Solitude.

We went quietly, so that we might hear the better; and when about half-way down the lane we heard something that made our pulses beat faster. Pulling up and listening, we fancied we could distinguish the tramp of horses, and either the ring of steel or the rattle of wheels.

As we went on these sounds grew louder, though intermittently, owing, doubtless, to the presence of trees and the inequalities of the ground.

"It is they! It is they!" cried St. Jean, excitedly. "Shall I go back?"

"Not until we see them," I answered. "Don't let us make a mistake, whatever we do."

"But cannot you hear? They have turned into the lane."

"It sounds like it. All the same, we had better make sure."

By this time we were close to the hollow way, which I have already described, and Candolle, who was a few yards ahead, had reached one of the many bends in the winding road.

"Hist!" he whispered, reining in his horse, and raising

his hand as a signal for us to do the same. "I can see them."

"Why not go on, then?"

"Because I am not quite sure; there are too many. The escort was not to exceed fourteen or fifteen; here are at least thirty, and it looks as though more were behind. Come and see for yourself, but keep in the shade."

I rode up and peered over Candolle's shoulder.

Day was breaking, and in the dim half-light I beheld a string of horsemen, riding silently, three abreast, down the hollow way. How many, there was, as yet, no telling—we could see only one end of the string; but more, I felt sure, than Candolle had said, and for aught we knew there might be a hundred behind them.

"Who are they?"

"Can you make them out?" I asked Candolle, who had the better position for seeing.

"I am afraid—by Heaven they are—gendarmes! Back to the house, Lebrun! Back to the house!"

"Wait a second. Will you stand by me, Candolle?"

"To the death."

"Good! Monsieur St. Jean, gallop back for your life. These are gendarmes—scores of them. We are betrayed. Gallop for your life! Let fly the disaster signal. Urge the count and our friends to escape at once by the other road. Candolle and I can hold this pass for an hour."

"And then?"

"Not another word. Go, I tell you."

St. Jean wheeled his horse round, and went off at full gallop.

13

CHAPTER XXVII

HOLDING THE PASS

THE gendarmes were riding slowly—perhaps that they might make the less noise; and as three cavaliers occupied the full width of the road, they rode knee to knee. Owing to the sinuosities of the lane, we could make only a rough guess at their numbers; but as twelve ranks were already in sight, they counted at least thirty-six—possibly twice that number.

We did not reckon on holding them in check more than twenty minutes or half an hour, for the odds were terribly against us; yet less so than might appear. The high banks and close-growing trees that rose on either side of the hollow way rendered deploying impossible, and the gendarmes were so huddled together that they could scarce wield their swords; moreover, the rear ranks would be unable to take part in the fight, except with their carbines and at the risk of hitting their own men.

Moreover, we had the better position and whatever advantage comes of taking your enemy by surprise, and hoped by a sudden attack and vigorous charge to unhorse the front rank and throw the rest into confusion.

As yet, though it grows lighter every minute, we have not been seen. Besides, being in deep shade, one behind the other, we are partly hidden by an overhanging bush.

When the head of the column is about half a furlong from our ambush, we see that the time is come, and, drawing our swords (pistols, by reason of the rain, might have missed fire), we rush down the hill.

The foremost Blues draw rein, making as though they would halt; but, being pushed on by those behind, and somebody calling out, "Charge! you imbeciles, they are only two," they spur on their horses to the encounter.

Yet, irresolutely withal, and too late; for before they are well under way we are at them, horse to horse, man to man, steel to steel; wild cries of fear and rage pierce the air, two horses roll over on the slippery ground, a third gallops riderless towards the manor-house, and the prostrate chargers struggle to their feet and follow. Of the three gendarmes, two have received their quietus from our swords; the third, in whom I recognize our friend with the red hair, crawls to the side of the road and there lies.

Then we engage the second rank, or, rather, they engage us, charging resolutely, while those in the rear let fly at us with their pistols and carbines; but as they are forced to shoot over the heads of those in front, and their pieces, by reason of the dampness of their powder, often miss fire, we take no harm, and, being on higher ground and having room to wield our weapons and manœuvre our horses, still keep the upperhand. Candolle, a fine swordsman, fights like a paladin; and my height, long arm, and big horse give me a vast advantage over the Blues, who, for the most part, are short men on small horses. Goliath carries me splendidly, and helps potently in the fight. A gendarme slashes him across the face with his sabre, whereupon the great horse rears, and, lashing out with his fore-feet, knocks the man and his mount clear over, and tramples upon them.

As fast as one rank goes down, another, thrust forward by those behind, comes on; and albeit the gendarmes are hampered by wounded comrades and hindered by fallen horses, some of whom, having been lamed by kicks, cause dire confusion by their ineffectual efforts to rise, we are forced to back inch by inch, stubbornly fighting yet, so far, though more than once touched, not seriously hurt.

The ground about us is like a shambles : the cries of the wounded and of the unfortunates who fall under their horses' feet, the yells and cries of the men whom the crush and the narrowness of the lane prevent from coming to the front, are maddening.

Still the foe gains on us ; and knowing that once we are out of the hollow way and beyond the crest of the hill, the advantage of position will be reversed, I tell Candolle that the game is nearly up, and we had better prepare for flight, when we hear a ringing cheer behind us, and our comrades from the manor-house come galloping to our help.

This is against my orders, but the brave fellows have too keen a sense of honor to leave friends in the lurch. Yet they had done better to obey, for at the very moment of their appearance there befell a disaster which I had feared from the first without being able to prevent.

A number of gendarmes, dismounting from their horses, had crept furtively through the wood, and now open fire on us from the top of the bank which overlooked the road. Candolle's sword-arm is broken by a bullet : and as I wheel my horse round and give the order to retreat, I am hit in the shoulder, and Goliath, shot through the head, falls in a heap and pins me to the ground.

While I am in this predicament a Blue strikes me with his sabre, and horse after horse passes over me.

" Done for at last," I think ; "they cannot all miss me." The thought is answered by a blow on the head, and I know no more.

CHAPTER XXVIII

CAPTURED

PITCH-DARK.

I thought at first that I had passed into another, though not a better, world; next, that I had wakened from a bad dream; then, recalling the fight and what followed, that I was still prone in the hollow way, pinned to the ground by the carcase of my dead horse, for I could neither turn my body nor raise my head; but it rested on something that felt like a pillow, and on groping about I found bed-clothes; also, that my right arm was bound to my chest and my body swathed in bandages.

And my legs! Good heavens! was it possible that one or both had been amputated while I slept? No; I could move my toes. And then I remembered having heard that people who had lost their legs could still feel their toes; but the doubt thereby engendered was speedily set at rest by shoots of pain in both my legs, and it dawned on my mind that they had been made fast with splints and other surgical appliances, and were benumbed by remaining long in one position.

So far good. Though badly crumpled up and nearly as helpless as though coffined and entombed, I was alive and in full possession of my senses and members, for the which I devoutly thanked God. But where was I? In prison? It could hardly be otherwise. I had been struck down just as I gave the order to retreat, and the fire from the bank was so hot and the pursuit so vigorous that I feared it had gone ill with my friends. They were, doubtless, all either captured or killed.

Yes, I must be in prison. But where, and in what prison? Was it possible that I had been taken to Paris without knowing it, and lodged in the Conciergerie, or the Madelonettes, or the Abbaye? Vain queries; I could neither see aught nor hear aught. It was either an exceptionally black night, or I was in an uncommonly deep dungeon.

I waited for the dawn with feverish impatience, and after what seemed a vigil of many hours the darkness became less dense, and presently a faint light shone on the wall and a silvery sunbeam fell on my face.

How I blessed that sunbeam. It came, as I soon saw, from a window which, though heavily curtained, had not been rendered altogether impervious to the light. As the sun gained power the room grew less darksome, and I saw that, whatever else it might be, it was no dungeon. It was well furnished, and my bed was of the sort usually found in good houses.

Soon I heard footsteps and voices, and after a while a woman in peasant costume entered, and, drawing aside the curtains, let in a flood of light. Then she looked at me, and asked whether I was right in my head yet.

"I hope so," quoth I. "Could you oblige me by telling me where I am?"

"At the manor-house of La Solitude, to be sure."

"But how?"

"It's no use asking me questions; I cannot answer them."

"Why?"

"Such is my orders;" and with that she quitted the room. Her manner left no doubt in my mind that, though not in jail, I was a prisoner. No gentleman's servant could have behaved so rudely. But where were the others (if any of them survived), and what had become of the Comte de Veridet and his family?

In about an hour, as nearly as I could judge, the door opened again, and there entered a little spare gentleman, dressed in sober black, and wearing a white peruke. He had a queer, puckered up, yet not unkindly face, a Roman nose, and bright eyes ; in one hand he carried a cocked hat, in the other a gold-headed cane.

" The doctor, of course," I thought.

" Jeannette tells me you are yourself again," he said, coming to my bedside. " How do you feel ?"

" Like a mummy who has been restored to life without being unrolled."

" Ah ! ah ! Not a bad comparison, and perhaps apter than you are aware of. You have been restored to life. If I were not an old army surgeon and a deft hand at human carpentry, though now only a village doctor, your mangled remains would long ere this have been consigned to your mother earth. Let me see ; two ribs and one leg broken, the other leg badly contused ; one bullet in the shoulder, another in the thigh ; a fractured collar-bone ; a crack on the skull that produced concussion of the brain ; and a few minor cuts and bruises. You were brought here in a sheet, Monsieur Lebrun. But you had your compensations ; if the Blues had not believed you to be dead, they would not have left you alive. And seeing that you killed and wounded a round dozen of them, no wonder. When I arrived on the field of battle and found you buried under that monster of a horse, I, too, believed you were no more ; but on discovering that the vital spark was not quite extinct, I said to myself : " Here is a man of fine physique ; I will try to pull him through. And I have pulled you through, though it will be some time before I can set you on your legs."

" So I am indebted to your kindness and skill for my life, Monsieur le Docteur—"

"Carouge."

"Monsieur le Docteur Carouge. I owe you my life, and I thank you with all my heart."

"Yes, I think I may say that I have saved your life—for the time being. But it is all labor in vain, you know. So soon as you are well enough to travel, you are to be taken to Paris, there to undergo amputation of the head; and that is an operation which I never knew any patient survive."

"I am condemned already, then?"

"Not at all. But you will be tried by the Revolutionary Tribunal, and that admirable institution is not likely to show mercy to a man who has been concerned in a plot to carry off Louis Capet and Madame Veto, and has killed with his own hand six or seven gendarmes. Yes, I am afraid you are destined to make the acquaintance of La Belle Guillotine. But you need not worry about it. I can promise you a long respite. You will not be out of my hands for three months, at the least."

"And how long have I been here?"

"Fifteen days, and unconscious all the time. Happily so. You were as motionless under the knife as if you had been in a cataleptic fit; and without the perfect physiologic rest which your comatose condition insured, it is just possible that my skill in human carpentry might not have availed to save your life."

"And the others, and the count?"

"Your fellow-conspirators, you mean. Three or four were killed in the hollow way; the others escaped, to the great enragement of the Blues, who say their cartridges were so damp that they could not shoot properly, their horses so tired that they could not catch the fugitives. The _ci-devant_ Comte de Veridet also escaped with his family, and there is reason to believe that they have succeeded in crossing the frontier. But the government has confiscated his property, and his house is in possession of the police."

" Do you know the names of the three or four who were killed ?"

"I have no idea. I take no interest in the dead. Apropos of names, yours is Lebrun, I understand ?"

"Yes; Jacques Lebrun."

"Commercial traveller for the house of Lafond & Co., clothiers and woollen merchants ?"

" Precisely. Do you know them ?"

" No ; neither do the police. They seem just a little mystified, those gentlemen of the police. One of them was here the other day for the purpose of identifying you. He thought you were the *ci-devant* Vicomte de Lancy. But when I pointed out that, according to his description, the gentleman in question is five feet five inches high, and that, according to my measurement, you are six feet and an inch, he was obliged to admit that he had made a bad shot. He said that the house of Lafond did not exist, and that your passport, which has been sent to Paris, was—slightly irregular, and wanted me, when you were able to converse, to ask you a few questions, and report your answers to him. But I told him that, though a good patriot, I was no spy ; and the gentleman went away very little wiser than he came."

" I am greatly obliged to you. I did not know you were a patriot."

"I am, though, with a big P., and I have the honor of being the president of our local Jacobin club." And then, taking a pinch of snuff and smiling ironically, he added : " I love France too much to leave it, and value my head too highly to lose it."

From which I inferred that Dr. Carouge was a time-server ; but I always speak of a man as I find him, and, de-

spite his sardonic humor, he had a good heart, and proved
a true friend.

He came to see me every day, and we had many pleasant talks; and when I was well enough to be shifted to a
couch, and the gendarmes, who had so far taken no notice
of me, proposed to keep guard in my room night and day,
lest I should, perchance, slip through their fingers, the doctor saved me from the annoyance by personally answering
for my safe custody, while I, on my part, gave my word of
honor that so long as I was under his charge I would not
attempt to escape.

This arrangement enabled me to take the air, greatly to
the benefit of my health, so soon as I could hobble about
on crutches. Nor was this all. He kept me at La Solitude
for weeks after I had become convalescent by reporting to
headquarters that I was still unfit to travel, and the gendarmes, who had the run of the count's cellar and were
having a fine time, did not say him nay.

But this was too good to last; and one day there came a
peremptory order from Paris to take me thither the following week, even if I died on the way.

The doctor was greatly disturbed.

"To think," he said, "that I have saved your life and
healed your wounds, and the fractured bones of your leg
have united so beautifully that it is stronger than the other,
yet not a hair's-breadth shorter. To think that I have
done all this in order that you may be made shorter by the
head! It is too bad. Word of honor, it is too bad. But
don't you want a pair of shoes, or, better still, two pairs?"

The irrelevancy of this question took me rather aback,
but as I did need shoes I said "Yes."

"Good! Rat, our village cobbler, shall come this day
and measure you. Have you money?"

"Yes, in the lining of my waistcoat."

"It is bad to have all your eggs in one basket, my dear sir. Paris turnkeys are capable of anything. They would rob a cripple of his crutches. Had you not better divide it? I think I can find a safe hiding-place. Rat is a man of confidence."

I knew what the doctor meant, and making a slit in my waistcoat lining I handed him twenty gold pieces and as much in paper.

The cobbler came and took my measure, and shortly afterwards the doctor brought the shoes.

"Be good enough to observe, Monsieur Lebrun," said he, "that between the welts and the soles of these shoes with buckles your money is hidden; in one of those with ties is ingeniously concealed a highly tempered little saw, warranted to cut iron, in the other is an amputating-knife, with which, in case of need, you might cut a throat—a turnkey's, for instance—as the alternative of having your own head cut off."

"I understand, Monsieur le Docteur. The saw for escape, the knife for defence, or, perchance, carving a hole in my prison door."

The next morning I was put in irons and driven away under charge of two gendarmes, both armed to the teeth.

At parting Dr. Carouge embraced me with great affection.

"You must escape," he whispered. "Stick at nothing to keep your head on your shoulders. You will never get another. Your destination is the Conciergerie."

CHAPTER XXIX

IN PRISON

THE Conciergerie, once a royal palace, now a prison and the Court-house of the Revolutionary Tribunal, was a vast building on the banks of the Seine, of terrible memories and forbidding aspect.

On the steps leading up to the principal entrance were a number of women, harpies of the guillotine, who, as I alighted from the carriage, shouted with joy, denounced me as an aristocrat, and assailed me with ribald abuse.

We entered by a wicket, or low door, in the great gate. Three or four yards farther on was a second wicket, guarded, like the first, by an armed porter, opening into a vestibule, where the governor of the house sat enthroned in a capacious chair. To the left was a room divided by an iron grating into two parts, respectively known as the "office" and the "back office." Here were three young men, bareheaded and divested of collars or coats. Their hands were tied behind their backs, and their hair was cut close to their heads.

I knew without asking that these unfortunates had been condemned to death, and were waiting for the cart which was to carry them to the place of execution.

"Your name and quality?" demanded the governor.

"Jacques Lebrun, commercial traveller."

"Age about twenty-five, I suppose?"

I did not contradict him. The trials of the last few months had increased my apparent age by years, and it might be an advantage to be thought older than I was.

After my name had been entered and my person and my valise searched and my fetters removed, I was handed over to two warders (or, as they were generally called, gate-keepers), who led me through many iron doors to a vaulted passage, damp and dark and evil-smelling, lined with cells, into one of which I was shown with scant ceremony.

"That is your billet, No. 17," said the senior warder, helping me forward with a push, and then shut and locked and barred the ponderous door.

It was a horrible hole, unfit for a wild beast's den, and, as I soon discovered, contained animals less cleanly and more ferocious than the worst of the carnivora.

The cell was half lighted by a small barred window, blurred with the dust of years; the walls streamed with moisture, the filth was unspeakable, the air so close and fetid that I nearly fainted.

On one of three wooden benches, covered with litter dirtier than I had ever seen in a stable, sat two men playing dice for coppers and drinking brandy—men of aspect so vile, and clad in garments so ragged and foul, that they looked less human than baboons.

As the door banged behind me they looked up from their game. "Hello! a pal!" exclaimed one of them. "What are you in for? murder or highway robbery? Come, don't be sulky. You are not the first bloke that's been lagged, by a long way. Have a drink; it'll warm your innards and lighten your heart."

I was going to answer with an indignant negative, when, reflecting that, as I was shut up with these ruffians, and could not escape from their companionship, it might be well not to offend them, I took the proffered glass, and let a few drops of the fiery liquid pass my lips. Then they asked me to pay my footing—*bienvenue* (welcome) they called it—whereupon I threw them an assignat, the worth of which

so far exceeded their expectations that they called me a
good prince, and insisted on shaking hands.

"Where do you sleep?" I inquired.

On this they laughed long and loud.

"Here, to be sure; these are our beds" (pointing to the
litter-strewn benches); "and here we are night and day,
and never go out. This is our world. Have you never
been in quod before? No! But you don't tell us what
you have been up to. Forging? Still no answer! Perhaps you are a royalist or counter-revolutionist?"

"Yes, something of the sort."

"Why the devil have they put you here, then?" said the
fellow, in a tone of contempt. "Thank goodness, we are
not royalists, the Angel and I. He is a maker of flash-
notes and counterfeit coin. I am a house-breaker. They
say, also, that I have committed a few murders; and the
name I go by is Coupegorge (Cutthroat).

And then Coupegorge, who was "forward in drink," as
they say in Lancashire, narrated some of his exploits, the
ferocity of which made my blood run cold. As he himself
said, with diabolic glee, he had committed enough crimes
to render him worthy of being broken on the wheel.

By nightfall Coupegorge and the Angel (probably thus
called because of his likeness to a fiend), having made themselves blind drunk, rolled themselves in their rotten straw.

Mine was too filthy to touch, much less to use as bedclothes, so, pushing it on the floor with my foot, I stretched
myself on the bare boards, and while sitting, while lying,
sometimes getting a few winks of uneasy sleep, got through
the night.

In the morning two of the warders on duty brought us
water and food, and replenished my fellow-prisoners' brandy-
bottle, for which they paid out of the money I had given
them for my footing.

Then things went on as before — Coupegorge and the Angel dicing, quarrelling, smoking, drinking, and dozing; myself watching them in dull apathy and deepening disgust.

Yet thinking it better to have their good-will, such as it was, than their ill-will, I treated them civilly; but when they demanded more money, and on my refusal became abusive and violent, I just knocked their heads together — no very difficult feat, the wretches being weak of body and sodden with drink.

After this they treated me with respect; but the ruffians were always with me, and their vile language and repulsive ways, the fumes of their bad brandy and worse tobacco, the poisonous air, the swarms of rats and other vermin still more pestilent, the moral and physical defilement of the place made No. 17 an inferno whose horrors will never be effaced from my memory. I grew so desperate, indeed, that had the ordeal lasted much longer I should either have gone mad, or, by way of ending it, attacked the armed warders who brought our food.

On the ninth or tenth day of my detention—I forget which, for I had lost count of time—two gendarmes and a warder came into the cell and said I was wanted "for an interrogation," and must go with them.

I would have gone anywhere to escape for a while from my hideous surroundings, and put out my hands willingly for the handcuffs, which, albeit there were so many to guard me, were deemed necessary for my safe-keeping.

Then I was marched between the two gendarmes, the warder following, through stony passages, till we came to a staircase, up which we went, and I was presently ushered into a room where two gentlemen, one of whom I took to be an examining judge, the other his secretary, sat at a table covered with books and papers.

" The prisoner Jacques Lebrun," announced the warder.

" Very well," said the judge. Then to me, after glancing at his papers: " You are described as a man of violent temper and great strength, prisoner; but if you will promise to refrain from violence during the interrogation, we will dispense with those handcuffs."

I promised, with a mental reservation that I would not be taken back to No. 17 without a struggle which should cost somebody his life.

When the handcuffs had been removed, the gendarmes and the warder were ordered to withdraw and wait within call, and I was provided with a chair.

The judge opened the interrogation with a little preliminary talk on things in general, and was so affable withal, and his questions, when he did begin to ask them, were so craftily put that had I not, remembering De Lancy's warning, been on my guard, I might have made damaging admissions unawares.

Not that my answers were likely to influence my fate— my fight with the gendarmes was quite enough to insure my condemnation. But for the sake of the friends who had sheltered me I meant to preserve my incognito as long as might be; I was also resolved to give no information that might compromise the vicomte and his fellow-conspirators.

When the judge found that fair words and guileful ways were lavished on me in vain, he knitted his brows and altered his tactics.

" You are a commercial traveller. Were you brought up to business?" he asked.

" Yes," said I.

" By your father?"

" Yes."

" Where is your father at present?"

"Not being a clairvoyant, Monsieur le Juge, I am unable to say."

"But you could give me his address?"

"I would rather not, though."

"Why?"

"You might send for him, and I should be very sorry to see my father here."

"But you can give me the address of the house—Lafond & Co.—by whom you say you were employed."

"Paris."

"That's too vague; and the police have sought all Paris in vain for these gentlemen."

"I am very sorry to say, Monsieur le Juge, that I can give you no further information on the subject than is contained in my passport."

"Your passport is a forgery, as you well know."

"Possibly."

"Where did you obtain it?"

"That I cannot tell you, nor aught else that might get anybody into trouble."

But this was mere skirmishing. The judge cared nothing about my father or the mythical Lafond & Co. His object, as presently appeared, was to obtain information touching the conspiracy, which, though detected and defeated, had not yet been thoroughly bottomed; neither had the police been successful in arresting or even identifying all the conspirators. This I suspected at the time and learned later on. The judge was particularly anxious to obtain a full list of them, and was so curious about De Lancy that I felt sure he was still at large.

But I would not admit that I had ever met the ex-vicomte, which so annoyed my questioner that he rated me roundly, saying that if I did not answer more frankly it would be the worse for me.

14

"How so?" I demanded. "You are sure to send me to the Revolutionary Tribunal, sooner or later, and the Tribunal will send me to the headsman. What can be worse than that?"

"If you make full confession you may not be sent to the Tribunal, while if you remain obdurate I can have you put in a less comfortable cell."

"That is impossible," I exclaimed, hotly. "There is no less comfortable cell than No. 17 on this side of the Styx. It is a stye at the best, and Coupegorge and the Angel make it a hell. A less comfortable cell, indeed! I would rather lie in a dog-kennel."

"And have they actually herded you with common malefactors? That is against the regulations; it shall be seen to."

The judge rang a bell which stood on his table, whereupon entered the warder and the two gendarmes.

"Why have you put the prisoner Lebrun in No. 17?" asked the judge.

"Because we were ordered," answered the warder.

"There must be some mistake. He ought not to have been put there. Take him to the governor and say I said so. Stay; I will give you a line."

"You may go, Lebrun," added the judge, when the line was written. "I hope that at our next interview you will be more communicative. It will be worth your while."

When we were out of the room the warder made as though he would handcuff me again. But as he was taking the irons from his pocket I whipped his sword out of its sheath, and put my back against the wall.

"Now look here," I said, quietly. "I don't want to give you any trouble, and I promise to go quietly; but if you try to put those things on again, I shall do somebody a mischief."

"Well, you are a queer customer," returned the gendarme. "However, let it be as you say; I agree."

"Word of honor?"

"Word of honor."

"Good! Here is your sword—and something else," slipping a five-franc piece into his hand.

"*Allons!*" says he; and we marched in the same order as before to the office, where we found the governor, or, more properly, head turnkey, sitting in his chair of state.

I had noticed previously, and I saw now, that everybody toadied to this man; and it struck me that if I took a rather different line it might be to my advantage.

When the warder had delivered his message and the judge's note, the chief referred to his register, and then, turning to me, said that there had been a slight mistake—I had been put in No. 17 instead of No. 71, and he inquired whether I would lie on straw or a mattress.

"Well, if the straw is as filthy as that in No. 17 I should prefer a mattress," quoth I.

"In that case there will be a charge of twenty-five francs a month," says he.

"Good! I will pay it. And if I can have a cell to myself I will pay double."

"A cell to yourself! Perhaps you would like a servant to wait on you?"

"I should. Can I have one?"

"A thousand thunders! I believe the fellow fancies he is in a hotel. Put him in 56, Marteau. I suppose he is a quiet prisoner."

"Very," answered the warder, with a grin; "only he rather objects to handcuffs."

"They all do. You will be doubled up with the *ci-devant* Marquis de Lasalle, prisoner. You can make a servant of him, if you like. It would be something new to have an ex-noble waiting on a commercial traveller. You may go."

This time Marteau was my sole escort, and I perceived that the tip had disposed him in my favor.

"It was rather cool of you to ask the governor for a cell all to yourself," he observed, familiarly, as we went along. "But, as I said before, you are a cool customer; and if you are willing to pay double, I don't see why, and—" hesitating.

"Stand something for the warder who stands my friend. Of course that goes without saying."

"Well, it can perhaps be managed—after a while. If we were full it could not be done at any price. I shall also say a good word for you to my colleagues."

"Thank you," I said, indifferently, as though I cared very little about it; for to show anxiety were to betray my purpose. I wanted to be alone, because I meant to escape. But unless my fellow-prisoner were either willing to keep my secret, possibly to his own undoing, or sufficiently resolute and courageous to take part in the adventure, escape would be impossible; and these being conditions on which I could not reckon, it was absolutely necessary, by hook or by crook, to have a cell to myself for at least a night or two.

CHAPTER XXX

WE MEET AGAIN

HAD I been put into cell 56 on my arrival at the Conciergerie, I should have called it, as indeed it was, damp, dirty, and pestilential; but after No. 17 it seemed an abode of luxury.

There were two beds, with mattresses, sheets, and coverlets (which, though far from clean, were better than a shakedown of rotten straw), two wooden stools, two barred windows, a three-legged stool, a table, and not much else.

But prisons never are pleasant places, and the revolution treated its victims with scant indulgence — anything was thought good enough for people whose destiny, in nine cases out of ten, was the guillotine. Yet I had been worse off, and, as I have already mentioned, I meant to escape. Moreover, I was no longer to be shut up with Coupegorge and the Angel, and I should be able to stretch my legs in the open air. Prisoners in the infirmary quarter, said Marteau, were required to quit their cells every morning at half-past nine, and stay in the yard assigned to them until evening; also the prisoners on this side were all politicians and mostly gentlemen, and their yard was divided from the ladies' yard only by a grating, through which they could talk, see each other, and even flirt and make love.

At least, so said Marteau; though I thought it sounded too good to be true. After telling me these things, Marteau went for my valise, and I, sitting down on one of the crazy stools, communed with myself, thinking, among other things, how much easier life can be made, even in a prison, by greasing men's palms, wondering whether and where I should see Angélique again, and how my father would regard my long silence. It troubled me sorely that there was no possibility of letting him know that I still lived and did not despair of regaining my liberty.

Dear busy old Lancashire seemed farther away than ever now—so far away, indeed, that there were moments when I got confused about my own identity, and realized only with an effort that Fritz Astor, Anatole Boucher, and Jacques Lebrun were one and the same person.

As night was closing in my musings were disturbed by a great uproar — shouts, oaths, the baying of hounds, the trampling of feet; then came a jingling of keys, a shooting back of bolts, a rasp of rusty hinges, the heavy door swung back, and a gentleman, two warders, both half-seas-over, and a couple of fierce-looking dogs entered the cell.

"Here is your companion, Lasalle, name of Lebrun," growled one of the turnkeys.

"I am glad to make your acquaintance, sir, though I wish it could have been made under happier circumstances. I hope we shall be good friends," says the gentleman, doffing his hat.

"I have no doubt we shall," said I, as we shook hands.

"Marteau told us about you," muttered one of the turnkeys, significantly.

"Yes, Marteau has a good heart. Here is something to drink my health," tipping them both liberally.

"Sacred name! you also have a good heart. Can we get you anything—a bottle of brandy?"

"Thank you, not to-night. I have been breathing brandy for the last ten days."

"Ah, Coupegorge and the Angel take kindly to their liquor, don't they? It is not quality they care for. Rapp

and I—my name is Botte—go in for both, don't we Rapp?
Good-night, prisoners."

"It is quite true," observed Lasalle, when the fellows
were gone; "they do go in for both, and a good deal of it.
They are drunk every night. You did wisely to grease their
palms. My stock of grease is unfortunately getting low,
but I dare say it will last until Monsieur Sanson"—the executioner—"adds my head to his collection of trophies.
Might I, without being deemed guilty of indiscretion, inquire with what offence you are charged?"

Coupegorge had said, "What are you in for?" However,
it came to the same thing.

"Espousing the king's cause, and killing a few gendarmes
—in fair fight, of course," I answered. "And you?"

"Nothing nearly so heroic, though the penalty is equally
death. I emigrated, I returned to see my mother, who was
like to die, and here I am."

"And you think you will be condemned?"

"I have not a doubt of it. The rascally sans-culottes are
so full of the king's trial that they are rather overlooking
their victims in the Conciergerie. But that won't last long.
We may be called before the Tribunal to-morrow, and that
means making the acquaintance of La Belle Guillotine the
same day; for I cannot deny that I visited my dying
mother, nor you, I presume, that you made mince-meat of
those Blues. But what does it signify? Everybody is under sentence of death. If we escape the guillotine it will
only be to perish of some painful disease, or, worse still, die
of old age. And really, you know, unless one is young and
rich and can enjoy it in Paris, life is scarcely worth living."

The Marquis de Lasalle was a fluent talker and a pleasant companion, yet I did not think we were likely to become close friends. The disparity in our ages was too
great, and we had few, if any, ideas in common. Moreover,

I gathered from his conversation that he was one of the recreant nobles, who, after encouraging the revolution until it became dangerous to their order, had left the country and joined its enemies.

This, not visiting his sick mother, was the offence for which he had to answer.

He was clearly not the man, even though he had been younger, to participate in the desperate enterprise which I contemplated, and until I knew him better it would be imprudent to take him into my confidence.

At eight o'clock on the following morning Botte and Rapp brought our breakfast, for which, as it was better than the ordinary prison fare, we had to pay at a rate that left the caterers a profit of at least cent. per cent. But, as the marquis remarked, when you are in the ante-chamber of death the cost of living becomes a secondary consideration.

Shortly after nine o'clock we were turned out of our cell and ordered to betake ourselves to the man's yard. It was a narrow, gloomy enclosure, bounded by great walls which shut out the sun; but we could move about and meet our fellow-prisoners, to most of whom Lasalle introduced me. All seemed to be in high spirits—laughing, joking, and telling piquant stories as unconcernedly as if they had been sipping coffee on the boulevards, or strolling in the gardens of Versailles.

Yet any one of them might be "called" on the morrow, since though there was just then a lull in the activity of the Revolutionary Tribunal, there was seldom a day on which it did not send at least one of the inmates of the Conciergerie to the guillotine.

When a prisoner failed to appear in the yard at the accustomed hour, none of his former associates were so ignorant as not to know that he would never return, or so ill-bred as to mention his name.

At noon the ladies appeared in great force, many of them in rich attire, none ill-dressed, and we dined practically in their company, our tables and theirs being placed close to the railing that separated the two yards, and the bars were so wide apart that a thin man might almost have slipped between them.

Never was I at a merrier party. We toasted each other —those of us who were rich, in wine ; those who were poor, in water—bantered each other, and exchanged more or less witty repartees. The conversation was brilliant—all seemed to have cast care to the winds, as though they had said to themselves : " Let us eat and drink, for to-morrow we die."

After dinner most of the men went up to the railing, and either stood or paced to and fro, talking between whiles to the ladies on the other side.

Not, as yet, knowing any of these fair prisoners, I was looking curiously on, when I spied among the throng an old lady leaning on the arm of a young girl.

"Poor old lady ! What is her crime, I wonder?" As this thought passed through my mind, she and her companion turned their faces towards me.

Merciful Heaven ! My brain reels, I rush up to the bars, and, in my excitement, exclaim, loud enough to be heard, " Mademoiselle de la Tour, Madame la Marquise !"

Angélique stops and turns pale, looking as startled as though she beheld a ghost. Then, recovering herself, she leads the marchioness to where I stand.

" You here, Monsieur—"

"Lebrun, Madame la Marquise," I put in.

"Of course, Monsieur Lebrun. I really think my memory begins to fail me. You here ! Yet why should I be surprised ? If you want to meet your friends come to the Conciergerie. I have met many already, some of whom I shall never meet again—here."

"I pray Heaven, madame, you are not here because of your kindness to me. If so, I shall never—"

"No; they arrested me because I sent money to my son, who is an emigrant. Holding communication with an emigrant is a capital crime under the republic. But they will have to be quick, or I shall anticipate the executioner. It does not take much to kill an old woman of eighty-four, and this prison life will soon make an end of me, I think. But for this dear girl, who comes every day and cheers me with her company, and brings me little comforts, I should have been dead long ago. Oh, she has a rare courage to traverse the streets of Paris unattended at a time like this."

Thank God! Angélique was not a prisoner, then.

"We heard you had been desperately wounded, and feared you were dead," she said, regarding me sadly with her beautiful eyes. "We little thought, when you set out on that ill-omened journey, that we three should meet again in a prison. Poor marchioness! Surely they won't have the heart to condemn her. But I don't know—they have guillotined ladies nearly as old. You see how she has aged; it is only occasionally, and on fine days, that she can come into the yard for an airing."

"And your uncle, what of him?" I asked.

"He is in hiding. You know how clever he is. He was warned in time, and slipped through their fingers. Was it you who sent off the pigeon with the danger signal?"

"I ordered it to be sent off."

"I thought it was your doing. And you were badly wounded?"

"Yes; but I am all right now."

"Have you been before the Tribunal?"

"Not yet. I have been interrogated once, and am to be again."

"And what do you think will be the result—I mean, have you any hope—"

"Of acquittal? Not the least. My offence is too fla-grant. But I have some hope of escaping — with your help."

"My help! Oh, if I could— But how?"

"As yet I am unable to say. I have not hit upon a feasible plan. But I shall, if they only give me a few days' respite; and as they have not done with their interrogations, I think they will. You come to the Conciergerie every day, don't you?"

"Yes, to see Madame la Marquise; but I come into the yard only when she can come, and that is not often."

"But you will come here every day, mademoiselle. I know it is a great deal to ask, and not quite the right thing for you to do—or would not be in ordinary circumstances. But these are extraordinary times, and this is a case of life and death. And the mere sight of your face does me good —gives me hope and courage. It is like sunshine—"

"Oh, monsieur!"

"Yes, it is like sunshine. And though I hope they will give me a few days, there is no telling, as you said just now about the marchioness. Any morning, even to-morrow—"

Angélique turned pale.

"Oh yes, I will come," she murmured.

Here the marchioness, who had been sitting on a bench which, though near, was out of earshot, rose from her seat and tottered to the railing.

"It is time for us to go; I am very tired. *Au revoir*, monsieur," she said, giving me her hand, which I reverently kissed.

Then Mademoiselle de la Tour gave me her hand.

"Angélique has been more to me than a daughter. She is the best girl in the world," added Madame la Marquise.

The thought that I might never see her again flashed through my mind and unsealed my lips.

"It is true, and I love her with all my heart!" I exclaimed, in a passionate whisper, heard only by Angélique.

Angélique's hand trembled, but it remained for a few delicious seconds in mine. When I looked in her eyes I saw that I had won her heart, and though I was in the antechamber of death, never in my life had I felt so happy.

CHAPTER XXXI

As yet, albeit I had suggested that Angélique might help me to escape, I was groping in the dark, and saw no way out. The idea I had first conceived of cutting through the bars of my cell window, letting myself down, and climbing over the outer wall, was obviously impracticable, even though I should make or otherwise obtain a rope. I had discovered that the window overlooked the yard, and that the yard was bounded by walls too lofty to scale without a forty-foot ladder, to say nothing of the sentries who were always on guard below.

The alternative to scaling the walls, after I got into the yard, was going out by the way I had come in ; but as this plan involved breaking through, or opening without keys, half a dozen iron-bound doors, at any of which I might encounter a brace of warders, and running the gantlet of the people in the vestibule and the Cerberus at the wicket, it was even more impossible than the other.

The idea of bribing one of the turnkeys was also conceived, only to be dismissed. The man who connived at my escape would do so at the peril of his life, and I doubted whether I had enough money to make it worth a man's while. Moreover, if the turnkey to whom I made the proposal were honest, he would denounce me ; while if he were dishonest, he might take my money and obtain credit and promotion by betraying me.

Too risky altogether, even had I the wherewithal.

Though I thought and thought till my head went round,

and cudgelled my brains in the watches of the night, I found no solution of the difficulty, and rose in the morning gloomy, despondent, and almost despairing.

Even the thought that I had won Angélique's heart failed to revive my drooping spirits. since if I were guillotined she might marry somebody else, and the possibility did not please me.

To make matters worse, Angélique did not keep her tryst. After dinner I was hanging about the barrier, watching for her, when a young woman with a pale face and black eyes beckoned to me—a call which I promptly answered.

"You are Monsieur Lebrun?" she asked.

"That is my name, madame. What can I have the pleasure of doing for you?"

"You are expecting Mademoiselle de la Tour."

"Yes, I am hoping to see her."

"And I have the advantage of knowing her. She was here this morning—I mean in our room, Madame de Malartie's and mine—but only for a few minutes, and desired me to tell you that, having some important business to attend to, she could not see you to-day, but hopes to do so to-morrow."

I thanked the lady for her information, and then, sick with disappointment, turned away and joined a group of prisoners who, being unacquainted over the border, were whiling away the time in conversation, which, judging by the laughter it evoked, seemed to be amusing. To hear them and look at them you would have thought they had not a care in the world.

The talk was about mesmerism, which a little time before had been greatly in vogue. Opinions were divided, some believed in it, some did not, the unbelievers being apparently in the majority. After the discussion had gone on for a while, one of the sceptics, who seemed to be somewhat of a wag, said that he knew of but one case of mesmerism in which there was neither deception nor illusion, and the operator's will prevailed over that of his victim. The case occurred in Italy, and he could vouch for its accuracy.

One day at high noon a banker, living in a provincial town, was called to his door by a stranger, who said he had an important and strictly private communication to make. The banker, scenting business, responded to the summons, whereupon the stranger, fixing him with his eye and slightly opening his cloak, bade him put on his hat and step outside.

The banker obeyed, the stranger took his arm, and the two walked through the town, the banker, at his companion's bidding, greeting all and sundry whom they met.

They proceeded for several miles arm in arm, and almost cheek by jowl, until they came to a wood, where they found several gentlemen whose many weapons and devil-may-care air suggested grave doubts as to the honesty of their calling. Nevertheless, they greeted the banker courteously and his conductor with profound respect. After this personage had refreshed himself with a deep draught of wine, he called for pen, ink, and paper, and requested the banker to sit down and write an order on his bank for the payment of ten thousand lira to the bearer.

The mesmerist then handed the paper to one of the gentlemen in question, and bade him go with all speed to the town, cash the order, and bring back the money.

" When it comes," he said, turning to the banker, and again fixing him with his eye, " you may go. Meanwhile, let us amuse ourselves with a game of cards."

The play went on, to the unfortunate banker's great disadvantage, until the messenger returned with the ten thousand lira.

When the bandit had counted the cash and found it right, he courteously dismissed his reluctant guest, and the latter returned to his home, a sadder and a wiser man.

The listeners laughed heartily, and said it was a capital story—all except one gentleman, who looked very serious and wanted to know how it was done.

"That," said the narrator, "I shall leave you to guess."

Whereupon more laughter, for everybody else had divined the secret of the mesmerist's power. I thought the tale of the banker and the bandit the best I had ever heard. It was the light I had been seeking—the light which should show me out of the Conciergerie, since, given certain conditions not impossible of attainment, I felt sure that as the bandit had mesmerized the banker with his dagger, so I could mesmerize a warder with my amputating knife, and make him my guide to liberty.

During the rest of the day and far into the night I was thinking out my scheme, nor did I sleep until it was complete in every detail. I rose in the morning full of hope and courage, and anxiouly awaited Ang lique's coming, for I wanted to tell her the good news, and her co-operation was essential to the success of my scheme.

Late in the afternoon she appeared at the railing, alone.

"The marchioness is very ill to-day or I should have come sooner," she said, as we shook hands.

"Why did you not keep your tryst yesterday?" I asked, reproachfully.

"For your sake, monsieur—"

"Fritz, not monsieur—if you love me, Angélique."

"It was for your sake, Fritz," she said, lowering her eyes, but leaving her hand in mine, "that I did not come yesterday. I went to see Uncle Claude, for he has a wise head, except where the king is concerned, and though in hiding, has still some influence in high quarters. He was much distressed when he heard of your great peril, and will do whatever he can. But unless you can escape, he fears—"

"The worst. So do I. Nay, I am sure of it. But I have thought of a plan, Angélique—a plan of promise ; and if you will give me your help—"

"If I will! Oh, Fritz," raising her eyes lovingly and pathetically to mine, "only tell me, and you shall see."

"You must first know, my dear Angélique, that the success of my plan is contingent on certain conditions, one being a full week's further respite—"

"That's arranged already. My uncle gave me a letter to Monsieur Dufour, which frightened him dreadfully—"

"To Dufour?"

"Yes. I am living at his house. He and his father were under obligations to the marchioness—she had been a valued customer of theirs for many years ; and when she was arrested and seals were put on the doors, and I had nowhere to go, Madame Dufour invited me to become her guest. Well, the letter had a great effect. Monsieur Dufour said he would endeavor to delay your appearance before the Tribunal as long as possible—as he hoped, for several weeks. More than this he could not do, even though you were his own brother."

I guessed what De Lancy had written. He had intimated to Dufour that if I were guillotined he would be denounced for having cashed the draft on my father, which seemed a base return for the money-changer's kindness ; but necessity has no law, and I knew that the threat would never be executed, even though I should be.

"You were to be interrogated again to-morrow," added Angélique ; "but Monsieur Dufour has seen Citizen Lemaire, the judge who has your case in hand, and he will not send for you again for five or six days."

15

" So far good, very good, my darling. Didn't I say you could help me ?"

" Oh, but this is not enough. It merely puts off the fatal day. What else can I do, and what are the other conditions you spoke of ?"

" One is having a cell to myself for a few nights; that, I think, can be managed by a little judicious bribery. Another is the possession of three or four yards of cord, about the thickness of your little finger, and a phial of laudanum, which you can bring to-morrow or the next day."

" Laudanum !"

" Don't be alarmed. I neither contemplate suicide nor murder. Then I must have some place to go to when I get out. Do you think I could join your uncle ?"

" I think you had better not. He may have to change his quarters any moment. I will speak to Madame Dufour. You once rendered her a service which she is anxious to repay, and she takes great interest in you. Between us we will devise something. Trust to a woman's wit."

" With all my heart; especially your wit, my Angélique."

And then we had some further talk which need not be repeated here. We talked at our ease, for my fellow-captives were far too courteous and discreet to interfere with, or even seem to observe, a lady and gentleman *en tête-à-tête*, and when the time for parting arrived, I profited by the darkness of the yard and the deepening twilight to bid the dear girl a tender farewell.

I hoped to see her again on the morrow; but in her stead came Mme. Dufour, to my great discontent; yet, when the lady explained the reason of Angélique's absence, I found that I had no cause for complaint, and was forced to admit that I had not thought of everything, and that woman's wit was better than mine.

"As you doubtless know," said Mme. Dufour, "there are here, as in every prison in Paris, spies in the employ of the police, or traitors who, in order to ingratiate themselves with the authorities, betray their fellow-prisoners, and report whatever they may deem strange or suspicious. Now, if Mademoiselle de la Tour pays you a visit every day, and you should, as I hope you will, escape, they might suspect her of connivance. That would compromise us all, for she is living with us, and is admitted to the Conciergerie as a favor to my husband. Moreover, you will have to come to our house, which is another reason why we must do nothing to excite suspicion."

"You are quite right, madame, and I am vastly obliged to you."

"Don't mention it, pray. I owe you a debt, remember, and I would do much more for our dear Angélique" (smiling); "she will see you to-morrow for a few minutes and bring you what you asked for, and then you will perhaps be able to tell her when we may expect you. Meanwhile, you will do well to pay some attention to these other ladies (of course as a blind), even to the extent of flirting with them. I don't think Angélique will mind. And now, monsieur, I think I had better go. A man with the furtive eyes that betray the *mouton*" (prison spy) "is prowling about. *Au revoir.*"

When Mme. Dufour was gone I acted straightway on her advice, and talked and joked with one of the fair prisoners, to whom Lasalle had introduced me, until we were dismissed to our cells — driven rather, the warders being always rude and often drunk.

I followed Lasalle up the steps that led to our room. Botte followed me.

"A word with you, Lebrun," he whispered, as we reached

the first landing. "You said something to Marteau about
a cell to yourself. Well, I think you may have exclusive
possession of this after to-morrow—if we can come to
terms."

"How? What—"

"You will know in the morning." Then, raising his voice,
he added, in his usual rough fashion: "Sacred name! go
quickly, will you? I am in a hurry, if you are not. Now,
then, in with you, Lasalle."

The heavy door banged behind us, the keys were turned,
the bolts shot home, and ourselves shut up once more.

Lasalle threw himself on his bed.

"I am getting tired of this, Lebrun," he said, wearily. "If
the sans-culottes don't let me out soon, or make an end of
me, I shall make an end of myself. At the best, life is a
mistake when you are past forty and have nothing to look
forward to but death and poverty, and I don't care how soon
I am out of it."

Being unprepared with a suitable answer, I kept silence.
If I had spoken my thoughts I should have said that the
Count de Lasalle was not likely to be much longer oppressed
with the life which he found so burdensome.

CHAPTER XXXII

A MESMERIZED WARDER

BOTTE's hinted forecast was not long in coming to pass.

As Lasalle and myself were at breakfast on the next morning we were startled by the regular tramp of heavy feet and the rattle of accoutrements in the corridors leading to our cell.

We both stood up, the count cool and self-possessed, myself in some trepidation, for the thought had crossed my mind that Botte might have played me a malicious trick, or made a mistake as to the man.

The door opened, and Botte and Rapp appeared at the threshold. Behind them were three gendarmes with fixed bayonets.

" Which is it?" asked the count.

" You, Lasalle," answered Rapp.

Save for a slight yet almost imperceptible twitching of the upper lip, the count showed no emotion whatever.

" I am ready," he said, cheerfully. Then to me :

" Farewell, my dear sir. Our acquaintance, albeit not long, has at least been pleasant, and will dwell in my memory—as long as I live."

" Farewell ; I am very sorry."

More I could not say, being deeply moved, for it is no light thing to see a brave man going to his death ; and though I had not taken Lasalle to my heart, I admired his courage and deplored his fate.

After shaking hands with me and the two turnkeys, the handcuffs were put on, and the gendarmes led the doomed man to the Tribunal, whence, after being tried and convicted, he was carried straightway to Revolution Place and there beheaded.

"You may as well go into the yard now; it will save me the trouble of coming again," observed Botte, who had not gone with the others. "You are alone now, and may remain so—for a while—if, as I said, we can come to terms."

"I don't think I care much about being alone," quoth I, with affected indifference. "Lasalle was an agreeable companion."

"But the next might be disagreeable. Besides, we could shove three or four in."

"Into this den?"

"A den, do you call it? Why, it is one of the best rooms in the prison."

"How much?"

"Twenty francs a day. Half for me, half for Rapp."

"That won't do at all, Citizen Botte. You want to ruin me. No, thank you. Everything considered, I think I would rather not be alone."

"Fifteen, then?"

"No."

"Ten."

"I'll think about it."

"You won't have the chance. It must be either yes or no, and now. You need not hesitate so much. It may not be for long."

"What do you mean?"

"We are to have an official visit this morning. A member of the Committee of Public Safety and a deputy, who is also a municipal, are going to look us up, and if they think the prisoners are getting too thick on the ground—"

"I understand; they may make a clearance. Very well;

I agree — ten francs between you and Rapp. Here's your first day's pay ; and you can get me a bottle of cognac."

"Good! May I taste ?"

"By all means ; first quality, mind."

"Good again. *Allons !* It is time for you to be in the yard."

Most of my fellow-captives had heard of the approaching visit, to which, by reason of the monotony and inactivity of their lives, they attached, as I thought, undue importance ; and Botte, I felt sure, had exaggerated, or more probably lied, to serve his own ends.

Be that as it might, Dufour having arranged for the postponement of my examination, I could look forward to the visit without misgiving.

So it came to pass that when the visitors arrived I was the only unconcerned individual in the yard, and instead of avoiding them like some of the other prisoners, I kept my ground and refused to budge.

As the inspectors were accompanied by the governor and surrounded by several minor officials, it was not easy to tell which was which.

"Whom have we here ?" I heard one of them say in a voice which seemed familiar to me ; and turning towards the speaker, I found myself face to face with Deputy Serin.

The recognition was mutual.

"I think we have met before," said he, in his harsh, grating voice. "You are the young man from Alsace, named Boucher, who made an appointment with me at the Hôtel de Ville, and did not keep it. A *ci-devant*" (noble) "I suppose ?"

The governor whispered something in his ear.

"So you are the *soi-disant* Lebrun, one of the royalist conspirators who tried to carry off Capet, and resisted the gendarmes at Flins. That is months ago, and you are alive yet !"

"He was so badly wounded that he could not be removed, Citizen Deputy, and has been here only three weeks," put in the governor.

"Three weeks too long. I must see to this. I shall speak to Fouquier Tinville"—public prosecutor of the Revolutionary Tribunal—"about him at once."

"His interrogation is not yet completed, Citizen Deputy."

"Interrogation! What is the good of interrogating a fellow like him? He is a born liar; he will lie to the judge as he lied to me."

This was more than flesh and blood could bear.

"If I were not a prisoner and you were less well guarded I would wring your neck, Citizen Deputy!" I exclaimed, wrathfully and recklessly.

"Oh, you would wring my neck, would you? Well, I promise you that by this time to-morrow you will have no neck to wring. I promise, and Serin always keeps his word, even to lying and malignant aristocrats like yourself. Wring my neck, would you? Let us pass on, Citizen Governor."

When the visitors and their suite were gone, my fellow-prisoners crowded round me, some to congratulate, others to condole.

"It was a gross insult; you did well to resent it. I felicitate you on your courage," said one.

"You will have to go before the Tribunal to-morrow instead of next week or next month," said another, "that is all. And I dare say two or three of us will have to bear you company; there is always an increase of executions after an inspection."

This by way of consolation!

My answers were brief, for I felt by no means proud of my exploit. I had lost my temper and wofully worsened my prospects.

Only one night between me and death ! I had intended to win the confidence and allay the possible suspicions of the two warders by giving them two carouses in my cell before attempting the enterprise which was to decide my fate. But now I should have to stake everything on a single throw of the dice.

It was that night or never ; and my plans were fortunately so far matured that if Botte and Rapp took the bait I was going to offer them, and Angélique kept her tryst, the odds, as I reckoned, were still in my favor, albeit less than they had been.

Angélique did keep her tryst, purposely and prudently coming late, in order that she might pass me the cord and the phial unobserved, which she did very deftly, and I put them away in my pocket. As spies might be watching us, we wasted no time in love - making. I told her at once that something had happened which rendered delay dangerous; that I purposed, with God's help, to make my escape that night, and inquired how I should obtain admission at M. Dufour's house.

" You know where it is ?"

" In the Rue St. Denis."

" Yes, but you must go round to the back ; and for your better guidance we shall leave a light behind a red curtain in the attic window, the highest of all. The door will be left unbarred and unlocked. You must open it noiselessly, shut and fasten it ; then creep softly up-stairs to the attic, which you will recognize by the light; and as the door will be left ajar, you can make no mistake. Go in and stay until somebody comes ; but don't enter the house before midnight. Deputy Serin comes to the Dufours two or three times a week and often stays till past eleven."

" Deputy Serin ! Oh, I remember him. He called when I was there, and the Dufours hurried me away."

" He is a wretch.   I hate him."

" Has he dared—"

" Don't ask me, Fritz."

I had no need to ask; Angélique had said enough.   I knew the deputy had been paying her odious attentions, and longed more than ever for an opportunity of wringing his neck.

And then my love and I parted—until the morrow, as we told each other, or forever, as I said to myself; but of the latter possibility I was careful not to speak.

Everything now depended on the two turnkeys, as, unless I could outwit and cajole them and make them my tools, my scheming was in vain.   In one sense Serin's threat might be an advantage; it would disarm their suspicions and serve as an excuse for the invitation I was about to give them.

Botte accompanied me to my cell, as usual.

" You will find the bottle of cognac on your table," said he.   " I profited by your permission to taste it."

" And found it good ?"

" Rather."

" Would you like another taste ?"

" Wouldn't I, just !"

" You shall have more than a taste ; but not now.   You heard what the Citizen Deputy said ?"

" Yes; you put your foot in it there, Lebrun.   And very sorry I am ; it will be money out of our pockets—mine and Rapp's."

" You think I shall be called to-morrow, then ?"

" Sure."

" Well, then, let us make a night of it.   It will be my last, and I don't like the idea of being all alone.   You and Rapp come here after you have done your work and had your supper.   Bring another bottle of brandy and three or four bottles of burgundy, some glasses, cards, and dice — just to pass the time and kill care."

" It is against regulations, Lebrun—against regulations ; and if we got found out we should get the sack. To you it would make no difference. They cannot do worse to a man than make him shorter by a head, and yours is as good as off already. However, as this is your last night on earth, and you have treated us so liberally, and that brandy is so toothsome, we will risk it for this time only. I answer for Rapp. Expect us in about two hours. *Au revoir.*"

"Good," I said to myself — " very good." And then I set to work.

The first thing I did was to empty the phial of laudanum into the bottle of brandy—or, rather, what remained of it, Botte having tasted freely.

Next I donned the shoes that contained the money, and ripped open the soles of the pair that contained the saw and the amputating-knife—broad and bright, and as keen as a razor. I placed it in my breast-pocket, and, taking the saw, began to cut the bars of my window, three of which it would be necessary to remove before a man of my girth could squeeze himself through. As they were deeply rusted, I needed only to nick them. That done, I should have no difficulty in wrenching the bars from their sockets or breaking them off short.

All the same, it was a tedious job; and before I had finished it my guests were at the door; so I must hide my saw and play the host.

" Hadn't we better blind the window ?" says Botte, as he and Rapp disburdened themselves of the bottles and glasses.

" By all means," quoth I ; and with great alacrity sprang up and curtained the window with a coat, which effectually excluded the light of the warders' lanterns.

" Now we are all right," said Rapp, unbuckling his sword, an example which Botte speedily followed.

Then the dilapidated table was drawn up in such sort that one of the beds could be used as a seat, the cell being ill provided with sitting accommodations.

After drinking to each other's health, we began to gamble at large, and I lost heavily in small change, purposely giving much less heed to the game than to the replenishing of my visitors' glasses; and so soon as they were on the right side of two bottles of burgundy, I proposed a nip of cognac, to which they readily assented, and during the rest of the carouse drank nothing else. Nevertheless (there being two bottles and myself acting as butler), I took good care to give Rapp at least twice as much of the sophisticated stuff as I gave Botte, whose services I should require later on.

After a while, and sooner than I expected, Rapp fell asleep, dropped from his chair, and rolled on the floor.

" Let him lie; he has a head not worth a row of pins," growled Botte. "*Allons;* it's your throw."

We resumed our gamble; but, in spite of himself, Citizen Botte soon began to nod, and presently joined his friend on the floor, thereby enabling me to complete my preparations at leisure.

I relieved Rapp of his coat, bound him hand and foot, and gagged him. Botte I merely bound. Next I broke his sword close by the hilt, and restored the broken pieces to the scabbard.

This done, I finished the nicking of the bars, tore them from their sockets, and made my bedclothes into a rope strong enough to hold a man, and long enough when let down from the window to reach to within five or six feet of the ground.

I had now only to wait until all was quiet, and Botte so

far recovered from the effects of the laudanum as to be able to understand plain French and find his way about.

When I thought the time had come, I tried to waken him; but kicking and pinching producing no result, I poured water on his head and down his neck.

This roused him.

"A thousand thunders!" he muttered; "it is raining — raining like a dog, and I haven't brought my umbrella."

"Are you quite awake, Botte?" I asked.

"Awake? Yes, certainly, of course. But where the devil? And what—what's this? I am corded like a trunk. I cannot get up. I—" (trying to rise). "Am I a warder, am I a prisoner, or am I dreaming?"

"At this moment you are a warder and my prisoner. Now listen, Botte. Do you understand?"

"Give me a nip, and then I shall."

I lifted him up, set him on a chair, and administered the desired nip.

"Now I begin to understand," said he; "but I didn't expect this of you, Lebrun."

"Never mind what you expected of me; let me tell you what I expect from you. Rapp lies there, bound and gagged, and, as you see, I have put on his hat, coat, and sword. Now I want you to show me the way out by one of the side doors you know of. If you agree, I shall give you a thousand francs effective, which means three thousand in paper. If you refuse, I shall slit your windpipe," exhibiting my mesmerizer, "and go by myself."

"Slit it, then. What's the odds? If I do what you ask I shall be sent to the guillotine within twenty-four hours."

"Not a bit of it. I have drawn three of those teeth in the window and made a rope of the bedclothes. All you have to do is to let me out—and as I shall be taken for a warder, nobody will meddle with us—then return hither, drop the rope from the window, waken Rapp, lock the cell door behind you, and go quietly to bed. When the rope is seen dangling outside in the morning it will be supposed that I have escaped that way."

" How will it be supposed you got over the wall?"

" That's no affair of yours. My cell was searched as usual during the day, and you locked me in at the customary hour. Nobody can blame you, and if you and Rapp keep still tongues, you will not even be suspected."

Still Botte seemed to hesitate.

"This knife is very keen," I added, letting him feel the edge of it on his windpipe, "and three thousand francs are not to be picked up every day of the year."

" I see," said he. " If I refuse, I die : if I agree, I may not be found out, and three thousand in assignats are a thousand effective—as much as the republic gives me for a year of honest work. I agree; so just unloose me, if you please. These cursed cords hurt."

"We shall walk arm in arm," I observed, as I undid the cord; "my left in your right. My right hand will be under my coat, holding the knife; and if you try to break away, give an alarm, or play any trick whatever, you are a dead man. You understand?"

" Perfectly."

"Good! Don your hat, also buckle on your sword; it will look better. And as I have broken the blade off short by the hilt, you cannot hurt yourself with it. So let us away."

CHAPTER XXXIII

I MAKE AN END OF DEPUTY SERIN

WHEN we were outside, Botte barred and locked the cell door, while I held the lantern. Then, returning it to him, I took his unoccupied arm, and we set out on our hazardous journey. As when I entered the prison with Marteau, we traversed several corridors divided into sections by iron-bound doors, all of which my guide opened with one of his many keys. But, instead of going forward to the main entrance, we turned to the right, descended a long underground passage like a cathedral crypt, and went on till we came to a heavy door, which was evidently not often used.

" Is this the door ?" I asked.

" This is the door. On the other side you are free," answered the warder.

" If I am not stopped. You haven't told me the password for the night."

" That is not in the bargain, and I'll be shot—"

" No you won't, you'll be guillotined. Suppose I am arrested by a sentry and tell by whose connivance—"

" Sacred name ! you are right. I never thought of that. The word is ' Marat.' "

" Good. Now open, Sesame," quoth I.

The hinges were so stiff, the door so heavy, that even after it was unlocked and unbolted, it was all we could do to pull it open.

" The coast seems clear," says Botte, peering forth. " I should be sorry for you to be caught; but if you are, you won't blab ?"

" Not though they tear me in pieces. Here is my hand
on it, and here your reward," giving him the stipulated
recompense.

" A thousand thanks. *Au revoir*, Lebrun."

" Heaven forbid ! I want to see neither you nor this
hideous prison again. Good-bye forever."

I looked up at the stars, took a deep breath, and stepped
briskly out, as became a warder taking his evening walk.
I had not gone far before I spied a sentry treading his
beat.

" Who goes there?" he cried, coming to a halt.

" Rapp, a warder of the Palace " (the name by which the
Conciergerie was best known).

" Advance, warder, and give the countersign."

" Marat."

" Good ! You can pass on."

And I passed on gladly, crossing the river by the Pont
au Change, which was in a direct line with the Rue St.
Denis. But I took at once to the back streets, at that time
almost deserted, where I knew there were no police-stations,
and I should run no risk of encountering a patrol.

Knowing my Paris well, and having a good eye for locali-
ties, I had no trouble in finding M. Dufour's house. A light
was burning in the attic window; but bearing in mind Angélique's warning, and as the clocks had only just gone eleven,
I thought I had better keep away for a while, so rambled on
northward as far as the King's Mews, and then retraced my
steps by another road.

The clock of St. Sauveur was striking the last quarter
before twelve, and I was within a few minutes' walk of
my destination, when I chanced to meet a man with a
lantern, the light of which, to my annoyance, fell full on
my face.

I stepped aside, and was about to pass on when he

uttered an exclamation that made me jump half-way across the street.

"A thousand thunders! Lebrun! You have escaped! Help! To me the police! To me!" cried Serin, for he it was.

Before the words were well out of his mouth, I had seized him by the throat and dashed the lantern from his hand.

"Silence, you scoundrel!" I said, in a fierce whisper. "Another word and I will bury this knife in your heart. Yesterday you insulted me, and, when I resented the outrage, threatened me with the guillotine. You are a murderer both in thought and deed, and deserve to die the death of a dog. But I will treat you better than you were going to treat me. I will give you a chance for your life. You are armed; draw and defend yourself, and we will fight our quarrel out, though, 'pon my soul, I do you too much honor."

Serin answered promptly to my challenge, and our blades crossed. He knew something of fence, and, to do him justice, showed no want of pluck; but I soon found that I was the better swordsman, and my length of arm gave me a decided advantage over him. As all was quiet, and the clash of our weapons might be heard by some passing gendarme in the next street, I pressed my adversary hard from the outset; yet it is ill fighting in the dark, and once he touched me; but the next moment I engaged his blade in *carte*, and, carrying my point behind his wrist and under his elbow, ran him through from side to side.

Serin fell without a groan, stark dead, and I felt that I had deserved well of France in ridding her of so pestilent a ruffian—I would gladly have served every other Terrorist in the same way. Nevertheless, it was not a deed to be proclaimed on the house-tops, and as a sword might be an

16

embarrassing possession when the deputy's death became known, and I was solicitous not to get my friends into trouble, I made straight for the nearest quay, rolled the weapon in Rapp's coat, and dropped both into the Seine, then returned to the Rue St. Denis, and, after reconnoitring the goldsmith's house, entered by the back door, as Angélique had directed.

So soon as I was inside I doffed my shoes, bolted the door, and crept softly up-stairs to the attic-chamber, where the light was still burning.

It was a cosey little room with a camp-bed, on which I lay down without undressing, and, being thoroughly tired, fell asleep as soon as my head touched the pillow, and did not open my eyes till long after sunrise, when I was wakened by a light tapping at my chamber door.

" Yes," said I.

" It is I, Madame Dufour.   Are you dressed ?"

" Yes ; I did not undress."

" I may come in, then ?"

"Certainly.   I shall be delighted."

Whereupon the lady entered.

"I am so glad," she said, taking both my hands—"so glad.   We were in an agony of suspense last night, Angélique and I, and until she came to my room, about one o'clock, and told me that she had heard footsteps on the stairs, and that the back door was bolted—which meant, of course, that you had come in—I could not sleep a wink. You must tell us all about it when Angélique comes.   I will call her in a minute.   She sent me to see if you were awake ; but, meanwhile, I have something to tell you— something very grave and terrible.   Serin has been assassinated.   His body was found in the Rue de Renard at three o'clock, but it is almost certain that he was killed not more than ten minutes after he left our house, which was between eleven and twelve. The police were here making inquiries an hour ago."

"Have they arrested the assassin?"

"They have not the least idea where to look for him. They think he is some personal or political enemy, who, knowing Serin was in the habit of visiting our house, lay in wait for him. And I should not wonder. He was himself an implacable enemy and a Terrorist, and, between ourselves, fully deserved what has befallen him. . . . But I must call Mademoiselle de la Tour ; she is dying to see you and hear the account of your escape. So am I."

And then my hostess left the room and in a few minutes returned with Angélique. The dear girl looked pale and worn, and when (disregarding French etiquette in such matters) I put my arms round her, all she could say was : "Oh, Fritz, thank Heaven !" and then, laying her head on my shoulder, fell a-weeping. But quickly regaining her composure, she bade me tell her and Mme. Dufour all that had happened me since last night, which I did, with the exception that I made no mention of Serin or of Rapp's sword and coat.

So soon as I had finished and answered a few questions in elucidation of my tale, Mme. Dufour was good enough to say she would fetch me some breakfast, and with that left the room.

"Has Madame Dufour told you about Serin's murder?" asked Angélique, when the lady in question was gone.

"Yes, but are you sure that it was a murder?"

"*Mon Dieu !* Can you . . . is it possible you know something about it? . . . I am sure you do. I can read it in your face. You met him ; you saw his body !" she cried, excitedly.

"I can have no secrets from you, dear," said I, taking

her hand. "It was done in fair fight. I will tell you all, and then you can judge whether I acted rightly."

Which I did, from the encounter in the prison yard to the duel in the street.

"It is a dreadful thing to take a man's life," she said, when I had done; "but if you had not taken Serin's he would have taken yours, and he was a bad man. You could not have acted otherwise, and I think you acted rightly."

From that time forth there was no further mention of Serin between my love and me.

Presently came Mme. Dufour with my breakfast, looking very serious.

"What is wrong? Have you heard bad news?" inquired Angélique, anxiously.

"Only that the town is ringing with the assassination of Serin and the escape of a certain Lebrun, *alias* Boucher, from the Palace. You are out of prison, Monsieur Astor, but you are not out of danger, neither is our dear Angélique, here."

"Angélique in danger? How? why?" I exclaimed, in dismay.

"She comes of a noble family, her father was bitterly opposed to the revolution, she is the particular friend of Madame de Malartic and niece to Monsieur de Lancy— more than enough to make her 'suspect;' and now that Serin is dead—"

"Good heavens! what has Serin to do with it?"

"Well, you see, Serin admired Mademoiselle de la Tour— admired her very much. His visits here were of late very frequent. It was easy to divine with what object, and I had to entreat Angélique, as she valued her life, not to treat him with the disdain and contempt which he inspired. You understand?"

I understood perfectly, and felt more pleased than ever that I had given the ruffian his quietus.

"His attentions were odious; that goes without saying," continued Mme. Dufour; "yet, being unaware of the fact, and as Angélique, in deference to my advice, did not absolutely reject him, he took care she was not molested. But now—"

"I see. His death increases her danger."

"Unquestionably, for the Jacobins, enraged by the deputy's assassination, will be more virulent and suspicious than ever. Unless Angélique departs quickly, she is sure to be arrested, and a domiciliary visit would lead also to your arrest—and ours. You must be out of Paris by this time to-morrow."

"Nothing would please me better. But how?"

"We have a plan, Angélique and I. We talked it over last night, and completed it this morning. You are to get yourselves up as tramps."

"Angélique and I?"

"You, Angélique, and the vicomte. It would not be right for you and her to travel by yourselves. Even with her uncle as guardian, I am not quite sure that the proprieties would approve. But these are times when the proprieties must take care of themselves. Do you play any musical instrument?"

"Not even a penny whistle."

"Nor sing?"

"Nothing in French."

"That is unfortunate. But the vicomte is a fair violinist, I believe, and Angélique sings. He will fiddle revolutionary airs, and she will sing them—whenever it seems necessary; and as you can neither play nor sing, you must enact the part of a blind beggar—Angélique being your sister, Monsieur de Lancy your father."

"I know I am only a stripling; all the same, I doubt whether De Lancy looks old enough to be my father, and anybody who looks at my eyes will see that I am not blind," quoth I, dubiously. But this objection Mme. Dufour brushed aside as unceremoniously as every other that I urged. She had not been on the stage for nothing; she could make the vicomte look old enough to be my grandfather; and by painting my eyelids and dropping belladonna in my eyes, I could be made to look as sightless as a marble statue.

"Leave that to me," she added. "You have been an employé in a fireworks factory, and lost your sight through an explosion of gunpowder. Your eyes look so bad that you wear a shade over them. Angélique will lead you by the hand, and you shall have a little dog that will lead you by a string. My husband will obtain your passports. It is all a matter of money; the forging of passports has become quite a trade. And if you want money for the journey, he will find it for you, on your simple undertaking to remit the amount to a correspondent at Amsterdam, whose name and address he will give you."

From which I inferred that M. Dufour was very anxious to be rid of us—and small blame to him.

To my inquiry whether all these preparations could be completed during the day she answered, "Certainly." Her husband would see to the papers, herself to the garments of disguise.

"England being your destination, you will, of course, make for Dieppe," observed my energetic hostess, "the more especially as you can go part of the way thither by water."

"Exactly what I was going to propose," said I. "You have thought of everything, Madame Dufour. I place myself gratefully and unreservedly in your hands."

. " You must not give me all the credit, though. The plan is as much Angélique's as mine," says she.

" Not at all. I merely suggested the idea of disguising ourselves as vagrants," put in Angélique, " and monsieur, your husband—"

" Monsieur, my husband, did nothing whatever—at least, nothing more than offer to provide you with passports and money," interrupted Madame Dufour. " It is our scheme entirely."

Angélique and I exchanged amused glances. Without passports and money, quitting Paris would be difficult ; getting to England impossible.

" It is our scheme entirely," repeated the lady. " And now we must be off to the Conciergerie. You seem surprised ?"

" And so I am, as much as if you had proposed to put your head into a lion's mouth."

" But don't you see that it is absolutely necessary ? For several weeks past I have gone to the Palace occasionally, Angélique almost daily, to see Madame la Marquise. If we omit going the day after your escape the omission is sure to be remarked, especially as Madame la Marquise was so ill yesterday that they did not think she would live through the night, and somebody might recall that the prisoner Lebrun and Mademoiselle de la Tour had been seen talking through the bars. On the other hand, her appearance will be regarded as proof presumptive of her innocence, and we shall hear no end of gossip about your disappearance."

" Well, it is perhaps one of those cases in which boldness is the best policy. All the same, I shall be on pins till you return."

" You will have to be on pins a long time, then ; for we have much to do, and shall not be back until late in the afternoon. But if either of us is arrested, you are pretty sure to be apprised of the fact within the hour—by a domiciliary visit.   So don't worry."

They went away smiling and full of courage, leaving me, however, in an agony of apprehension, since, despite Mme. Dufour's confidence, I knew they were running a terrible risk, and I could not divest myself of the fear that Angélique might be detained—and then !

CHAPTER XXXIV

BY LAND AND SEA

My anxiety, which waxed as the day waned, taught me for the first time in my life that danger impending over those you love is harder to bear than a danger that threatens yourself—above all, when you are obliged to remain quiescent, and apprehension is intensified by suspense.

"If Angélique is taken, what shall I do—what will become of us? It will be impossible to leave her to perish, equally impossible to save her. But one thing I can do: I can die with her; and I will. If I hear that she has been detained, I will return to the Conciergerie and give myself up."

Thus ran my thoughts, and bitterly did I rue having killed Scrin; for if he had lived, Angelique had been safe. But as the leaden hours crept on I grew more tranquil, since in existing circumstances no news was essentially good news. After a while the door opened and in came the man of the house, looking so ill at ease that my fears revived, and without answering his greeting I put the question that was uppermost in my mind.

"If any harm had befallen Mademoiselle de la Tour or my wife I should have heard before this," said he, taking from his pockets half a bottle of wine and some bread and cheese, which he had smuggled out of the kitchen. "One cannot be too cautious. If the maids were to get an inkling that we had a guest in the attic-chamber it might be fatal. I count myself a good patriot, but patriotism has ceased to be a protection. Let a secret enemy or a treacherous domestic denounce you and you are doomed. Serin's death makes a great difference to me, monsieur. He may have been a bad man—indeed, between ourselves, I think he was—but he was a good friend to me, and while he lived I had little to fear. Now I am in no better case than any other body. The mere fact of entertaining Mademoiselle de la Tour is enough to make me 'suspect.' And my wife, monsieur, has a tongue—she has a tongue which I fear will get us both into trouble one of these days. But I am not come to talk about my affairs; I am come to talk about yours. How about money?"

I told Monsieur Dufour how much money I had left. It was very little; and though our journey to Dieppe would be inexpensive, I should doubtless have to pay heavily for conveyance from Dieppe to the English coast; so by way of making ample provision for this eventuality, he agreed to let me have the equivalent of one hundred pounds, and I on my part undertook to remit the amount of the loan to Van Loon, Vandam & Co., his correspondents at Amsterdam.

This point settled, we discussed the scheme for our flight, of which M. Dufour fully approved. He thought that once out of Paris we should encounter no serious difficulty until we got to Dieppe, where, and I fully agreed with him, we should need to be exceedingly wary. The passport which he had procured for us seemed to be quite in order. It described us as the family Bopp: Jacques (father), itinerant musician, Jean (son), ex-employé in a fireworks factory (eyes seriously injured and sight all but destroyed by an explosion of gunpowder); Marie (daughter), cantatrice.

" I thought it better to say 'eyes seriously injured' than stone blind," explained M. Dufour. " It might be convenient to admit that you can see just a little."

This relieved me of an anxiety. It would be easier to play the part of a purblind than of a wholly blind man.

We were still talking when the door opened again and Madame Dufour entered smiling. All had gone well. Even the death of the poor marchioness, considering her great age and recent sufferings, and that, had she lived a few days longer, she must have died on the scaffold, might be regarded as well. They had stayed at the Conciergerie only a short time, yet sufficiently long to learn that the officers of the prison were still quite in the dark as to the method of my escape, and Botte and Rapp at large and unsuspected.

The old clothes, wigs, and the rest were already in the house, and M. Dufour undertook to transfer them from his own room to the attic-chamber. Angélique had gone to look for her uncle, who kept himself so well hidden that even with the clews she possessed there was some difficulty in finding him. But as he was dying to get out of Paris, there could be no question that he would profit by the present opportunity.

Having imparted this information and made a few observations of a general character, Madame Dufour left us to ourselves, only, however, to return an hour later accompanied by Angélique.

I was amused to observe how faithfully (notwithstanding the serious business she had on hand) our hostess played the part of chaperon. Only once did she leave us for a few minutes to our own company. Wherefore our greeting was not very lover-like, according to English notions. I took both my sweetheart's hands in mine, pressed one of them respectfully to my lips, and then prayed her to be seated.

She had found her uncle, albeit not where she expected to find him, for he seldom remained in one hiding-place more than three days. As Madame Dufour had anticipated, he was more than willing to accompany us in our flight and accept the rôle assigned to him. He would come at eleven o'clock, suitably attired for the occasion, enter at the back door, and share my room. Angélique had bought and brought with her a second-hand fiddle, which seemed just the thing for an itinerant musician.

Our plans prospered. Shortly after eleven De Lancy stole into the attic - chamber carrying his shoes in one hand and a small bundle in the other.

If I had not expected him I should not have known him. His clothes were as shabby as any beggar's. He wore a white peruke, which fitted him like his own hair, and a pair of horn - rimmed spectacles. He had shaved off his eye-brows, and anxiety and long seclusion had made him so wan and lantern-jawed that I thought he would easily pass for my father without any artistic touches from the prac-tised hand of Mme. Dufour.

We did not talk much—there would be plenty of time on the road for telling each other the tale of our late advent-ures — but got us quickly to bed, and at four o'clock we were up and dressed — I, of course, in the garments pro-vided for me by Mme. Dufour, as to which I need only say that they were a good match for De Lancy's.

Our next proceeding was to descend to a room on the first floor, where we found M. Dufour and the two ladies. Angelique's face, hands, and arms had been dyed nut-brown with walnut - juice, and for all that she wore a com-mon linsey gown, short by the ankles, a shabby jacket and clumsy shoes, and her *coiffure* was nothing more than a red kerchief twisted round her head. I thought she had never looked more charming; she was surely the prettiest beggar-maid I had ever set eyes on.

Mme. Dufour took me in hand at once, dropped bella-donna into my eyes, and painted the lids and brows in such sort that Angelique declared she could not bear to look at me, and turned away shuddering. Then the shade was adjusted, and my disguise completed.

Being the strongest, I had naturally to carry the family belongings, which were bestowed in a capacious wallet.

The idea of taking a dog had been dropped, M. Dufour fearing that the creature's barking might waken the servants, and, perchance, disturb the neighbors.

My money was stitched in my waistcoat lining as before, and for weapons I had a stout stick and the amputating-knife—the latter handy, albeit well concealed. Angélique's jewelry, of which she had a good deal, was hidden in her clothing.

All being ready, we bade the kindly pair to whom we owed so much a grateful farewell, and slipped out of the house while it was yet dark.

De Lancy, with his fiddle-bag under his arm, went first, Angélique and I following hand in hand. We went on our way in sombre silence; for the route we took (past the Carrousel, the Tuileries, and Revolution Place, where still loomed the terrible guillotine) was haunted by memories that paralyzed our tongues and depressed our spirits, and between us and England lay the ordeal of the barrier and a perilous journey.

As the sun rose we stepped out more briskly, and by the time we reached the Arc de Triomphe it was full daylight.

"What can you sing, Angélique?" asked the vicomte.

"I learned the words of 'Ça Ira' and the 'Marseillaise' yesterday; I can also sing 'Malbrook,' and a few other things."

"Good! That is enough for the present; and if you are required to sing any of their infernal republican airs, look as though you were pleased, and put your heart into it. . . . *Allons.* If we go with a confident air, they may let us pass through without question."

Which they did, but only to call us back the next minute.

"You are in a hurry, I think," said the officer on duty, gruffly. "Whither are you going?"

"On a professional tour," answered De Lancy.

"Which means a begging expedition, from the look of you. Your passport?"

De Lancy produced it.

"Hum! the Bopp family — father, son, and daughter. Son nearly blind—or supposed to be."

And with that he raised my shade (through which I could see dimly), and I fixed my eyes in a stony glare.

"Poor devil! Blind enough," he murmured. "Pity, though; you would make a fine recruit. Could you give us a bit of music, Citizen Bopp—you and your charming daughter?"

"With pleasure," responded De Lancy, uncasing his fiddle. "We will give you the 'Ça Ira.' Now Marie!" flourishing his bow.

They gave it so well that the gendarmes were quite delighted.

"It is all right; you can go on," said the officer. "And you won't need to beg; only play like that, and you will come back with pockets full of money."

"A good omen," observed the vicomte, *sotto voce*, as he put up his fiddle.

Resuming our journey with lightened hearts, we reached St. Germain towards sundown, and passed the night at a little river-side inn, where, hearing that a boat was to start early next morning for Rouen, we took passage by her, with the intention, however, of landing before we got thither; that city, like Paris, having barriers and prying police-folk whom we had no wish to encounter.

This design we carried out, disembarking about a league to the eastward of Rouen, and gaining the direct road to Dieppe by a long détour.

Mostly walking, occasionally getting a lift on a country cart, and making such stages as Angélique could easily accomplish, we were nearly a week on the road between Rouen and the coast. Now and then my companions gave a performance at the villages through which we passed, and at one place De Lancy and his fiddle were requisitioned for a rustic fête, whereby we lost a whole day.

During our last stage we fell in with a tramp who gave us a useful wrinkle. Dieppe, he said, was just then a hard place to get into, and a bad place to be in. So many fugitives had escaped that way that the police scrutinized passports with great severity, were very rough on wayfarers like ourselves, and, as likely as not, would either turn us back or lock us up.

But he could show us a by-road by which, at the edge of dark, we might obtain access to the town through the suburb of Le Pollet (a quarter inhabited by sailors and fishermen) without incurring these risks.

This meant a tip and a bottle of wine, which we gladly gave him. It would have been worth our while to give him a good deal more. In Le Pollet dwelt Blondin, the smuggler captain, to whom I had been introduced by Von Affry.

So at dusk we wended thitherward, and were taken by the friendly tramp to a lodging suitable for folk of our condition.

After we had supped, De Lancy and myself set out to look for Blondin, whom we were lucky enough to find at home. He received us gruffly, remembering neither my name nor face, and not until I reminded him of what had passed at our previous interview did he recognize me as Von Affry's friend and throw aside his reserve.

He was a brave old salt, had no political opinions, and cared not a button-top for the police; yet he knew how to drive a bargain. Not for a centime less than twenty-five hundred francs effective (£100) could he run us across the Channel, but at that price he would undertake to land us safely in England (wind, weather, revenue-cutters, and warships permitting) the next day but one.

I offered to make the price one hundred and twenty pounds if he would say the next day.

"That means setting sail to-night," quoth he, thoughtfully. "Well, if you will put up with a rather small and not very well-found boat, I think it may be done."

"We will put up with anything that will convey us safely across," said I.

"Done! Be here at ten o'clock, sharp, and you will find somebody to show you where the *Beautiful Star* is berthed," said he.

On this hint we hied us back to our inn to inform Angélique how we had fared, and, presently returning, found two sailors at Blondin's door, who, after conveying us to the water-side, led us across half a dozen vessels moored side by side, at so great a pace that, the night being dark and the decks slippery with recent rain, we could scarce keep up with them.

"Behold her!" exclaimed one of the fellows at last, to my great satisfaction, for in trying to help Angélique I had tripped over a coil of rope and barked my shins.

The *Beautiful Star* was not a big vessel—only about half the size of a canal-boat, as far as I could judge. But little time was given us for inspection, since no sooner were we aboard than Blondin opened a trap-door and bade us go below and hide under a spare sail we should find there, adding that we might have a visit from the police, or from some of the harbor-master's people before we got outside.

So down we went and there we hid. Soon, however, the boat began to move, and after a while the trap-door opened again and we were allowed to go on deck.

There was a small cabin aft, where sleeping accommodation had been prepared for Angélique. De Lancy and myself preferred to stay on deck. Save the hold, there was nowhere else for us, and, besides being pitch-dark, it was as evil-smelling as my first cell at the Conciergerie.

Though the weather was dirty, the wind was fair, and shortly before six o'clock we sighted the white cliffs of dear old England.

I could have shouted for joy; and, despite the wetness of my clothes and the sickness of my stomach, should have done so had not De Lancy looked so woe-begone and the sailors so serious. For by this time it was blowing a gale of wind, and the sea was so rough withal, and the old hooker so rotten, that Blondin made no secret of his fear that we might go to the bottom or drive against the cliffs. To prevent this catastrophe he let go both his anchors. Whether wisely I am unable to say, not being skilled in seamanship. But the result was unfortunate; for when we had been riding about an hour, the cables parted, the mast snapped, and we drifted helplessly shoreward, grounding at last on a sand-bank between Newhaven and Brighton, as luck would have it, not more than fourscore yards from the strand, where several people, fishermen and others, were watching us.

We had no boat, and it is doubtful whether a row-boat could have won through the breakers that raced over the sand-bank and dashed against the smack, which lay on her beam ends exposed to all the fury of the storm. But Blondin was equal to the occasion; he knotted a rope to a spar, which, being launched into the sea, was swept ashore and caught by the fishermen.

The rope was then made fast, and the other end of it being held taut by the people ashore, we were all enabled to land. Angélique would have ventured alone, but I insisted on carrying her, and though we were a good deal buffeted, I

17

succeeded in placing her on terra firma, save for cold and exhaustion and a thorough drenching, none the worse.

We received a warm welcome from the unknown friends among whom we found ourselves, and when they learned that we were fugitives, and that one of our number was an English officer, late of the Swiss Guard, who but ten days previously had escaped from a French prison, they gave us a hearty cheer and took us to a little inn hard by.

Angélique and her uncle, who had been very sick, and were both perishing with cold, went straight to bed while their clothes were dried. But I had an imperative duty to perform, and, borrowing from the landlord a suit of clothes which, though a tight fit, served passably well, sat down to write to my father.

I gave him, first of all, a brief account of my adventures, with promise of a fuller account when we met. Next I mentioned that one of the companions of my flight was a young lady of noble family, who, besides saving my life on the fatal 10th of August, had helped me to escape from the Conciergerie, and to whom I was devotedly attached. After asking my father's forgiveness for falling in love without his knowledge or consent, I besought him not to accuse me of recklessness until he heard the whole of my story, nor to pass judgment on my choice until he saw Angélique, who, as I took care to observe, was in charge of her uncle, the Vicomte de Lancy.

Then I informed him that we proposed on the following day to make for London, and should alight at La Belle Sauvage, in Ludgate Hill, where he himself was in the habit of staying when he went to town. But as my wardrobe needed replenishing, and I could not leave Mlle. de la Tour until I had seen her comfortably lodged, and ascertained whether any of my comrades of the regiment had succeeded in reaching England, he must not expect to see me much under a week. In the meantime I hoped he would let me have a line in reply, saying how it fared with him and my mother, not forgetting the shop and old Wiggin.

Though I carefully refrained from saying so, I was not without hope that they might invite Angélique to make our house her home.

On the next morning we went to Brighton, and after exchanging our beggars' garb for garments more befitting our condition, travelled post to London (I was too happy to be cheese-paring), and put up, as I had proposed, at La Belle Sauvage.

The following days we spent in ordering clothes, disposing of some of Angélique's jewels (which brought her a nice sum), and in making inquiries about missing friends, several of whom we were so fortunate as to find in London.

As we returned from one of these excursions, some four days after our arrival, a post-chaise, bespattered with mud and drawn by perspiring horses, rattled into the Sauvage yard. When the carriage stopped, who should step out of it but my father! He was turning round to offer my mother his hand when I ran up and received her in my arms.

What happened next I can scarce tell. The arms of both seemed to be round me at once. I heard my father say, "Fritz! Fritz! Oh, my dear boy!"

My mother murmured, weeping, "My son who was dead is alive! Thank God! thank God!"

Then, recovering her composure, she spied Angélique, who was looking on in glad surprise.

"Is that the dear lass that saved your life and stole your heart?" asked my mother.

"The same, mother."

"God bless her bonny face!" says she, and taking my sweetheart in her arms, gave her a hearty Lancashire hugging and kissing.

But as all this was in public, and the people in the inn yard were staring at us in open-mouthed wonder, I invited my father and mother to accompany Angélique, her uncle, and myself to our sitting-room. There we had a long and pleasant, albeit somewhat lively talk. My father, though naturally and by habit abstemious. ordered champagne, and became quite hilarious. My dear mother was quietly happy, sitting between Angélique and myself, holding a hand of each.

The result was all I could desire. Our betrothal received parental sanction on the spot, and Angélique accepted an invitation to go with us to Lancashire and make our house her home until she had one of her own.

My tale is told, for, although I was only at the beginning of my career, and since that time have fought in many campaigns, and met with many stirring adventures, it is no part of my present design to narrate any other than those which arose out of my service with the noble regiment of the Swiss Guard, where I learned that honor is more precious than life, and a stainless name better than riches.

THE END

By W. D. HOWELLS.

THE COAST OF BOHEMIA. A Novel. 12mo, Cloth, $1 50.

THE WORLD OF CHANCE. A Novel. 12mo, Cloth, $1 50; Paper, 60 cents.

THE QUALITY OF MERCY. A Novel. 12mo, Cloth, $1 50; Paper, 75 cents.

AN IMPERATIVE DUTY. A Novel. 12mo, Cloth, $1 00; Paper, 50 cents.

A HAZARD OF NEW FORTUNES. A Novel. 2 Volumes. 12mo, Cloth, $2 00; Illustrated, 12mo, Paper, $1 00.

THE SHADOW OF A DREAM. A Story. 12mo, Cloth, $1 00; Paper, 50 cents.

ANNIE KILBURN. A Novel. 12mo, Cloth, $1 50; Paper, 75 cents.

APRIL HOPES. A Novel. 12mo, Cloth, $1 50; Paper, 75 cents.

CHRISTMAS EVERY DAY, AND OTHER STORIES. Illustrated. Post 8vo, Cloth, $1 25.

A BOY'S TOWN. Illustrated. Post 8vo, Cloth, $1 25.

CRITICISM AND FICTION. With Portrait. 16mo, Cloth, $1 00.

MODERN ITALIAN POETS. With Portraits. 12mo, Half Cloth, $2 00.

THE MOUSE-TRAP, AND OTHER FARCES. Illustrated. 12mo, Cloth, $1 00.

FARCES:—*The Unexpected Guests.—Evening Dress.—A Letter of Introduction.—The Albany Depot.—The Garroters.* Illustrated. 32mo, Cloth, 50 cents each.

MY YEAR IN A LOG CABIN. Illustrated. 32mo, Cloth, 50 cents.

A LITTLE SWISS SOJOURN. Illustrated. 32mo, Cloth, 50 cents.

PUBLISHED BY HARPER & BROTHERS, NEW YORK.

☞ *The above works are for sale by all booksellers, or will be sent by the publishers, postage prepaid, to any part of the United States, Canada, or Mexico, on receipt of the price.*

WALTER BESANT'S WORKS.

We give, without hesitation, the foremost place to Mr. Besant, whose work, always so admirable and spirited, acquires double importance from the enthusiasm with which it is inspired.—*Blackwood's Magazine*, Edinburgh.

Mr. Besant wields the wand of a wizard, let him wave it in whatever direction he will. . . . The spell that dwells in this wand is formed by intense earnestness and vivid imagination.—*Spectator*, London.

There is a bluff, honest, hearty, and homely method about Mr. Besant's stories which makes them acceptable, and because he is so easily understood is another reason why he is so particularly relished by the English public.—*N. Y. Times*.

ALL IN A GARDEN FAIR. 4to, Paper, 20 cents.

ALL SORTS AND CONDITIONS OF MEN. Illustrated. 12mo, Cloth, $1 25; 8vo, Paper, 50 cents.

ARMOREL OF LYONESSE. Illustrated. 12mo, Cloth, $1 25; 8vo, Paper, 50 cents.

CHILDREN OF GIBEON. 12mo, Cloth, $1 25; 8vo, Paper, 50 cents.

DOROTHY FORSTER. 4to, Paper, 20 cents.

FIFTY YEARS AGO. Illustrated. 8vo, Cloth, $2 50.

FOR FAITH AND FREEDOM. Illustrated. 12mo, Cloth, $1 25; 8vo, Paper, 50 cents.

HERR PAULUS. 8vo, Paper, 35 cents.

KATHERINE REGINA. 4to, Paper, 15 cents.

LIFE OF COLIGNY. 32mo, Cloth, 40 cents; Paper, 25 cents.

SELF OR BEARER. 4to, Paper, 15 cents.

LONDON. Illustrated. 8vo, Cloth, Ornamental, $3 00.

ST. KATHARINE'S BY THE TOWER. Illustrated. 12mo, Cloth, $1 25; Paper, 50 cents.

THE BELL OF ST. PAUL'S. 8vo, Paper, 35 cents.

THE HOLY ROSE. 4to, Paper, 20 cents.

THE INNER HOUSE. 8vo, Paper, 30 cents.

THE IVORY GATE. 12mo, Cloth, $1 25.

THE REBEL QUEEN. Illustrated. 12mo, Cloth, $1 50.

THE WORLD WENT VERY WELL THEN. Illustr'd. 12mo, Cloth, $1 25; 4to, Paper, 25 cents.

TO CALL HER MINE. Illustrated. 4to, Paper, 20 cents.

UNCLE JACK AND OTHER STORIES. 12mo, Paper, 25 cents.

PUBLISHED BY HARPER & BROTHERS, NEW YORK.

☞ *Any of the above works will be sent by mail, postage prepaid, to any part of the United States, Canada, or Mexico, on receipt of the price.*

By CONSTANCE F. WOOLSON.

HORACE CHASE. A Novel. 16mo, Cloth, $1 25.

JUPITER LIGHTS. A Novel. 16mo, Cloth, $1 25.

EAST ANGELS. A Novel. 16mo, Cloth, $1 25.

ANNE. A Novel. Illustrated. 16mo, Cloth, $1 25.

FOR THE MAJOR. A Novelette. 16mo, Cloth, $1 00.

CASTLE NOWHERE. Lake-Country Sketches. 16mo, Cloth, $1 00.

RODMAN THE KEEPER. Southern Sketches. 16mo, Cloth, $1 00.

Delightful touches justify those who see many points of analogy between Miss Woolson and George Eliot.—*N. Y. Times.*

For tenderness and purity of thought, for exquisitely delicate sketching of characters, Miss Woolson is unexcelled among writers of fiction.—*New Orleans Picayune.*

Characterization is Miss Woolson's forte. Her men and women are not mere puppets, but original, breathing, and finely contrasted creations.—*Chicago Tribune.*

Miss Woolson is one of the few novelists of the day who know how to make conversation, how to individualize the speakers, how to exclude rabid realism without falling into literary formality.—*N. Y. Tribune.*

Constance Fenimore Woolson may easily become the novelist laureate.—*Boston Globe.*

Miss Woolson has a graceful fancy, a ready wit, a polished style, and conspicuous dramatic power; while her skill in the development of a story is very remarkable.—*London Life.*

Miss Woolson never once follows the beaten track of the orthodox novelist, but strikes a new and richly-loaded vein which, so far, is all her own; and thus we feel, on reading one of her works, a fresh sensation, and we put down the book with a sigh to think our pleasant task of reading it is finished. The author's lines must have fallen to her in very pleasant places; or she has, perhaps, within herself the wealth of womanly love and tenderness she pours so freely into all she writes. Such books as hers do much to elevate the moral tone of the day—a quality sadly wanting in novels of the time.—*Whitehall Review,* London.

PUBLISHED BY HARPER & BROTHERS, NEW YORK.

☞ *The above works are for sale by all booksellers, or will be sent by the publishers, postage prepaid, to any part of the United States, Canada, or Mexico, on receipt of the price.*

By MARY E. WILKINS.

JANE FIELD. A Novel. Illustrated. 16mo, Cloth, Ornamental, $1 25.

YOUNG LUCRETIA, and Other Stories. Illustrated. Post 8vo, Cloth, Ornamental, $1 25.

GILES COREY, YEOMAN. A Play. Illustrated. 32mo, Cloth, Ornamental, 50 cents.

A NEW ENGLAND NUN, and Other Stories. 16mo, Cloth, Ornamental, $1 25.

A HUMBLE ROMANCE, and Other Stories. 16mo, Cloth, Ornamental, $1 25.

The pathos of New England life, its intensities of repressed feeling, its homely tragedies and its tender humor, have never been better told than by Mary E. Wilkins, and in her own field she stands to-day without a rival.—*Boston Courier.*

It takes just such distinguished literary art as Mary E. Wilkins possesses to give an episode of New England its soul, pathos, and poetry.—*N. Y. Times.*

The simplicity, purity, and quaintness of these stories set them apart in a niche of distinction where they have no rivals.—*Literary World,* Boston.

The author has the unusual gift of writing a short story which is complete in itself, having a real *beginning,* a *middle,* and an *end.*—*Observer,* N. Y.

A gallery of striking studies in the humblest quarters of American country life. No one has dealt with this kind of life better than Miss Wilkins. Nowhere are there to be found such faithful, delicately drawn, sympathetic, tenderly humorous pictures.—*N. Y. Tribune.*

The charm of Miss Wilkins's stories is in her intimate acquaintance and comprehension of humble life, and the sweet human interest she feels and makes her readers partake of, in the simple, common, homely people she draws.—*Springfield Republican.*

The author has given us studies from real life which must be the result of a lifetime of patient, sympathetic observation. . . . No one has done the same kind of work so lovingly and so well.—*Christian Register,* Boston.

PUBLISHED BY HARPER & BROTHERS, NEW YORK.

☞ *The above works are for sale by all booksellers, or will be sent by mail, postage prepaid, to any part of the United States, Canada, or Mexico, on receipt of the price.*

BEN-HUR: A TALE OF THE CHRIST.

By LEW. WALLACE. 16mo, Cloth, $1 50. *Garfield Edition.* Two Volumes. Twenty Full-page Photogravures. Over 1000 Illustrations as Marginal Drawings by WILLIAM MARTIN JOHNSON. Crown 8vo, Printed on Fine Super-calendered Plate-paper, Uncut Edges and Gilt Tops, Bound in Silk and Gold, $7 00. (*In a Gladstone Box.*)

Anything so startling, new, and distinctive as the leading feature of this romance does not often appear in works of fiction. . . . Some of Mr. Wallace's writing is remarkable for its pathetic eloquence. The scenes described in the New Testament are rewritten with the power and skill of an accomplished master of style.—*N. Y. Times.*

Its real basis is a description of the life of the Jews and Romans at the beginning of the Christian era, and this is both forcible and brilliant. . . . We are carried through a surprising variety of scenes; we witness a sea-fight, a chariot-race, the internal economy of a Roman galley, domestic interiors at Antioch, at Jerusalem, and among the tribes of the desert; palaces, prisons, the haunts of dissipated Roman youth, the houses of pious families of Israel. There is plenty of exciting incident; everything is animated, vivid and glowing.—*N. Y. Tribune.*

From the opening of the volume to the very close the reader's interest will be kept at the highest pitch, and the novel will be pronounced by all one of the greatest novels of the day.—*Boston Post.*

"Ben Hur" is interesting, and its characterization is fine and strong. Meanwhile it evinces careful study of the period in which the scene is laid, and will help those who read it with reasonable attention to realize the nature and conditions of Hebrew life in Jerusalem and Roman life at Antioch at the time of our Saviour's advent.—*Examiner, N. Y.*

The book is one of unquestionable power, and will be read with unwonted interest by many readers who are weary of the conventional novel and romance.—*Boston Journal.*

One of the most remarkable and delightful books. It is as real and warm as life itself, and as attractive as the grandest and most heroic chapters of history.—*Indianapolis Journal.*

PUBLISHED BY HARPER & BROTHERS, NEW YORK.

☞ *The above work will be sent by mail, postage prepaid, to any part of the United States, Canada, or Mexico, on receipt of the price.*

THE PRINCE OF INDIA;

Or, Why Constantinople Fell. By Lew. Wallace, Author of "Ben-Hur," "The Boyhood of Christ," etc. Two Volumes. 16mo, Cloth, Ornamental, $2 50; Half Leather, $4 00; Three-quarter Leather, $5 00; Three-quarter Calf, $6 00; Three-quarter Crushed Levant, $8 00. (*In a Box.*)

General Wallace has achieved the (literary) impossible. He has struck the bull's-eye twice in succession. After his phenomenal hit with "Ben-Hur" he has given us, in "The Prince of India," another book which no man will say shows the least falling off. . . . It is a great book.—*N. Y. Tribune.*

A great story It has power and fire. We believe that it will be read and re-read.—*N. Y. Sun.*

For boldness of conception this romance is unique of its kind. The amount of research shown is immense. The mere *mise en scène* necessary for the proper presentation of the Byzantine period alone involves a life-long study. . . . There are incidents innumerable in this romance, and all are worked up with dramatic effect.—*N. Y. Times.*

Its human interest is so vivid that it is one of those historical novels laid down reluctantly only with the last page with the feeling that one turns away from men and women with whom for a while he lived and moved. . . . A masterly and great and absorbing work of fiction. . . . Dignity, a superb conjunction of historical and imaginative material, the movement of a strong river of fancy, an unfailing quality of human interest, fill it over-flowingly.—*N. Y. Mail and Express.*

Politics, romance, religious discussion, war, statesmanship, and love, all have their part as elements of interest, and one may be sure that not Bulwer himself could have treated a notable epoch in history with greater fidelity to established fact or more splendor of constructive imagination.—*Boston Beacon.*

In invention, in the power to make mind-impressions, in thrilling interest, "The Prince of India" is not inferior to "Ben-Hur." The visit to the grave of Hiram, King of Tyre, with which the story opens, at once arouses the reader's keenest interest, which culminates in the closing pages of the second volume with the downfall of Constantinople.—*Philadelphia Inquirer.*

Abounds in scenes that have few rivals outside of the "Arabian Nights." —*N. Y. Herald.*

"The Prince of India" is a succession of Oriental pictures, faithful and ample in detail. It is beyond question an able historical novel, an absorbing theological novel, a refined and lofty love story. . . . Its qualities are thought-arousing, educating, pictorial, spiritually analytic.—*St. Louis Globe-Democrat.*

Published by HARPER & BROTHERS, New York.

For sale by all booksellers, or will be sent by mail, postage prepaid, to any part of the United States, Canada, or Mexico, on receipt of the price.

R. D. BLACKMORE'S NOVELS.

His descriptions are wonderfully vivid and natural. His pages are brightened everywhere with great humor; the quaint, dry turns of thought remind you occasionally of Fielding.—*London Times.*

Mr. Blackmore always writes like a scholar and a gentleman—*Athenæum*, London.

His tales, all of them, are pre-eminently meritorious. They are remarkable for their careful elaboration, the conscientious finish of their workmanship, their affluence of striking dramatic and narrative incident, their close observation and general interpretation of nature, their profusion of picturesque description, and their quiet and sustained humor. Besides, they are pervaded by a bright and elastic atmosphere which diffuses a cheery feeling of healthful and robust vigor. While they charm us by their sprightly vivacity and their naturalness, they never in the slightest degree transcend the limits of delicacy or good taste. While radiating warmth and brightness, they are as pure as the new-fallen snow. . . . Their literary execution is admirable, and their dramatic power is as exceptional as their moral purity.—*Christian Intelligencer*, N. Y.

LORNA DOONE. Illustrated. 12mo, Cloth, $1 00; 8vo, Paper, 40 cents.

KIT AND KITTY. 12mo, Cloth, $1 25; Paper, 35 cents.

SPRINGHAVEN. Illustrated 12mo, Cloth, $1 50, 4to, Paper, 25 cents.

CHRISTOWELL. 4to, Paper, 20 cents.

CRADOCK NOWELL. 8vo, Paper, 60 cents.

EREMA; OR, MY FATHER'S SIN. 8vo, Paper, 50 cents.

MARY ANERLEY. 16mo, Cloth, $1 00; 4to, Paper, 15 cents.

TOMMY UPMORE. 16mo, Cloth, 50 cents; Paper, 35 cents; 4to, Paper, 20 cents.

PUBLISHED BY HARPER & BROTHERS, NEW YORK.

☞ *Any of the above works will be sent by mail, postage prepaid, to any part of the United States, Canada, or Mexico, on receipt of the price.*